# love
## water
### memory

Also by Jennie Shortridge

*When She Flew*

*Love and Biology at the Center of the Universe*

*Eating Heaven*

*Riding with the Queen*

# love
## water
### memory

Jennie Shortridge

## GALLERY BOOKS

new york    london    toronto    sydney    new delhi

G

Gallery Books
A Division of Simon & Schuster, Inc.
1230 Avenue of the Americas
New York, NY 10020

Copyright © 2013 by Jennie Shortridge

First Gallery Books hardcover edition April 2013

GALLERY BOOKS and colophon are registered trademarks of Simon & Schuster, Inc.

For information about special discounts for bulk purchases, please contact Simon & Schuster Special Sales at 1-866-506-1949 or business@simonandschuster.com.

The Simon & Schuster Speakers Bureau can bring authors to your live event. For more information or to book an event contact the Simon & Schuster Speakers Bureau at 1-866-248-3049 or visit our website at www.simonspeakers.com.

Designed by Davina Mock-Maniscalco

Manufactured in the United States of America

10   9   8   7   6   5   4   3   2

Library of Congress Cataloging-in-Publication Data

Shortridge, Jennie.
Love water memory / by Jennie Shortridge.—1st Gallery Books hardcover ed.
p. cm.
1. Self-realization in women—Fiction. 2. Memory—Fiction. 3. Psychological fiction. I. Title.
PS3619.H676L75 2013
813'.6—dc23
2012026951

ISBN 978-1-4516-8483-4
ISBN 978-1-4516-8485-8 (ebook)

*Love is so short, forgetting is so long.*

Pablo Neruda

S he became aware of a commotion behind her, yet it seemed important to keep scanning, searching for something out over the water, toward low mountains, a skiff of clouds. A bridge in the distance, familiar. And something else, something that shimmered on the periphery of . . . what, the horizon? Her vision? No, her mind. Something she was looking for. Voices called out; the people behind her. Seagulls shrieked from the pier on the right. Just past them, the masts of tall ships creaked slowly back and forth as though they'd been there forever, only she was just now seeing them.

"Hello?" A distinct male voice, closer. She tried to turn to see him, but her legs felt numb. No, they were cold. Ice cold. Dead legs. Was she dead? Where was she? What was this place?

She looked down and saw dark water to her knees. She held high heels in one hand and shouldered a large purse that made her neck ache. Her skirt was wet at the hem.

"Excuse me, are you okay?" Closer still.

"I don't know," she said, turning her head. That she could do, at least.

The man waded toward her from the beach, wearing only a skimpy bathing suit and a black swim cap strapped beneath his chin. She tried to move away from him—who was he? Why was he dressed like that? He was so exposed—his chest, his arms, his midsection—freckled and sun weathered, a thick white scar on his abdomen she didn't want to see. Why was he so naked here with her? And then she noticed a crowd of people dressed similarly standing at the shore, men and women, some in wet suits, others in swimsuits. All with those black caps. All looking at her.

"I can't feel my legs," she admitted.

"I bet," he said. "You've been in here nearly half an hour and the water's only sixty degrees." He stopped a few feet away. He seemed friendly, like someone's brother, maybe. Laugh lines creased his face, but his smile was tentative. "Do you want to come out now?" He looked at her in a way that said she really should, so she nodded.

"What's your name?" he asked.

She opened her mouth to tell him, but didn't know what to say. He waded closer, slowly, carefully, like someone would approach a hurt dog or a crazy person.

"Do you live around here?" he asked. "Or did you come down from the cable car?"

Did he think she was crazy? She wished he would quit asking her questions. It hurt inside, trying to figure out how to answer. Her head throbbed now, or maybe it had all along.

She let him come right up to her and take her by the arm. His hand was warm, and his arm and body, and she realized she was freezing, even though the sun lit everything around them into a sharp, bright world she didn't know.

"Want to try to walk back to the shore?" he asked, gently rotating her until they faced the crowd on the sand, a banner behind them that read Alcatraz Open Water Invitational. They were all going swimming, she guessed. All at once.

"Is she all right?" someone called.

"I think we'd better call 911," he answered.

"Already did," another replied.

"It's only my legs," she said. "They're so cold. I'll just put my shoes back on."

"Okay," he said, slowly walking her toward shore. "Let's keep moving."

She slid her feet like blocks across sandpaper. They hurt now. Everything hurt now. Something was changing inside her, trying to speed up to catch the cog, but there were only broken gears grinding against each other. She wanted to turn back and stay looking across the water, to find what she came for, but the man kept guiding her toward the crowd. Behind them were too many buildings, and behind those, a hill of more buildings.

She looked up and saw letters against the sky. Ghirardelli. Oh, she would love some chocolate.

A tall woman in a black swimsuit waded out and wrapped an arm around her shoulders as the man kept hold of her arm. They were so warm.

"You're going to be okay," the woman said, but she wasn't sure. She heard a siren now, and shuddered.

An ambulance screamed down the pier next to the beach. Red lights, blue lights. Such a horrible loud sound. It hurt almost as much as trying to answer questions. She hated sirens, maybe the most of everything.

Others rushed forward with towels, swaddling her inside them, taking her shoes and bag away from her. People in uniforms pushed through the crowd, insisting she lie on the sand. Yes, that was good. She was exhausted.

"What's your name?" they kept asking while checking her heart, her pulse, putting an oxygen mask on her face. "Where's your ID? What day is it? Do you know where you are? Who's the president of the United States?"

"Obama," she finally murmured into the mask. It was the only answer she had, and as good as it felt to know her president, it was nowhere near enough.

# lucie

t he color orange, the sweet of strawberries. The sound of women's laughter in another room. It was the nurses, but they seemed to be friends, too, and all but one were nice to her.

Butter on bread. Hot showers. The silence of sleep. These were things she knew she liked immediately upon experiencing them. Had she always felt this way, or were these affections new?

The calendar on the dayroom wall said it was July 6, but this she found hard to believe. Clue one: the sky hung heavy and gray on the other side of the windows. She'd checked for latches, for sliders, wanting to let in some air, some normal life. The oxygen here got sucked away by outbursts of shouting, the crying jags that followed, the too-busy spinning of obsessive minds, and the thick, dull breathing of the sedated. But of course, the windows were not the kind that could be opened.

Clue two: none of the magazines on the coffee table were

dated later than April, and some were years old. She rummaged through them, then noticed the address labels, all different and to private residences. Good Samaritans had donated them. Regular hospital waiting rooms surely didn't have to rely on the kindness of others for magazines, but this was a psych ward. The only people waiting here were nuts, and they were waiting to get out. Which was why she would not be disagreeing with the nurses about what month it was, all evidence aside.

She sat thumbing through old news, desperate for distraction as the other patients acted out their various syndromes and maladies. The wandering mumbler with no teeth, the head jerker who stared into space. A guy so young he had pimples, who talked incessantly to no one in particular about God and his demons, one piston leg jumping to a beat no drummer could hear.

After three days of talking with doctors and police officers, it had finally sunk in: she was an amnesiac. She had absolutely no autobiographical memory, not in a general sense (name, rank, social security number) and not in a personal sense (Who am I? Where am I from? What happened to me?). Liking bread and butter held no secrets to her past, just as hot baths and deep sleep didn't. They weren't memories. They were pleasures, pure and simple.

The only parts left of her conscious memory were random chunks of useless information. How did she know, for instance, that the decor in this room was straight out of the early 1990s? The blue upholstery on the chairs was dingy and dull, the white laminate end tables scuffed. They had to be nearly twenty years old, but how did she know that, exactly? She didn't even know her name.

Lucie Walker. That's what her doctor had told her just that morning, coming through on rounds. One of the crackpot callers turned out not to be a crackpot after all, and everyone at San Francisco General now called her Lucie, which was better than the "ma'ams" and "misses" of the past few days. The Walker part was ironic, given that she'd apparently walked away from her life. Her "fiancé," a man from Seattle, had now identified her from a photo shown on the TV news, the announcer having said, "Can you help us find Jane Doe?" Couldn't they come up with something a little more clever than Jane Doe? And she'd been found; she just needed to be claimed.

So now this man from Seattle was coming all the way to San Francisco to retrieve her, like a piece of lost luggage with no ID tag. His name she forgot. Greg? Garrett? Something with a G. She didn't think she knew anyone whose name began with G. Especially not a "fiancé."

And that was the worst part of all of this. She didn't know who she knew, or if she knew anyone at all. She didn't know if anyone loved her or counted on her or might be missing her.

Inside her rib cage, sinew ripped from bone, steel fingers tearing her open. She gasped, an awful, crazy sound, and the incessant talker stopped talking. The mumbler let out a shout. The head jerker said, "Are you all right?"

Lucie dropped her head into her hands. What was happening? She knew this pain, this tearing open of something, but she had no knowledge of where it came from. Who did she miss? Who missed her? How could she not know that?

The man-whose-name-began-with-G had told the shrink he missed her, and even though she didn't remember him—didn't quite believe he was who he said he was, to be honest—she wondered if he was causing the tears. Or could it be her parents, her siblings? Her kids? *No*, Lucie thought. *Please don't let me be someone who abandoned her own children.* Surely the man would have said something to the authorities if she had.

If she was a mother, she was a stylish one. The business suit she'd been wearing was Armani, the handbag Gucci, and the pumps Prada. Her short haircut had odd colors streaked through it: a flaxen white, an unearthly purple-red. The plain brown, she assumed, was hers.

And the makeup! Inside the massive, gaping leather handbag were several smaller bags, the largest containing enough makeup to paint a Las Vegas showgirl. Exactly how did she know about Las Vegas showgirls? Was this part of her history or brain fluff? *Brain fluff, brain fluff*, she thought, willing it to be so.


LUCIE HAD FIRST met Dr. Emma Gladstone (Dr. Emma, she called herself, like a TV personality) at the end of day one in the hospital. The doctor had sat on the edge of Lucie's bed and explained that Lucie had a rare disorder—dissociative fugue. Dissociative. Wasn't that what they called people with multiple personalities? Fugue, in addition to being some kind of amnesia, was a style of music composition, a melody played over and over in many voices. How did she know that? Many voices, multiple personalities. Did this mean something? Clue or random information?

"Here's why we believe we have the correct diagnosis," Dr. Emma said. "You have the classic markers: sudden, purposeful travel for no reason; not remembering details of your personal life; not knowing your identity."

She looked up from her notes. The not-yet-named Lucie glanced away.

"With no evidence of head injury or physical trauma." The doctor paused. "Meaning, we believe it was brought on by some kind of emotional trauma."

Lucie shrugged. The only thing traumatizing was not remembering anything.

Dr. Emma put down the clipboard and sighed. "This is a really serious condition. Most people with it get most or all of their memory back, in time. With work. But a small percentage never do."

"Well, that sucks." The enormity of Lucie's predicament was so vast all she could do was say something as dumb as that and look out the inoperable window. Whatever else Dr. Emma had told her that night filtered through without comprehension. She was transparent, a ghost. No identity. No past. No life.

This morning, the six o'clock sunrise had woken her as it had each morning at the hospital, and once the noises entered her consciousness—the banging of breakfast carts, the chorus of toilets flushing, the too loud voices of patients and nurses alike—she could no longer sleep. Dr. Emma appeared not long after, hooded sweatshirt beneath her white doctor's coat (*clue three,* Lucie thought, feeling stubborn about the whole "July" thing), large pink sunglasses parked on her head. Dimpled, rosy, fresh as a buttercup, probably just out of med school.

"You really have to be at work this early?" Lucie asked from her bed, groggy, out of sorts. She sat up and eased her legs around so that she was sitting at the edge of the bed, blanket wrapped around her waist.

"I've been on for hours," Dr. Emma said, reaching for her buzzing phone, punching a button, then dropping it back in her white coat pocket. "I have wonderful news for you."

Lucie tried to swallow, to breathe, as she learned that she did indeed have an identity, a name, and a home. Not to mention a fiancé. She nodded and attempted a smile. She knew she should feel happy at this news, overjoyed, in fact, but her heart knocked out of rhythm, once, twice.

"When's he coming?" she asked.

"He wasn't quite sure what flight he'd get on, but he was hoping to be here by noon or so. You might even be able to have lunch together."

"And have we determined he's legitimate?" she asked, hoping for a small portal of uncertainty to escape through.

"He scanned and e-mailed your birth certificate and pictures of you two together. Your wedding invitation. He got the DMV to send us your info. We've run a police background check on him to make sure he's who he says he is, and he checks out. I mean, I suppose you could have a twin out there who's also gone missing, but . . ."

The doctor smiled and leaned her head to the side. "What's up?" she asked. She didn't speak the way Lucie would have thought a psychiatrist would. She should be more formal. She should ask, "How are you feeling?" or "Does this make you uncomfortable?" But she just said, "What's up?" and all of the terror and confusion Lucie had been stifling volcanoed to the surface.

"What if I'm not who he thinks I am?" Lucie heard the anguish in her voice and was surprised. Where did that come from? Why was she so emotional? She was a blank slip of paper, but she was acting the way a person with a past, present, and an identity would. It was as if she were watching from outside her body, feeling someone else's pain as gut wrenchingly as if it were her own.

But it was. Clue one.

"After the two of you have had a chance to reconnect," Dr. Emma said, "we'll see how you're feeling. Then we'll need to sit down and talk—you, me, your fiancé—about your next steps." After a shoulder squeeze and an encouraging smile, she left to continue her rounds.

Next steps. They assumed she'd be leaving; she must not be too crazy.

Lucie sighed, then stood and walked into the small bathroom. She'd been avoiding the mirror since she arrived. It was too disconcerting to stand in front of it and see a stranger staring back. Now, however, now she was actually someone. She needed to know the gory details. She turned on the light, stepped forward, and gripped the cool porcelain.

The hair was still alarming, but hair grew. She reached to touch the lines across her forehead. They were permanently etched. Lucie was glad she wasn't a person who had succumbed to Botox. (Okay, she knew about Botox! That had to be a good sign.) She wasn't young and she wasn't old. She was somewhere in the middle.

Her features were acceptable, if plain: high, arching brows; a long, straight nose; freckles. A wide mouth, generous lips but crooked teeth—a picket fence knocked askew. She shook her head and stepped back, pulling off her gown to look down at her body. A few more freckles on her chest and arms, small breasts, a mole near her navel, a pinkish brown mark on her right thigh that reminded her of crop circles. That was enough for now. She quickly showered, pulled the gown back on, and returned to her bedside to ring the call button. The nice Filipino nurse from the night before was no longer on duty; the surly nurse of the day shift was back.

"Yes?" the mean nurse said from the doorway, as if stepping inside would admit defeat. It seemed to Lucie that the woman would be better suited to driving trucks.

"I need my clothes today," Lucie said. "This morning, actually." They'd taken her filthy suit and blouse and all her undergarments to launder them. All she had left were the scuffed pumps and bag.

"They're in your closet." Annoyed, the nurse shook her head and turned away, calling over her shoulder, "Have been since yesterday."

"No one told me," Lucie said, not loud enough for the nurse to hear. They must have returned them while she slept. She walked to the clothes cupboard, took out the plastic-covered clothing, and laid it on the bed.

The suit was structured unusually, cut in hard angles. An

ecru kind of white, but they'd gotten all the stains out. She undressed and pulled on each piece of clothing she'd removed
upon arriving at the hospital: the ivory silk bikinis, the body
shaper–slip with built-in bra. Her body didn't have any fat on
it; she wasn't sure why she needed the shaper, but Lucie had
to wear something beneath the blouse, which was as thin as
onionskin.

Then she attempted the makeup, but didn't get very far before stuffing it all back in its bag.

And now it was almost one o'clock, and no fiancé. Lucie
drew a deep breath and released it. Yes, he was flying all the
way from Seattle. No, he couldn't be held responsible for flight
schedules and taxi availability and San Francisco traffic. Was
this impatience part of her personality or just nerves? *Nerves,*
she decided. After all, she was blank. Maybe she could now
choose any personality traits she wanted to. She picked up another magazine and tried to relax.

*National Geographic,* November 2006, older than the
*Newsweek*s and *InStyle*s she'd been thumbing through, information dispersing as quickly as she took it in. What good did it
do her to know that Congress had rejected the latest eco-jobs
bill or that chunky heels were back in fashion, if it was all old
news? Did she care about things like this, anyway, she as in
"she"? Clothes? What Congress was up to?

It was the cover of the *National Geographic* that attracted
her. "Lucy's Offspring Found!" it proclaimed, and she felt a stab
of panic again, shame at the thought that she might have left
behind her own offspring, even though no one had mentioned
she had any. She couldn't shake the fear that she was some kind

of horrible human being. What if this man from Seattle knew that about her? If he was who he said he was, he would know all kinds of things about her, and he could use them against her without her even knowing if they were true. And then she had another thought: What if he was some kind of pervert, or abusive, and she wouldn't remember that, and then—

*Jesus,* she thought, heart pounding. *I have to get a grip.* They'd checked him out. They did this sort of thing all of the time, right? Released crazy people to family members? To fiancés? She had to trust someone, she decided, because she could no longer trust herself.

Lucie settled back to read the story about her namesake—a pile of bones that lived over three million years before in Ethiopia. Something fluttered inside her as she read. She remembered this story. She remembered that the small ape-like human had been called "The Mother of Man," had been the first ape discovered that walked on two feet, and that in those days, the 1970s, a surprising number of people had been upset to think they might have been descended from an African, much less an ape.

Lucie must have been a child when she first read about her, perhaps in school. Had it been just the name that intrigued her, knowing she shared it with the first woman found on earth? And now that they'd found the little hominid's descendants, Lucie felt a wave of unexpected emotion. Lucy the ape was indeed a mother; Lucie the woman did indeed have roots, primal ones anyway. She blinked her eyes, swallowed salt.

This was not just a clue. It was real pain at thinking about family she'd left behind.

The double doors at the end of the hall opened, and Lucie looked up. A couple walked onto the ward, looking nervous about the Careful: AWOL Risk signs. She relaxed. Not her fiancé. At least she didn't think the man was. He carried a video camera, and the woman had a workbag strapped around her shoulders and wore a suit not unlike Lucie's. They strode busily to the nurses' station, talked with the nurse behind the desk, who shook her head and pointed toward the door. A quiet disagreement ensued, and the supervising nurse appeared, joining in the heated discussion, all in sotto voce tones. They kept looking at Lucie.

"What?" she finally called across the room, exasperated, and again, the incessant talker shushed. The head jerker, this time, remained silent, as if he, too, wondered what was going on.

Wait. *Sotto voce.* How did she know about that? It was a musical term, wasn't it?

The nurse walked out from behind the desk toward Lucie, the man and woman at her heels.

"These people are from the TV station that ran your photo," the nurse explained. "Somehow"—here she glared at the two people—"they got someone to let them in. They know about your fiancé coming today and are requesting an interview. We're about to kick them out of here, but if you want to talk to them, you can, as long as it's off hospital grounds. Or you can say no."

The woman ignored her and turned to Lucie, smiling in a too eager way, extending her hand.

"Ann Howe, Bay News Eight. And this is my cameraman."

Lucie didn't shake her hand. Was this all just a big hoax,

like the crackpot calls that came in after the TV newscast? She'd overheard the nurses talking about it; they didn't seem to realize how their voices carried along the tile corridors.

They'd gossiped about all of the things Lucie had supposedly been up to during her time in the city. People had reported seeing her riding the bus and eating in a diner. Picking fruit from trees on Russian Hill. Giving money to panhandlers near Fisherman's Wharf. But worse were the weirdos who claimed Lucie was the female Antichrist, a yuppie Cassandra, a murderer's daughter.

Was the fiancé just someone's sick idea of a joke, and now they were going to spring it on her for one of those cruel TV shows? She backed away from the woman, trying to escape.

The reporter looked excited. "We were so happy to be instrumental in helping your fiancé find you, and our viewers have taken a special interest in your story. Has Mr. Goodall arrived? The traffic on 101 was a nightmare, so we're running a little—"

The nurse moved in front of the woman, arms up as if to shield Lucie, and the ward door opened once more.

A man entered alone. He was tall and lean with a mess of black hair, tanbark skin, the broad cheekbones of someone descended from Native people. He appeared to have dressed in a hurry, or without thinking: baggy cargo shorts hanging from his hips, a wrinkled white business shirt misbuttoned. He ignored everyone else and looked only at Lucie, and though she didn't know his face, she felt a shift inside at the sight of him—an easing up, a sense of relaxation for the first time in three days. He saw her, really saw her. He strode quickly to her side.

"Roll, roll, roll," the woman murmured to the cameraman. "My god, are you getting this? It's incredible."

The nurse ran to the desk and picked up a phone. "Security on eleven, please. Security on eleven." Her voice echoed from overhead.

The dark-haired man was oblivious to the commotion, to everything but Lucie. His face twisted in emotion, his hands reached out as he arrived in front of her. She flinched, she must have, because he pulled back and wrapped his arms around his torso, saying, "Oh, Luce, oh god. I'm . . . I'm sorry." Tears filled his eyes. It was extraordinary, she thought, and it made her own eyes well.

Lucie looked into his face. She saw intelligence there, tenderness in the expression lines and subtle creases at the corners of his mouth. She knew he wanted to comfort her, but he seemed to be the one who'd been hurt.

"It's okay," she said, more to make him stop crying than because it was. "Am I really . . . her? Me?"

"Lucie, of course it's you." He looked at her in disbelief. "God. Jesus. How can I . . . ?"

She didn't know him at all, and yet, there was something that told her she did. "It's okay," she said again and reached out to embrace him, to let him embrace her. They stood together as if connected; their arms knew where to go, their bodies how to shift to accommodate the other. His cheek rested against her hair. Her head knew where to nest along his smooth neck; she inhaled and knew his scent. Lucie marveled at this, that their physical selves seemed to know each other so well, even though her mind was still trying to find clues to make it all fit.

Two security guards busted through the doors as if in a barroom scene of a Western, moving immediately to the cameraman and blocking his lens. The news reporter argued, the nurse yelled over her, and the man wept silently into Lucie's ridiculous hair. He was real. He knew her. He loved her. And he was the only one who could help her figure out who she was.

"*Shhh,*" she whispered, stroking his back, letting her hands traverse the hills and valleys that were his shoulder blades and ribs and vertebrae. As if by instinct, the fingertips of her right hand fit themselves into a deep notch formed by the muscles just above the waistband of his shorts. Outside, while she hadn't been looking, the fog had rolled back, leaving the sun to burn the city white as ash.

"*Shhh,*" she said again.

# grady

"What's your name again?" she asked, her voice familiar and soothing against his ear. He'd just stopped crying, finally, but at that he lost it again. Lucie really didn't know who he was.

"Uh, Grady," he said, wondering if he should quit hugging her and shake her hand instead. Shake her shoulders, yell, "Lucie, wake up! It's me!"

But he just said, "Goodall, Grady Goodall," and stepped back.

She looked at him the same way she had five years before, when they first met at the aerospace job fair: that curious look women have when a man has been staring at them too long. And he had been staring at her that day, although nothing about her had been very descript until he got up close, and then everything was: the way light glowed from beneath her skin, the sea glass green of her eyes. She was taller than most women, slim and elegant. He hadn't thought of another woman since, even when things were difficult between them. Lucie wasn't the easiest person to love, but Grady had a feeling he wasn't, either.

"How old am I?" she asked now, her fingers drifting to her forehead. She was the same, so much the same, even without her hair fixed or her makeup on, her freckles exposed. She'd lost weight; her clothes were no longer formfitting, but still. She looked like herself, only she wasn't.

"Your birthday's in two months. September fourth." *Oh, man,* he thought. How would she take this? For the past five years, she'd been increasingly freaked out about turning forty. "We're having a big party, because, well . . ."

Lucie leaned her head at him in a way he'd never seen before. She was curious, that's all, curious why he'd paused.

"Because it's your fortieth," he continued, "and, well, because that's our wedding day." They'd scheduled a happy event to counteract the dreaded birthday, though it hadn't worked out that way. That's why she'd run, as far as he knew—to avoid the whole thing. To put as much distance between the two of them as she could. It was the only reason that made sense to him.

Lucie's brows rose. "Oh," she said.

She was surprised, but he couldn't tell if this made her happy or angry, if she thought it was a good thing or a bad one. Here he'd spent five years trying to learn her every expression and squint and lip tightening, so he'd know how to react, how to please, how to love her best, and he could no longer even pretend to read her face. Dissociative fugue was what she had, according to the doctor on the phone, a serious disorder brought on by emotional trauma, but this Lucie seemed far less emotionally traumatized than he'd ever seen her.

A woman and man were being hustled out of the ward by

uniformed guards. Grady had never been on a psych ward, but he'd expected this kind of thing. The woman yelled, "Grady! Tell your friends and family how it feels to have found Lucie safe and unharmed!"

"What?" he asked, looking from the reporter to Lucie as it dawned on him. How the hell had they found out he'd be here? But it figured. The media had latched on to his story like big fat ticks, like the bloodsucking vampires they were.

Lucie turned toward the reporter. "This is private. Please, leave us alone." There was none of the old Lucie ire in her voice, but it was a forceful enough statement. The two disappeared through the door, and Grady wished he'd been able to be that effective with reporters for the past week.

The nurses turned away, shaking their heads, clearing the other patients out of the room. Then they, too, found other places to be.

Finally, he was alone with Lucie for what felt like the first time.

She walked to a chair with an open magazine lying on it, picked it up, and sat down, indicating for him to sit as well. Should he sit next to her? Across from her? No, that was too far for private conversation. He chose the chair at a ninety-degree angle.

"Anything interesting in there?" he asked, nodding at the magazine, trying to contain his legs so that his toe didn't touch her foot, or his knee bump her knee. It was an old *National Geographic*, definitely not her kind of magazine. Lucie loved design, loved fashion and highbrow stuff. What she was doing with him, he'd never known.

"Yes," she said, but didn't explain. "May I ask you questions?"

"Yeah. Yes. Of course." His voice rose and sank; his fingers flexed and released. He was missing his swim; it was the hour he always swam. He longed for the cool blue void, embracing him in the silent way that calmed him. Water had been his place for as long as he could remember, a quiet escape from the loud family of women he loved but would never understand. Growing up, he'd spent most of his free time swimming in the community pool and, in summer, swimming in the bone-numbing waters of the Puget Sound. In high school he'd been on the swim team, and he went to the University of Washington on a partial swimming scholarship. For the past week—when he wasn't out looking for Lucie, or making phone calls, or tacking up flyers—he'd submerged himself in the lap pool at the gym, staying under as long as he could, coming up only when his lungs screamed for air.

"How long have I been gone?" she asked.

A lifetime, he could have said. An eternity. "Eight days, almost nine," he answered, like it was a casual thing. *Eight days, twenty-two hours, and sixteen minutes,* he didn't say.

She startled, her cheeks flushing. "Really? But I only got here three days ago." Her brows pinched together and down, a more familiar look: Lucie dismayed. "This is all so . . ." She closed her eyes, and when she opened them, they were filled with tears. The old Lucie didn't cry. "I'm sorry," she said. "This is all just happening so fast, and I have no idea where I've been, or . . ." She drew a breath. "Do you know why I came to San Francisco? Why I was in the water?"

He shook his head; if only he did. He put his hands over his heart. "You've been right here," he said, feeling idiotic and corny, but it was true and the words were coming out before he could reel them back. It was as if some inner version of him had woken to soothe this seemingly gentle and sad person. "You've been here with me the whole time, Luce. I swear."

She looked at him the way a dog might look at its owner: with caring and curiosity, but also with the detachment of another species. "This has been hard for you," she said. "My being gone."

But not hard for her, he realized. Her pain now came from not knowing herself. As far as their relationship went, she'd been wiped clean, no sorrows or regrets or pain or even anger anymore. He was almost jealous.

Embarrassed, he pulled out the photos he'd brought. The doctor had said they might help her remember. "They said I should bring these. There's a few of you and me at a fund-raiser we went to for your work . . ."

She took them, and he noticed she wasn't wearing her ring, the full-carat number that was so expensive she'd offered to go in on it with him. She hadn't parted from it since she opened the little blue box the previous Valentine's Day, but now it seemed to be gone, unless the hospital had it in safekeeping.

She was going through the pictures too fast. She'd loved the photos of them all dressed up at that big gala, and now she just shuffled them to the back without really looking.

"And that's you with all my family, and then one with just my mom, and, uh, yeah, that's my niece . . ."

"Are you—is your family Native American? Or . . ."

She knew this, he thought, then shook his head. She didn't.

"My dad was from the Puyallup tribe. My mom's Irish. The rest of us are mutts." He attempted a smile.

She looked up. "Where's my family?"

He hadn't thought this through. Of course she'd ask that. He drew a breath.

"Your parents died when you were fifteen." He had to tell her. She needed to know.

She flinched, but didn't ask for details. "How about other relatives? I must have some—"

"Your aunt. She raised you after that, but you don't like her and you're not in touch anymore. I've never met her." He knew nothing about her past, really. These were the only things she'd ever divulged about her childhood.

"Oh," she said, swallowing, then straightened the photos into a neat pile. "I have to ask you something more personal."

Like none of this had been. "Yeah, sure," he said. "Shoot."

She leaned her head at him again in that new way. "Do I have a birthmark?"

His eyes went hot again. "The top of your right thigh. Three dots in a row." Three scars, Grady knew, pink and raised, each the size of a cigarette tip. "It's not a birthmark, but you won't talk about it. You get mad when I ask, actually, so I quit trying."

"Oh," she said, her eyes widening, then "oh" again, but she kept asking questions.

Lucie didn't seem nearly as disoriented as Grady felt, talking about her as if she were some other person. Of course she wanted to know everything that had happened the day she went missing. He told her, as best he could, leaving out a few parts. He wasn't proud of that, but she'd returned to him in a way that suggested a new beginning, even though it might all go wrong again. For now, though, he could hope.


THE DAY SHE disappeared should have been a happy one for them. Lucie was going downtown to have her first fitting at Lana Tang's, the designer she'd always dreamed would make her wedding dress.

Now, Grady considered how much he should tell her about the fight they'd had. He'd been stupid and gone out drinking after work the night before with a couple of Boeing underlings, had too much, and come home late and fallen asleep on the couch. When he woke she was staring at him, angry.

"Do you want out of this thing or what?" She meant the wedding. She meant being with her. The worst part was she was right; that's what he was thinking. They'd been fighting almost constantly as Lucie freaked out over every wedding detail, and he'd seriously wondered if they should just call the whole thing off. Hence the drinking. Hence the sleeping on the couch. But he decided not to tell her that now, not here, when they'd just been reunited and she looked so fragile and tired.

Instead he said, "We were stressed out about the wedding, and everything else, and we got into an argument before you left." It was a form of the truth, an extreme minimization of the events. He couldn't risk losing her again—his time alone without her had set in concrete his desire to be with her, to love and honor and cherish no matter what, and all of this had been a pretty damn big what. Absence hadn't just made his heart grow fonder; it had made him realize that every good thing in his life had happened because of Lucie—he'd become more of a man with her in the past five years than in all the thirty-seven years before he met her.

In spite of her faults, her sharp tongue and impatience with him, he knew the soft Lucie beneath, too, the Lucie who'd somehow been so damaged in childhood she couldn't even talk about it. That was the Lucie he'd always loved and wanted to make happy, and he wondered if maybe that was the Lucie who'd emerged from the harder shell of the old one. Grady had always been an honest man, honest to a fault, but he'd never been given such a free pass at a second chance. He wouldn't lie. He'd just be selective about which parts he told her, and not only in his favor. Hell, no. Lucie had gone berserk before she left.

"So, we had a fight, and you left early for your appointment. I should have made you stay, Luce, that's what I should have done, until we worked it out." Saying it, he realized it was true. He should have. "But you left so fast, and I wasn't thinking. I was mad."

"What day was it?"

She cared only about facts, it seemed, but it was a relief.

"Tuesday."

"I mean the date."

"June twenty-eighth." Grady still felt sick at those words. "Tuesday, June twenty-eighth."

"Did I make it to the appointment?" Lucie asked. "With the dressmaker?"

Grady shook his head. "Her assistant called about an hour later to ask if you were still coming. That's when I knew something was wrong. You love that designer, man. You drive by her store downtown just to look in the window and see what's new, and you slow way down"—here he couldn't help smiling—"and the other cars get all pissed off and honk, but my Lucie, she doesn't care, she just—"

"What's the designer's name again?" she asked, and Grady felt his shoulders slump.

"Lana Tang."

"Oh. Right." She stared at a spot in the carpet, then looked up. "I'm really into all that stuff, huh? Like this?" She plucked at her suit jacket.

He shrugged. "Yeah. You like nice things."

"Like what else?"

He shifted in the chair. The seat cushions were thin, and the chair too small, and the space between him and Lucie too close not to touch, but he kept his legs tight against the chair frame.

"I don't know. You just love shopping. You always say it's cheaper than a psychiatrist." *Shit*. Why had he said that?

She grimaced but continued. "So, then what happened? When you heard I hadn't gone to the dress shop?"

*Dress shop.* It was something his mother would say.

"I got in my car and drove the route I thought you would have. I should've called the police right away, but I thought maybe you'd broken down or something, had a flat tire."

She nodded. "That would make sense."

He sighed. He'd known she'd left him. He did drive around looking for her, leaving text and voice messages on her cell phone, knowing it was futile, but he couldn't think of anything else to do. You don't call the police because your girlfriend leaves you, when you've been a complete asshole and deserve every ounce of her fury. It wasn't until they found her car that he realized something even worse had happened.

"And then the police called. Your car was abandoned in a loading zone, unlocked, and your wallet was on the passenger seat, but it had been stripped." He knew she'd withdrawn six hundred dollars for the designer. Her credit cards were over-extended; they always were, but Grady didn't mention that.

Lucie gasped. "I was robbed? Abducted? I keep thinking something like that must have happened, that maybe I was hit over the head or something, or . . ." Her voice faded. They both knew she had no injuries, no physical trauma of any kind. She'd had every kind of exam and test available, it seemed, to check her brain, her internal organs. *Her heart and her head,* Grady thought. Uninjured but not unaltered.

He continued. "Well, that's what we thought happened, too, at first. The weird thing was that they found the car by the train station. Not the designer's."

Though Grady had wondered if she'd boarded a train to somewhere, it just seemed too illogical. Why take a train when you have a perfectly good car? It made no sense, but nothing that had happened did. So while both dreading and waiting for whatever horrible news was to come (*Had she been kidnapped? Was she injured? Jesus Christ . . . alive?*) he scoured the train schedules and tables to keep the uglier thoughts at bay. He tried to remember if she'd ever talked about taking a trip any-where, but they'd only discussed going to Hawaii that winter for their honeymoon. Did she have friends elsewhere, in other cities? Not that he knew of. The only relative she had was her aunt, who lived up near Everett, and Lucie had never expressed desire to see her again. Just the opposite, in fact.

After five long days, the police finally tracked her through Amtrak records to Sacramento. Why had it taken them so long, he demanded, but got no satisfying answers. Although they didn't say it, he knew they thought she was just trying to get the hell away from him. Their interest in the case waned. There was no other suspicious activity. Her credit cards had not been used, by her or anyone. Grady hadn't canceled them, just in case she needed them, but he'd kept a close eye on their activity. Nothing. Her driver's license was discovered the next day in the lost and found at Seattle's King Street Station. She'd only needed it to purchase the ticket, not to board the train.

Grady immediately called the Sacramento Police Department to report that his missing fiancée might be there, just in case the Seattle authorities hadn't. The next available flight to Sacramento wasn't until the following day—should he drive? Take the (*dear god*) train? And then what? Wander the city, calling "Lucie, Lucie," as if he were looking for a lost dog? *Fuck,* he thought. *What the fuck am I supposed to do?*

He was beginning to wonder if maybe she *had* just run away to start a new life, and so he did what he always did when life felt beyond hopeless: he called Dory, his youngest and most understanding sister. Should he let Lucie go or keep looking for her? he asked her on the phone, but thank god, Dory said, "*Kahkwa pelton,*" the old Chinook phrase their father had used when he thought they were being too silly or stupid. Very little of his language had stuck with his offspring, but this expression resounded often at family gatherings.

"Of course you have to keep looking for her," Dory said. "I'll go to Sacramento with you. We'll get on the news there, so people know to be looking for her," she said, even though he knew she couldn't get the time off at work. "We'll find her, Grady, we will."

And he'd booked the tickets for the next day, and printed hundreds more flyers to post in Sacramento. Just two hours before they were scheduled to leave, the Seattle detective called Grady with news of a woman who'd been found in the San Francisco Bay.

At first Grady thought the woman had drowned, hearing that, and had grim visions of having to visit a morgue to identify the remains. But of course, the woman had only been knee-deep. Grady didn't believe it could be Lucie. She'd never do that. Not his Lucie, who was always in such control of, well, everything. And then he clicked the link to the Bay News 8 story and saw the green-tinged police photo that was Lucie but not Lucie: disheveled, dirty, scared. He grieved almost as deeply as if she had drowned, seeing her that way, frightened and alone. It had taken an interminable day and a half to convince the authorities that he was her fiancé.

"Do you remember being on the train?" he asked her now.

Lucie looked at her lap and shook her head.

Surely she'd taken the bus from Sacramento to San Francisco. She'd done a lot of things after leaving their house, and it seemed impossible she couldn't remember any of it, but Grady needed to believe her.

Her hands fidgeted, picking at the edges of the suit jacket sleeves. For the first time, he noticed broken fingernails, the raw skin of her palms. He tried to imagine what she'd had to do to survive and couldn't let himself. All Grady knew was that he needed to take her home, to draw a hot bath, the way she liked it, with bath salts and almond oil. To feed her soup. To hold her and whisper to her that she would always be safe with him, always, from now on.

"Can you come back tomorrow?" She looked up. "Maybe we could talk more then."

Her upper lip had beaded with sweat. She stood.

"Oh." Grady stood, too. "I thought you'd want to get out of here. Go home." He had to stop himself from taking her arm and steering her out of that place into fresh air, away from the other patients, who were disturbed and maybe even violent, but she shook her head.

"I just need a little . . . time."

"Oh," he said. "Okay. So, tomorrow. Maybe nine, ten in the morning?" Lucie was an insomniac, usually falling asleep in the predawn hours.

"Make it seven," she said. "I can't sleep once the sun's up. It's too weird." She leaned close to whisper, "The people in here are all crazy."

He closed his eyes at the smell of her skin. It was her smell, her skin, her voice, and he reveled in it. In so many ways, she was still his Lucie.

He opened his eyes. He was alone.

# helen

the children shouted and ran about the room, more boisterous than usual this afternoon, and Helen knew her days working with them were numbered. She no longer had the strength or stamina to chase down the troublemakers, or lift a crying child out of the fray. It used to be it was the boys who were unruly, but these days the girls were just as wild.

The Tulalip Boys and Girls Club relied on volunteers like Helen: retired schoolteachers and professionals, many who'd fled the city for tall trees and blue water in the smaller towns of northwestern Washington. Helen had lived near the Tulalip Reservation most of her adult life, however, settling there with her late husband, Edward Ten Hands, nearly forty years before. She'd miscarried five times, then stopped trying, her sister telling her it wasn't such a bad thing to be a favorite aunt instead. With no children to raise, Helen got her teaching certification, like a booby prize, and taught kindergarten through second grade at Tulalip Elementary for nearly thirty years.

Now she hadn't taught in fifteen years, and cashiered at the casino part-time to supplement her pension, but she still enjoyed spending afternoons with the five- to eight-year-olds at the Boys and Girls Club. She could not stomach the adolescents. They were not the most grateful of creatures, not like the little ones, who wanted to hug and kiss you just for reading them a story, who called you "Miss Helen" with a certain reverence, and were not yet aware of the concept of disdain.

"Oh," Helen muttered, feeling the twist inside, the place that had gripped and ached over all the years of wanting her girl back. She should have known better than to call that hospital. Why had she even tried, just to be shunned again? And yet she knew she would keep trying. She owed her sister as much, and blood was blood. She could no more stop loving her niece than she could stop the decay of her decrepit body, even though both had betrayed her.

The old woman inhaled into her chest, coughed at the constriction, then clapped a cha-cha-cha rhythm—one, two, one-two-three. Magically, the children stopped and quieted and turned toward her with upturned faces, dutifully clapping their hands in a rhythmic answer: "We are list-en-ing."

"Thank you, boys and girls," she said, smiling at their obedience. "Now, everyone find a place to sit on the rug for story time. Raelene Coy, would you like to be my story helper today?"

The little girl nodded. Every year, it seemed, there was one girl Helen fell breathlessly in mother-love with, yet she kept her distance. Today was the first time she'd asked Raelene to be story helper. She didn't want the girl to feel uncomfortable or singled out. Helen kept her feelings to herself, having learned the skill from her late husband all those years ago, when Lucie left them. Now the old woman was content simply to feel the welling of emotion at the sight of such curious eyes, such dimpled cheeks and unguarded affection.

"Come on, then," she said, taking her seat on the stool at the front of the group. "Stand here beside me and you can show everyone the pictures."

Young Raelene stood close beside her, so close Helen could feel the heat radiating from the little girl's body.

The old woman pulled a tissue from between her bosoms, hand shaking, and daubed at her dry lips before beginning to read.

# grady

When the taxi had dropped Grady outside of San Francisco General earlier, he'd hesitated. The building loomed large and ugly, hard white concrete, with people outside in wheelchairs and on crutches and in various states of distress. He'd had to retreat across the driveway to a grassy garden area, trying to breathe, looking out past the finer, old brick buildings that encircled the newer, ugly one, past the old iron gates below, to the hills that rose in the distance, the sunlight bleaching the city to dirty white. He'd yearned for Seattle's green.

It had taken him twenty minutes to gather the courage to turn around and walk in through the automatic glass doors, through the shiny white halls, to search the directory because he'd forgotten to bring the notes he took at home, and press the elevator button for the floor that housed only psychiatric patients. His Lucie. He'd started crying before he even saw her.

Now, back outside, Grady had no idea what to do, where to

go. He walked through the garden again, down a long bank of steps toward the gate. On the other side was a grimy boulevard, choked with traffic, noisy with the day.

He'd expected to fly home later that day with Lucie. He'd bought tickets for both of them on the 4:10 Alaska Air flight. He hadn't brought luggage, a toothbrush, anything. What was he supposed to do now?

*Swim,* he thought. If only he could swim. He would find a hotel with a pool.

With no cabs in sight, Grady turned north, toward what looked like a promising clutch of buildings on the horizon. There had to be hotels near the hospital for out-of-town family. A walk would help clear his head.

The medical complex sprawled to the right, ornate brick buildings offset by dirty parking lots and an occasional small garden. The sun beat on Grady's head; already, he'd sweated through his shirt. He passed an unkempt man urinating on the street, in full view of traffic, splashing the bumper of a parked car. And all he could think about was Lucie, locked in a place she didn't belong.

Only she wasn't a prisoner. The doctor had said she could be discharged when he got there. Patients apparently went AWOL all the time, if you believed the warning signs. And Lucie chose to stay.

The hospital buildings gave way to run-down storefronts, each seedier than the last. After about a mile of sun bearing down on him, Grady crossed under a noisy freeway, the shade a relief but the sound deafening. Here the streets angled off, and he turned up Ninth, curious about a small building painted solid blue. Studs, the sign read. It took him a moment to comprehend, but then he noticed the presence of rainbow flags and banners in the storefronts, on the lamp posts, the vintage clothing shop with studded leather–clad mannequins in the windows. He almost turned back, but a block ahead he spotted it: a motel marquee that read Free Cable, Pool. The final *l* tilted precipitously, as if it might fall, just the way Grady was feeling. Rather than search any further or try to find a taxi, he walked toward it. It was most important to be as close to Lucie as possible.

Across the crumbled asphalt parking lot, he caught sight of a sliver of aqua. It was a small pool but looked clean. It would do. It would more than do.

He stepped inside the office to check in, immediately overwhelmed by the competing smells of mildew and unchecked body odor.

A squat blob of man sat behind the counter, thin hair pomaded over dull scalp. The glass door eased shut behind Grady, but the man didn't stop reading what looked to be a cheap detective novel. Grady cleared his throat. The body odor was now almost unbearable.

"Hello?" Grady tried. "Do you have any rooms available for tonight? Just one night?"

Without looking up, the man said, "Credit card," then took Grady's card, ran it through his machine, and pushed the card and receipt toward Grady to sign. Grady could now see he was reading not a detective novel but an ancient copy of *The Stranger* by Camus, a book Grady had tried to get through in college but found confusing and bleak, yet it still sat in a box with his college textbooks in the basement. Why had he never thrown them out? He shook his head. His opinion of the clerk had been wrong, just as his assessment of Lucie had been. Before June twenty-eighth, he'd never have guessed she'd leave him, first physically, and now in every other way imaginable.

Grady signed the receipt, pushed it back, then took the key the clerk slid to replace it. The man hadn't once looked up. He could be renting a room to anyone, Grady thought, then realized that might be the point.

The moldy smell was also present inside his room, coming from an air-conditioning unit spitting tepid moisture. Grady switched it off and slid open the window, then sat on the bed. Traffic noise bleated from outside; an airplane droned overhead. The mattress gave about as much as a department store display bed would, as if bolstered by cardboard and stuffed with newspapers. Grady sighed. This was not how he'd thought this day would go.

He jumped from the bed, electricity zinging through his left glute. "What the—" he said, then realized it was his cell phone. He pulled it from his back pocket. Yet another text from yet another sister; they'd been leaving messages and texting all morning: "Is it really her? Is she okay? Does she remember you?" They'd been so distraught about Lucie, but strong and capable, organizing search efforts and coming into Seattle to help, always with their positive outlooks and upbeat pep talks. He'd wished they'd stay away and let him be alone in the punishing silence so he could feel the heaviness of what he'd done, but his sisters never wanted him to feel anything less than chipper.

He would call Dory, his favorite, first. At the sound of her voice mail, he relaxed. He could leave her a message, and she would relay it up the Goodall chain, from youngest sister to oldest: Dory to Renie to Nan to Izzy to Floss to Eunie. Eunie would call their mother, who would in turn call him at some point, but at least he could cut out all the middle women in the process.

"Hey, Dor," he said. "It's her. I mean, I knew it was, but you know. Until I saw her . . . Anyway, she's fine. Well, she definitely seems to have amnesia, but she's kind of . . . okay. In a weird way. I mean, she's not stressed out or anything. Can you imagine? Luce not stressed? Anyway, other than being a little too thin, she's doing fine, no major injuries or anything. So, could you let everyone know? I just want to concentrate on getting Lucie ready to come home. Okay? Love you. Love to the rest."

Grady clicked off the phone and sat staring at the wall, then checked his watch. It wasn't even two thirty.

If he'd known Lucie would make him wait, he'd have brought his laptop so he could work, but he'd scrambled as quickly as he could to get the flights arranged and to Sea-Tac on time. What he wished he had more than his computer, though, more than a toothbrush, was a swimsuit. He stood and slipped the room key into his pocket, then stepped outside. The parking lot was empty. It was past checkout time and before check-in. He walked to the pool and breathed in: car exhaust and chlorine. A gaggle of rusted lounge chairs lazed along the far edge of the pool.

After having woken to cool drizzle in Seattle, Grady felt

suffocated by the unusual heat in San Francisco. His skin tingled with the anticipation of water, of blue nothing. The nervous excitement that always preceded a swim surfaced like seltzer through his pores. He looked around, then quickly undressed, toeing off each shoe, tossing his shirt and shorts onto a chair. He left on his underwear, of course; if anyone saw him from afar, they'd think he was wearing bike shorts.

Positioning his toes at the edge of the pool, Grady windmilled his left arm, then his right, then both. He drew a deep breath, shaking his hands briskly. His pre-swim rituals calmed him almost as much as the swim itself. He'd normally have adjusted his goggles just before diving in, but of course they were in his gym bag at home with his suit. He'd have to swim blind.

One more deep breath and he rose slightly off his heels, then dove in, focusing on a tight streamline that would take him to the other end of the pool without a stroke. The underwear slipped only a tad; he tugged them into place as he dolphin-kicked his way toward the bottom of the pool.

The sudden inundation of water, the dulling of sound: these things moved Grady from uncertainty to knowing, from awkward to graceful. He slit open his right eye and saw the concrete wall. Keeping his arms at his sides, he threw his heels over in a flip turn, then counted his strokes to the other side of the small pool. He stretched his right arm as far forward as possible, rotating onto his side. Reach and pull, right then left; after just seven strokes he'd arrived at the other end. He pulled his arms to his sides and accelerated his kick, making another flip turn, pushing from the wall to glide back in the opposite direction, eyes closed now, counting strokes, looking up only as he knew the wall was approaching. It was a sixth sense, knowing just where the wall was, just when to execute each turn.

As a kid, he'd wished he could be some kind of amphibian boy, not a mammal, who required air for oxygen. The real world was filled with noise and too many sisters, a mother who was too busy raising her huge brood to pay enough attention to a quiet, sad boy. He'd practiced holding his breath endlessly at the public pool, only to be ridiculed by other kids in their scrappy mill-town neighborhood.

Back then, Grady got picked on constantly for reasons he never quite understood, but he thought they had something to do with either his being Indian or his being quiet. He was often poked, prodded to fight, only he never raised a fist, no matter that he was generally taller than most of his classmates, with a reach they would have killed for. It wasn't that he didn't feel the anger, the rage they provoked. He just had no idea how to fight, how to throw a punch without looking like a sissy. He'd had no practice, except for fending off rowdy sisters who wanted to tickle him until he peed, and he couldn't exactly punch them. How was he supposed to know how to fight like a real man, without a dad around to show him? So, he'd sported a few black eyes, suffered aching ribs, but there'd been no lasting damage done to anything but his ego.

But some moments made up for everything. On summer Saturdays, his mother would take Grady and his sisters to the muddy sand beach at Dash Point State Park, and Grady would hightail it to the shore, running and jumping into the Puget Sound as if into someone's arms.

After the accident, Grady could feel the presence of his

father underwater, especially in the icy cold of the sound. The fishing boat had gone down in Alaskan waters, the same ocean that filtered through and around all the islands and islets and peninsulas to this place. His father's guardian spirit, the salmon, swam in both salt and fresh water, though, and Grady could find some solace even in the chlorinated water of the public pool.

When Grady was little, his dad had told him that he would find his own guardian spirit, too, when he became a man, but then he'd gone and died just a couple years later. Grady didn't know who else to ask about it. He couldn't ask his mother. She had enough on her hands, and besides, what would she know about guardian spirits? She was white. His father had often talked of cousins, but not brothers or sisters, and Grady eventually realized that to an Indian, *cousin* meant "friend" or "buddy," just like *auntie* meant "friendly older woman"—not necessarily related because they were all related. Their families knew no bounds, but Grady realized they knew no actual family on his father's side, and his own Indianness went with his father into the deep. Because Grady looked the part, though, people assumed he had some ancient tribal connection to all things Native American. For the most part, though, a devoutly Catholic Irish American mother had raised him. To her disappointment, he didn't find the comfort she did in church or in the words of the Bible.

Still, with all of his doubts, he reckoned his spirit was somehow aligned with his father's. As an adult, he swam nearly every day at lunchtime, and could cover two full lengths of the twenty-five-yard pool at the gym without breathing. Lucie had never understood his obsession with swimming but, as a runner, assumed it had to do with fitness or endorphins. He felt guilty for never inviting her to join him, but swimming had always been his place to be alone. To be completely himself and at ease.

The motel pool was probably only ten yards, and Grady completed several laps before his lungs begged him to breathe. He surfaced, then settled into a definitive rhythm, lap after short lap. The mechanization emptied his mind, freed him from the panic he'd felt every morning upon waking in the past nine days, every moment upon remembering.

He thought instead of fluid dynamics, of surface tension and the drag created by his torso in the pool. With correct body position, he could optimize laminar flow, water easing around him as smoothly as wind over an airfoil. It was all about the streamline, in swimming and in aircraft design. Hell, in life. Smooth on smooth, no interruptions or irritations between surfaces. The trick was to avoid turbulence, chaos, unpredictability. In his family, at work, and most especially, with Lucie, who challenged him most of all with her strong opinions and need for perfection. Just like they say: go with the flow. It had been the guiding principle of Grady's life, right up until Lucie ran.

He'd swum thirty-one laps when he saw them, two bodies on the steps at the shallow end. He slowed and veered to the other side, wishing he could swim out through a hole somewhere at the bottom of the pool. He stayed along the opposite edge, and sneaked a glance at a dark young woman in a maid uniform and a small girl in a frilly, pink swimsuit, flip-flops on the concrete beside them.

Grady quickly turned his head back underwater, but he'd
lost count of his strokes. He couldn't let this woman and her
child see him in his underwear. His forward hand was suddenly
at the wall—there was no room for a decent turn. At the last
moment he scrubbed the kick turn and scrunched into a ball to
find purchase on the wall with his feet, pushing weakly off in
the other direction. He had to get out of there; he'd make a
dash for it. They were having so much fun they'd probably
never even notice him.

Grady stopped at the far side of the pool, wishing for a ladder, but there was none. Hauling himself up too quickly on his
arms, he felt the boxers slip as his hips emerged from the water.
He scrambled to his feet, yanked up his underwear, and strode
quickly around the edge toward his clothes. The man from the
office was now stomping his short, fleshy way toward the pool,
surely to give Grady shit for swimming in his underwear. Grady
kept his eyes riveted to the concrete as he pulled on his shorts
and picked up his shirt and shoes.

"Hey," the man yelled. "What the hell do you think you're
doing?"

Grady turned to apologize, then realized the man was yelling at the maid.

"You can't bring your kid to work, and you can't use the goddamn pool."

"It's okay," Grady said. "I don't mind." He smiled at the
woman, but she was busy toweling off her daughter and consol-
ing her in a foreign language.

"Stay out of it." The man continued marching toward the
maid, the fat around his middle bouncing with each angry step.

"Come on," Grady said. "Look, it's fine. They're out of the pool. No harm done." The little girl stared at Grady with wide, deadpan eyes. She wasn't unaccustomed to such things, he realized.

"Everything isn't fine." The man had reached the woman's side and grabbed her arm when she tried to hurry away. "You are el-fired-oh, got it? Get outta here and take your brat. There are a dozen more like you where you came from." He let her go and turned back toward the office.

"Jeez, not in front of the kid," Grady said, but the woman picked up the girl, who still stared at Grady. "I'm sorry," he said to them, but the mother rushed past without looking up.

It wasn't fair. Nothing was ever fucking fair. Grady sighed and walked back to his room, slamming the door when he got inside.

# lucie

imi, the nice Filipino nurse, was back on duty
by dinnertime.

"I've brought something special for your last
supper," she announced, bustling a tray into Lucie's room.

Lucie sat in a blue chair near the window, back in her comfortable hospital gown, looking out at buildings, phone wires, a
slice of bay in the distance.

"They're kicking me out?" She knew she should have gone
with Grady earlier in the day, but she'd chickened out at the
last minute. Now she wasn't feeling very sure about anything.

Mimi laughed. "Oh, now. I hear your fiancé is a really nice
guy, and very concerned for you. And handsome."

Lucie nodded. It was true. He was all of those things.

"I just have a hard time imagining my name could actually
be Lucie. Lucie? That just doesn't sound right. And Seattle?
Rain?"

The nurse ignored her. "Tomorrow will be an adventure,"

she said. "You get to rediscover your home, your life, and a man who loves you. Yes?"

Lucie sighed. If only she could wake as someone different the next day, as the Lucie she used to be. The Lucie that Grady obviously loved and had come to fetch. He'd been good about not rushing her, though. He seemed patient. Lucie wondered if she was a patient person. He was clearly kind. Was she? What about her had made him love her? If only she could know that.

Mimi whisked a stainless-steel cover from the plate, releasing aromas of garlic and meat. "Adobo pork. I noticed you haven't been eating much, so I brought extra. And some veggies, some rice. Completely against hospital rules, so don't tell anyone, okay?"

As enticing as it smelled, Lucie said, "I don't want to get you into trouble."

Mimi shrugged. "You just remind me of my sister. Don't worry, I made sure no one would know."

Her sister. Lucie closed her eyes. She had no family. Of all the news she'd received in the past few days, this was the worst.

"You okay?" Mimi dropped the lid with a clang and rushed to Lucie, taking her face into her hands. "Open your eyes," she commanded, and Lucie complied.

"I'm fine." Lucie looked up into the nurse's small, pretty face. "Just . . . Did you hear I don't have any family?"

Mimi dropped her hands. "Of course you have family. Your husband-to-be came all the way here to get you. That's family."

"But I don't have a sister." Lucie knew she was being pathetic. "Or a mother or father. Or anyone. Except some aunt I don't like."

Mimi shook her head. "No one likes everyone in their family. It doesn't mean they're not family."

Lucie nodded; she had a point. She stood and walked to the bed. "What's it called again?"

"Adobo. The Filipinos' gift to the world. Enjoy. I'll be back for your tray in a little while, and you better have cleaned your plate." Mimi smiled. "And maybe I'll have another surprise for you, if you're good."

"Dessert?" Lucie had discovered an obsession for sugar, longing for the Red Vines and gummy fish in the vending machines, the Famous Amos cookies and Oreos. Unfortunately, she had no money, so she'd had to satisfy her cravings with the ubiquitous Jell-O and pudding that accompanied her meals, the occasional square of yellow cake with flavorless, sweet frosting.

"Better than dessert," Mimi said as she walked out. "You'll see."

The pork was, indeed, delicious. Succulent and tender, just spicy enough, the edges crispy from grilling. Paired with forkfuls of moist rice and buttered vegetables, it was the perfect comfort food. Lucie hadn't realized how hungry she was; she'd been avoiding the dreary hospital meals. Within minutes, the plate was empty.

Even after three days of rest, Lucie was exhausted, and her body still sore from who knew what. Sleeping on the ground? Walking great distances? She could only guess. Lucie lay back against the pillows and closed her eyes, waiting for the adobo magic to have its way with her.

When she'd first arrived in the ER downstairs, she'd thought for sure she'd suffered a stroke or aneurysm. Why else would she have stood in the water like that, letting herself get nearly hypothermic? Why else wouldn't she remember anything?

As she'd sat on the edge of a gurney in the exam room, a variety of scrub-attired people palpated her head, the back of her neck, checked her eyes, her pulse, her heart. Then they trundled her off to lie beneath machines that scanned her from this angle and that, infiltrating her skin and skull and brain tissue with invisible rays. They even gave her a pelvic exam. She should have told them her brain was quite a bit higher than that, but she'd still felt so out of it that first day, as if her body wasn't hers. She didn't care much what they did with it. They did report she showed no signs of abuse, sexual or otherwise, no sexually transmitted diseases, and no pregnancy. This news was clearly meant to comfort her, but it opened a new avenue of fear for Lucie: what had happened to her body while her mind had gone astray?

And the questions! Everyone asked her questions, every step of the way. She could answer anything that had to do with current events, history, geography. She could perform all of their odd requests to show her teeth, to raise her arms, to repeat or complete silly sayings: "Don't cry over spilled milk." "How now, brown cow?" "I left my heart in San Francisco."

She just couldn't say who she was, where she was from, or how she had ended up in the water. She had the general sense that she'd been in San Francisco before, at some point in her life, but the information felt cordoned off and obscured, as if far in the past. Someone else's past. But she'd been looking for something—that much she knew; this information didn't impress the doctors as important.

After a while they'd changed their tactics, asking her questions about problems in her life, recent traumatic events. "If I don't know who I am, how would I know that?" she asked, so frustrated that she wanted to shake someone, to say: "Just tell me who I am! Don't make me keep guessing!"

And then they'd given up, checked her into the psych ward upstairs, issued her a cotton gown and footie slippers, and a tray with a toothbrush and toothpaste, hotel-size soap and shampoo. She'd thought, *Well, this is the worst hotel I've ever stayed in,* knowing that should be funny. The problem was, she didn't remember staying in a hotel, but she knew she had, somewhere along the line.

As the ward door had closed behind her, she'd felt inexplicably comforted by the sound of the lock clicking solidly into place.

A CLATTERING SOUND woke Lucie with a start.

Mimi held the dinner tray at a precarious angle. She whispered, "Sorry! I dropped a spoon. Go back to sleep."

"No, that's okay." Lucie smiled at the young nurse. "You were right. The dinner was delicious. Thank you."

Mimi nodded. "Ready for your next surprise?"

Lucie shrugged. Why not? Every single thing that happened was a surprise.

"Follow me," Mimi said, stealth and mischief in her voice.

It wasn't yet late, only nine or so, but the dayroom was dark, the nurses' station empty. Lucie followed Mimi down the tile hall on slippery footies to the food preparation area. After depositing the tray into a tub, Mimi beckoned Lucie to follow her toward the locked ward doors. She turned and whispered, "We're going AWOL."

Lucie didn't want to leave the ward. She didn't know anything about how to live outside of it. Was this just Mimi's way of testing her, somehow, proving that she could leave the next day? "Listen," she said, "I don't really—"

"Hush," Mimi said. "I was right about the adobo, yes? Trust me."

Mimi held her badge up to the plate at the side of the door, releasing the lock. They passed the warning signs about lunatic escapees.

"Won't you get into trouble?" Lucie felt dizzy, the wide hallway expanding and shimmering around her as they walked out into it. It seemed to be the longest hallway she'd ever seen. From here she could go . . . anywhere. She could flee. Mimi was small; Lucie had a feeling her own long legs could easily outrun the nurse's. She could find her own way in the world, figure out some new way to be and not have to face the man and the past she no longer remembered. She must have some skills. She knew how to type, she was sure of it. Her fingers searched and found letters in the air; she sensed rather than saw the keyboard beneath them. An office job would be fine, and she could rent a cheap apartment somewhere, and—

"I'll only get into trouble if you tell." Mimi held her badge up to another plate next to another door. "Here we are," she said. The lock clicked, and the nurse pushed into a small, dark room. "Come on, hurry up."

Lucie stepped into the muffled space, smelling, what? Other people, the smell of too many other people. As Mimi shut the door and turned on the overhead fluorescent light, Lucie realized they were in a large closet. Long bars lined the walls at upper and lower levels, crammed with the circus colors of hundreds of garments: skirts, blouses, suits. Sweaters were folded upon high shelves; cubbies held undergarments, baby clothes. Shoes lined the floor beneath.

Mimi looked at her expectantly. "You don't like the clothes you were found in, right?"

Lucie nodded, wrapping her arms around the hospital gown she'd grown so fond of.

"This is the clothing bank. We're going to find you a new outfit for tomorrow!" Mimi clapped her hands together, delighted. Lucie felt nauseated by the smell of so many different kinds of body odor mingling in such a small air space.

"Are they . . . clean?" Lucie knew they must be, but clothes took on the lives of the people who'd inhabited them. Spots wore thin where people protruded or bulged, where anxious types rubbed sleeve hems, or lazy ones didn't hem pants. Smells were just part of what became embedded in a piece of clothing, no matter how many times you washed it. Lucie, with no reminders of her past, felt emptier than all of the stretched-out sweaters and faded Levi's.

"Of course they're clean! Everything has been laundered. There's some good stuff in here. We just have to dig through it a little. Haven't you ever been thrift-store shopping? It's like that."

Lucie shrugged. Had she?

"What about my clothes?"

Mimi nodded at a row of suits, all abandoned, waiting for suit-loving people to adopt them.

To shed that uncomfortable thing! That truly was a gift. Lucie reached to hug the nurse. "Are you this nice to every mental patient?"

Mimi shrugged.

"Fine," Lucie said. "I think I'd like something . . . casual."

The man, Grady, had been the epitome of casual. He looked comfortable, like he didn't pay a lot of attention to clothes, which appealed to Lucie. And as much as she was fighting all of this, she knew that he was telling the truth. He knew her. He'd come all this way for her. He must love her.

"Casual but cute," Mimi said. "You can wear anything, you're so tall and slim."

Cute didn't seem quite right, but Lucie let her hands reach toward the swirl of color. She clacked hanger after hanger along the bar until she came to a tangerine-colored T-shirt that proclaimed in small block lettering: "I am a noun." It also had a sales tag still attached. Donated by Good Samaritans. No one else had ever worn it.

Mimi narrowed her pretty, dark eyes, shaking her head, but to Lucie, it was a start. She could be a noun. For now, that was enough.

# grady

early the next morning, Grady stood outside San Francisco General in still-damp underwear. Fog had rolled in again overnight, dank and obscuring the upper windows of the hospital where Lucie might be looking out into the yellowish gray, wondering if he was coming, hoping he wasn't or, by some miracle, hoping he was. Or maybe she was still the old Lucie and lay sleeping on her side in a tight knot, head beneath the pillow to block out light and sound.

She wasn't expecting him until 7:00, but she said she woke with the light. He looked at his watch again. It was 6:44 a.m. He'd ignored the incoming call from his mother the night before, but heard the disappointment in her message: "She doesn't even remember *you?*" Like somehow it was his fault. He closed his eyes.

This was turning out the way he'd always expected it would, eventually. He'd had a chance at something real, at a happy life with Lucie, and he'd blown it. He didn't want to think about that.

Grady turned and walked away from the hospital, back toward the verdigris gate.


HE'D NEVER UNDERSTOOD what Lucie saw in him, even though it was clear she was attracted to him from the start. Maybe it had been purely physical, the excitement of his brown hand on her pale skin, or having a boyfriend who looked so different from other professional men in Seattle. Lucie and Grady didn't have much in common at first. She liked the finer things. He couldn't care less. She was a city person. He was a small-town bumpkin.

Seattle had always felt massive and imposing, with its skyscrapers looming over Elliott Bay, the loud viaduct bisecting city from nature, concrete from open water and cloud-thick sky. He'd avoided the so-called Emerald City most of his life, preferring the outskirts of his hometown of Tacoma. Even though it was less than an hour south of Seattle, it felt worlds away.

It had been dumb luck that got him to Seattle the day he met Lucie. He hadn't even been looking for a job, having grown used to working for an aircraft parts manufacturing business, as boring as it was. But Dory had e-mailed him the notice about the aerospace job fair at the Washington State Convention Center. She knew he'd always dreamed of designing airplanes for Boeing; he'd studied their commercial aircraft from the time he was a kid and loved going to the factory for the tour. In her e-mail, Dory wrote, "Go for your dreams!" in that exclamation point way of hers, the way she and all of his sisters had been cheering him on since they were young and lost their dad, and then when he tried out for basketball in junior high and wasn't chosen (even with his height). And then, again, when he got Virginia Vountclaire pregnant in the last year of high school and they ran down to the courthouse and got married the day after graduation.

"Congratulations, baby brother!" they'd all exclaimed, as if it was a happy thing, even though Virginia had moved into Grady's room at home, where she stayed in seclusion, crying most of the time. When Virginia left him before the kid was even born and went back to her irate family, his sisters' enthusiasm barely dimmed. "Wasn't meant to be," they sang. "When one door closes, another one opens!" But he'd never let that door open again, not to commitment, not to marriage—not until Lucie. She was different. She made him want to achieve things he'd never thought he could before; her self-assurance and belief in Grady had helped him succeed at his new job. It had been so easy to imagine sharing a life with her.

He hated that he'd always have to use the phrase "first wife" for someone he'd barely known, even though Lucie said she didn't mind being the second. She was pragmatic that way, but he wished she could be his first. Worse, though, had been living with the knowledge that a boy was growing up somewhere hating Grady, assuming he didn't want to be his father, when the truth was that the Vountclaire family had ordered him not to make contact. The checks he'd tried to send the first five years had all come back unopened, so he'd started a savings account for his son. If only the kid knew that Grady understood exactly what he was going through, that his father had abandoned him, too.

Grady had almost ignored Dory's e-mail that day in his cubicle, almost deleted it out of habit—just another sappy, encouraging note from a sister—but he'd hesitated. This time, she was right. If he ever got the chance to meet his son—who was now basically a grown man and capable of making his own decisions—wouldn't it be better to be the kind of father who was doing the thing he felt put on earth to do?

He called in sick the next day and drove north to Seattle, navigated its confusing freeway loops and exits and found the convention center parking garage. He paused before pulling open the glass doors, ran his hand through his hair, wondering if he should have had it cut, straightened his tie, then soldiered on. This company had designed his favorite aircraft. He had to try, at least once in his life. To really try.

After filling out forms, passing out résumés, shaking hands with people whose names he immediately forgot, he was directed to join a group of other engineers who looked as uncomfortable as he felt, grunting like corralled buffalo in a holding pen of folding chairs and tables. One by one they were called to slaughter, each looking back awkwardly as he or the occasional she was led away to be interviewed.

When his name was called, Grady startled, then threw that same pathetic look over his shoulder at the others as he was led away. Why hadn't he prepared better? He knew everything there was to know about Boeing, of course, having been a devotee since childhood, but maybe he should have read up on fault-tolerant design practices or active flow control. He had visions of a panel of senior engineering staff staring down at him from a stage, throwing him technical questions he couldn't answer, and his mouth went dry.

In the small conference room, however, there was just one person, and if she was an engineer, Grady thought, he'd eat the faux-leather briefcase his mother had given him seven Christmases ago. This woman was tall and regal in a gray suit, pinstripes outlining her waist and slight curves above and below. Her hair was short, almost boy short, but her face was a woman's. A beautiful woman's, in Grady's eyes, even though he knew not everyone might view her that way, with her crooked teeth and athletic frame. Beneath expertly applied makeup he detected freckles. Behind green eyes he suspected a dry sense of humor and intelligence beyond his own, a sense of how things should be that he would never quite grasp. Her glossed lips spread into a wide smile when she saw him.

"Mr. Goodall, I presume?" She looked surprised, as though he hadn't been what she was expecting, either. She later told him that she'd fallen for him in that moment, had seen him and thought, *There he is,* but he'd always had a hard time believing it.

They'd laughed, awkwardly, then turned straight to business. She was a high-tech recruiter, and became his advocate, coaching him and mentoring him through the rigorous process of landing a job with the product development team at Boeing. Sure, it wasn't the design job he'd hoped for—his engineering bachelor's degree precluded that, she said—and she'd collected a nice finder's fee from the company once he was hired. Miraculously, though, she'd kept in touch long after she'd actually needed to; it had been Lucie, in fact, who'd finally asked him out to dinner, and he'd liked that about her. Strong women had raised him, after all. He didn't mind Lucie taking the lead.

Well, he hadn't minded until the wedding date was set, and the military-style planning launched in earnest. He'd never have guessed that Lucie's need for perfection and control would be so overwhelming that he'd wonder if he even wanted to be married to her. He'd freaked out. He'd blown it. And now, here he was, sitting on a bench in front of a hospital in San Francisco, trying to figure out what to do next. And Lucie, the once all-powerful goddess of his life, sat broken and alone inside. The worst part was, he didn't know how to help her. He'd failed her, damaged her, and lost her. Now that he'd found her, would he just fail her again?

"Man up," a gravelly voice said, and he turned to look at the next bench over.

"Excuse me?"

Staring at him was an older woman wearing three coats and mismatched rain boots. She had six plastic grocery bags at her feet, filled with everything but groceries. He'd misheard her, of course. She was probably just talking to herself, as the street people in San Francisco seemed to do. In Seattle, for the most part, they simply asked for change, then said "Thank you" when you either gave them a few coins or said "Sorry." At least she wasn't urinating.

"I said 'Be a man.'" She looked at him with heavy-lidded eyes. "Grow up. Nobody likes going in those places to visit, but,

trust me, living in them is worse. Go on now. Go see your person, see if you can't cheer 'em up."

"Yes, ma'am," he said, the way he'd been trained to address
older women from childhood, then looked at his watch. It was
7:02. Lucie was waiting.

ONCE IN THE hospital lobby, Grady wondered if he should
bring Lucie a present. He decided to give the small shop a quick
once-over. Lucie didn't much go for the typical gifts men gave
women. She didn't eat sweets and didn't like anything too cutesy.
He bypassed the chocolates, the teddy bears and figurines, and
walked toward the cards. Maybe just something simple with
a nice sentiment. He scowled. Right. "I'm sorry you lost your
mind"? "Please come back to me even though I was a jerk"? He
sighed and turned to leave.

Just entering was a young woman in a tight orange top and
short denim skirt, headed straight for the candy section. Grady
averted his eyes so as not to appear to be staring, even though
he sensed she was beautiful. As hard as he tried to avoid her,
though, they met head to head in the narrow aisle.

"Excuse me," he said, head down.

"Do you have a dollar I can borrow?"

He looked up in surprise. It was Lucie. Of course it was
her; she looked just the way she always did when she first
woke: fresh and clear-eyed. It was almost disorienting how
much the same she looked, especially dressed this way, as if
she were the twin sister of the woman he loved.

"Sure, of course," he said, fumbling in his pocket. "I was just on my way up to see you."

She took the bill he handed her, closing her hand around it, knuckles brushing his fingers.

"I thought I'd save you from having to do the whole loony bin thing again." She shrugged and smiled the smile he loved, one side curved higher than the other. That smile had always made him want to kiss her. "And I was dying for some candy. I was hoping to either bump into you or work up the nerve to shoplift."

He laughed. Lucie had often made him laugh, but not with this light, off-key banter. She had a fierce, smart wit, thought before she spoke, constructed each sentence carefully.

"Uh, you don't actually eat candy," he told her, watching her select peanut M&M's, then linger over a packet of red licorice.

"I love candy," she said, turning to him. "I mean, I would know, right?" She bit her bottom lip, looking worried, so he shrugged.

"Sure. Of course." He hated the false sound of his voice, the little "heh heh" that trailed after. He hated the feeling that this was not really his Lucie after all, just some new person who would eventually figure out that he was no good for her. Of course, the old Lucie had already figured that out. He reached back into his pocket for his wallet. "Looks like you might need a little more," he said, handing her a ten.

"Thank you. Grady." It sounded like she'd been rehearsing his name.

He nodded, wondering what had become of the six hundred dollars. He could read her T-shirt now. It said in small white letters: "I am a noun." She wore flat sandals and carried a little bag over her shoulder, made of some colorful ethnic fabric. The old Lucie would hate the entire ensemble.

And still, no ring. Where was it?

Grady studied her as she busied herself with her selections. Wearing flats like this, she came only to his collarbones. And she was so thin—her wrists were frail, her cheeks not quite sunken, but not full, either.

"Are you hungry?" he asked. "Have you eaten breakfast?" He had no appetite, even though he hadn't eaten dinner, but she should be eating something besides candy.

"I'm starving," she said. "Hospital food is not exactly, well . . . food. Who eats Cream of Wheat?" Lucie smiled again. He could see she was trying. The day before she'd embraced him, but her expression had been inscrutable, her words unsure. Something had changed, but he tried not to let his hopes cast out too far.

He cleared his throat. "How about we get the hell out of here and get something to eat?" A meal. They'd start with a meal. If that went well, maybe they could take the next step, whatever that might be. Spending the day together, talking about their old life. Maybe even making plans to return to Seattle.

She nodded, and gathered the M&M's, red licorice, Starbursts, and a roll of fruit Life Savers. "Sure," she said. "Let's go. I'm already discharged."

"But," Grady said, then faltered. He couldn't swallow, couldn't catch a decent breath. She walked toward the counter to pay, and he followed her. Had she decided to come home? Was she going back to their house with him? To their . . . bed?

"What about your stuff?" he asked instead. "Where are the rest of your things?" Where was the Armani suit, the Gucci bag she'd loved? The twelve-thousand-dollar ring? How could he ask her that without making her feel bad if she'd lost it? And she wouldn't remember, anyway. It had probably been stolen somewhere along the way, or maybe she'd given it to some lucky son-of-a-bitch panhandler.

She loaded the pile of candy onto the small glass counter, smiled at the elderly woman behind it, then turned to him. "Oh, this is it. I've got everything I need with me." She patted the small, seemingly empty bag at her hip, then loaded the candy into it as the clerk rang it up, piece by piece.

# lucie

T he pancakes lolled pillowy and warm against her tongue, and Lucie slithered each forkful through a pool of syrup before devouring it. She and Grady weren't saying much, other than polite small talk—*How was your hotel? Did you sleep well?*—and he seemed not to be hungry; his egg-white omelet looked cold and forlorn, just one corner missing. She was starving. The sensation of food in her mouth, flavors that were familiar and sweet and satisfying . . . these things felt like life. As she'd taken the first taste, tears had come to her eyes and she'd pretended to have a wayward eyelash as she rubbed them.

Lucie knew that she must not have eaten much during the week she was gone. Her old clothes had been loose fitting and her ribs and hip bones jutted out, but she'd survived at least. It seemed she'd never catch up, now. When she'd tasted Mimi's sister's cooking the night before, she'd found a way to be human again.

"These are the best pancakes I think I've ever tasted," she said, then laughed. "Like I'd know."

Grady's mouth twitched, but he said nothing.

"Aren't you hungry?" Lucie asked. "Did you already eat?"

"No, I'm eating," he said, poking his fork at the anemic omelet. "It's just not like you to be eating pancakes. You seem to have developed quite a sweet tooth."

He looked up at her in such an earnest way that she laughed again. It felt good to laugh; it felt good to be sitting in a restaurant with a paper place mat and a white coffee mug and a nice, handsome, if quiet, man across from her. How had she gotten this lucky in her previous life? She could imagine other women swooning at the sight of him. Why had she wanted to stay at the hospital?

Her heavy mood was lifting, cloud layer by cloud layer. With each small step forward—choosing her own clothing, her own food—she felt more herself. Even if she didn't know what that meant yet.

"Was I not always such a pig?" she asked, feeling comedic, on the verge of something familiar, as if maybe this was a style between them, this banter, and she was remembering it.

"Well." He paused, his serious expression suggesting that was not the case. "I mean, you just never used to eat sugar, or white flour for that matter." He shrugged. "Not that I'm saying you shouldn't or anything, but you're kind of, well, you've always been a pretty light eater, and fastidious about what you do eat."

"Fastidious?" That didn't sound good. "Am I . . . anorexic?" Had she been this thin before she ever left?

"No, no, no. You're . . . health conscious." He cut a bite of omelet with his fork, raised it. "You got me to eat these things, for example."

"Why?" It looked bland. "Why would I make you eat that?"

This time, Grady laughed. "You didn't make me, Luce. You just encouraged me to eat healthier. High cholesterol runs in my family. I guess you wanted"—they both heard the stab of the past tense—"what was good for me."

Lucie leaned back in her chair, pushed her plate away. How could she not know this, the most basic of things, about herself? It didn't sound like her, didn't feel like her at all. No wonder he'd looked at her strangely when she'd pawed over all that candy.

"I didn't mean to ruin your breakfast," Grady said. He seemed genuinely remorseful. How weird for him, Lucie thought, to suddenly find that his girlfriend—fiancée—was so very different than she'd been just ten days before. Had he actually liked her suit? Should she have worn it? Did he like the way she looked in makeup? She'd given the entire makeup bag to Mimi for her nieces, and the big purse now sat on the clothing bank shelf. All she'd kept from it was a calendar the size of a credit card with a website address printed at the bottom—TechSource.com—and a nail file and lip balm. And now some sweets. She couldn't fathom ever eating the stale blanched almonds she'd found in the bag, or using the travel-size hair spray, the cuticle cream, the spot stain remover pen, the tweezers, the package of pantyhose. Why pantyhose? Who would lug those around?

Grady cleared his throat. "I'm surprised they checked you

out already. I thought we were supposed to have some kind of meeting with the doctor, to talk about your treatment in Seattle, and what we do now and stuff."

Lucie sat up straighter in her chair, squared her shoulders. The food sat heavy in her stomach. "Well, I have a piece of paper with all of that on it. Dr. Emma had an emergency to deal with and the guy taking her place just said to follow the in-structions, and discharged me. So, here I am." Had Grady wanted to talk to the doctor? She'd never thought about it. She'd thought he'd be happy that she was discharged.

"Here you are," he said, his mouth twisting. He was trying to smile, but Lucie knew he was fighting tears.

"I'm sorry I flaked out on you yesterday, but today is a new day."

Grady nodded.

"And I need to know more. That's part of how I get better."

"Okay then. What do you want to know?"

"Um, well. I don't know!" This made her laugh, though ner-vously this time. What did she want to know, exactly?

Grady pushed his plate away. "Let's start with the basics, then."

Grateful, she nodded, and they began. Her birthplace (Boise, Idaho), birth date (September 4, 1971), siblings (just to make sure, and "No," once again, was the answer). She switched gears, not wanting to hear again about the dead parents and es-tranged aunt. "Oh, do I have a job?"

Grady perked up. "God, yeah. You're a headhunter, Luce, a really good one."

She squinted at him. "Pardon?"

"A recruiter. You have your own business finding jobs for people, tech jobs, all over the country. Do you remember?" He looked at her expectantly, wistfully almost. Was her job that important to him?

It sounded deadly dull, this career, but it explained the calendar, TechSource.com. She shook her head. "Not really," she said, then to make it sound more hopeful she added, "Not yet."

"No, I know." He cleared his throat, looked down at the table. "I shouldn't be pushing you." His voice broke.

Her eyes filled at his emotion. Deeply buried love or garden-variety empathy? "May I see the photos again?" she asked, for his sake. It had been unsettling to her the day before, seeing a person who looked like her firmly ensconced in a world she knew nothing about, in relationships she knew nothing of, but she knew he wanted her to see herself in their old life together.

"I left them at the hospital," he said. "For you."

"Oh, no." Lucie sighed. "They must still be in my room. I'm sorry, Grady." She reached across the table to put her hand on his. Their hands rotated smoothly, automatically it seemed, until hers was resting inside his. Muscle memory; bones and nerves and muscles knowing more than her mind did. His skin was warm, the color of her creamed coffee, and his arms nearly hairless, considering the crop on his head.

"Let's talk about you for a while, okay?" she said, and he shrugged, rubbing his neck. Lucie noticed for the first time a long scratch beneath his right jawbone. It didn't look deep or particularly life threatening, but she shivered. "How'd you get that, for instance? Does the other guy look worse?" She tried to

make light of it, but he dropped his head, covering the wound
with his hand.

*Stupid,* she thought. She changed course. "Tell me about
your family. Did you grow up in Seattle?" She couldn't remember which tribe he'd said he was from; there were many in
Western Washington. She knew this, she did. Salish, Du-
wamish, Suquamish. She knew these names, but not why she
knew them. She was clearly white, whiter than white with her
freckles and the bluish tinge beneath her eyes.

Slowly, he opened up. He told her about growing up in Tacoma. His dad had been a fisherman—the Puyallup had
salmon rights in the sound—but he'd died in an accident at sea
long ago. His mom still lived in Tacoma and had never remar-
ried. Grady had six older sisters, whose names he rattled off but
Lucie didn't quite catch.

"And you need to know something else," he said, cheeks
flushing, "I've been married before, but that was right out of
high school, and it didn't even last a year."

"Okay." Lucie shrugged. "Are you, we, still in touch with
her?"

"No." He glanced sideways, jaw tensing, then looked back
at her. "I have a son, but I've never met him."

"Oh, that must be so hard," she said, but he looked away
again and they fell silent.

Early that morning, when the doctor had discharged Lucie,
he'd looked concerned. "Now, you're going to have to go
through treatment when you get home. Dr. Emma has written
the contact information for the psychiatrist you'll be seeing in
Seattle on your discharge papers, and we should have sched-

uled you an appointment, but it doesn't look like that's happened, yet. This is a very serious condition, and you'll need to be under a psychiatrist's care, as I'm sure Dr. Emma has told you."

*Endlessly,* Lucie wanted to say. She nodded, but she had no desire to see another shrink. "But she also said my memory should come back, eventually."

The doctor's mouth tightened, then he said, "Well, that's a very individualized thing. Most patients with this condition, yes, over ninety percent of them, retrieve some or most of their memory, but you'll probably never remember those days you were missing."

"I won't?"

He shook his head. "I'm sorry, no. It's rarely if ever reported with dissociative fugue."

Dr. Emma hadn't mentioned this peculiarity of the condition, and it nauseated Lucie now to think there was a chunk of her life she'd never have access to. Strangers—the people who saw her on the bus, or picking fruit—would remember her during that time. What had other people witnessed but not reported? It was a big city, and Lucie had been roaming it for days.

The doctor made notes in her chart, then looked up. "In addition to treatment, you should make a concerted effort to talk with people who know you, look through photos, go to places that were familiar to you before. But"— he looked at the discharge papers—"it's imperative that you see Dr. Seagreave. I'll have our staff make your first appointment with her before you leave."

Lucie shook her head. "I'll do it as soon as I get home, to make sure it's a good time for my . . . for me and my fiancé." The doctor looked hesitant, so she smiled. "I'd just like to make sure he can drive me. I don't think I'll know how to find my way around, yet."

He nodded and signed the paperwork, then handed it to her. "Well, then, Ms. Walker, you're good to go. Good luck."

Now, as Grady paid the check, as they stood to walk out into the sun-streaked mist the fog had become, Lucie breathed in short, shallow gulps, adrenaline sparking. She felt like running, wanting the pounding of pavement to give way to earth; she wanted to pump her arms and let wind fill her eyes with tears. She had no baggage, she had no history. She had absolutely nothing.

They walked to the nearest street corner. Grady turned to her, his face wary, weary, prepared for the worst.

"So," he said. "What's next?"

Lucie breathed in. Air filled her lungs and belly, expanded her rib cage and widened her shoulders. "Well," she said, "Grady." She felt the essence of his name rise from the back of her throat, then the consonants against her teeth, the vowels strong and able. She liked his name. She liked this man. She had no one else in the world. "Why don't we just go home?"

# grady

a flyer remained on the telephone pole at the end of their block, in full view as Grady made a left onto Meridian Avenue and drove toward their bungalow two doors up on the right. He'd tried to make sure the signs were all down before they arrived; he'd even called the coffee shop and market and library from the airport in San Francisco that morning, thinking how it might feel to Lucie to arrive home and find wanted posters plastered all over the neighborhood. Rain would eventually take down the dozens in the rest of the city, but he'd hoped to spare her in her first few days back home. How the hell had he missed this one? He glanced at her in the seat beside him as he parked at the curb in front of the house. She hadn't seemed to notice.

He'd let his sisters talk him into putting up the flyers, and that had kept him busy for the first couple of days, but he'd known as he tacked, taped, and stapled up every one that a simple sign, or hundreds of them, would not bring her home.

Thankfully, Grady did have the good sense to refuse to go on television and implore her hypothetical captors, or Lucie herself, to relent. "But anyone who sees you, who sees what this is doing to you," Dory had tried, her soft mare eyes almost convincing him. For once, though, he'd stood firm. Still, the local news shows had run Lucie's professional photo from her website at every opportunity (Attractive white woman missing!) and called him constantly to check on progress.

Lucie and Grady sat in the car, neither one moving. They'd missed lunch, and now it was early afternoon, but there'd been no mention of eating again. *Does she recognize our house?* he wondered, but she wasn't looking at it, just staring ahead. Grady wondered if she could hear his heart pounding. Did she remember choosing the gray paint when he'd wanted green? Asking him to remove the gnarled cherry tree that no longer bore fruit but still produced showers of white blossoms each spring? Did she remember that he'd done everything he could think of to make her happy?

Finally, Lucie opened her car door and got out. Rather than walking toward the house, though, she walked back down the street as Grady watched in the rearview mirror. He stopped breathing. She'd lost it again and was walking away. Should he chase her? Call out her name? Could he wake her from the trance? Or should he just let her go this time and not look for her, just let her do what she seemed so determined to do?

When she stopped at the corner, he snapped to his senses and jumped from the car to bolt after her, then stopped. She'd simply walked to the telephone pole, and was now studying the flyer. She touched her fingers to her cheek, then reached to remove the paper from the staples Grady had shot through the corners. She folded the flyer three times and put it in her little bag with the remains of the candy, then turned and walked back toward home.

"Hi," she said when she reached him on the sidewalk, just as she usually said hi, like it was any normal day and she'd been out for a run. All of this was bringing her back to reality: being with Grady, back in Seattle, in front of the home they'd lived in for nearly five years. They'd go inside and she'd drop her purse on the chair in the dining room, then she'd grab the mail and look through it, then maybe go into their home office to check her e-mail. The doctor had said most patients retrieve their autobiographical data once back in familiar surroundings with their families and loved ones; it was just a matter of time.

He wanted to hug her, but he left his arms at his sides. "I'm really glad you're home."

She nodded and glanced around the block, then tilted her head. "So," she said. "Which one is ours?"

LUCIE HAD NOT yet ventured upstairs to their bedroom in the converted attic. He'd left her to wander when they first arrived, and she'd gone straight into the kitchen, running her hand along the soapstone countertop. She'd pulled open the Sub-Zero and stared at the mostly empty shelves—he hadn't done much grocery shopping after she left—then closed it. Next she'd gone into the bathroom, pulling the door shut behind her.

Grady tried to busy himself, checking e-mail in the office, catching up on the previous days' events at work to give her space and time alone in the house, but he found himself straining to hear her footsteps, her movements as she stole from room to room like a cat just adopted from the shelter.

Overnight, a serious problem had cropped up at work and Grady now felt even guiltier about not having taken his laptop to San Francisco. As team lead, he should have been on top of it, should have been riding herd over the socially awkward engineers he managed. None of them had even tried to call his cell phone. They'd all known where he was going; they'd all watched helplessly as events unfolded over the previous week. In their own geeky way, they'd been taking care of him, but now he was home and Lucie was home and he needed to act like everything was all right. He needed some kind of normalcy.

He closed his eyes and imagined the thrumming silence of water against his ears, the cool slipstream over his skin. If only he could sneak away to the pool, even for just a quick swim, but no. He had to be here, for Lucie. *Right,* he imagined the old woman outside the hospital saying. *You need to be there for you, chickenshit. You think she's gonna do it again, don't you?*

His cell phone buzzed against the desktop. Dory. Not only was she his favorite sister but she was a shrink, of sorts. A licensed mental health social worker, Dory had always wanted to save the world and everyone in it, but all she got to do at Pierce County Human Services was evaluate her clients and refer them on.

"Hey," he answered, walking to press the door closed. "Hi."

"Is it a good time?" she asked. None of his other sisters would even think to ask.

"Yeah, sure." Grady glanced at the door, keeping his voice

low. "As good as any. She's walking around the house, kind of . . . well. Getting to know it, I guess."

"Jesus."

"I know. Unreal."

"So, what's the scoop? What did the docs in San Francisco tell you?"

"Well, I didn't really get to talk to anyone. I mean, on the phone they told me it's pretty serious, but over time she'll probably get most of her memory back."

"Hmm." She sounded dubious. He could hear the clicking of computer keys, and he pictured her in the small cubicle she spent her days in. "Any diagnosis with the word *dissociative* basically means a break from reality, you know? Not psychosis, but, well. You've heard of dissociative identity disorder, what they used to call multiple personalities?"

"Oh, god," Grady said.

"No, no, no. It's not the same thing. I'm just saying they're right. It's serious. And it's really rare. They gave her a treatment plan before releasing her, right?"

"Yeah, she's supposed to see a shrink here who specializes in this stuff." Grady had asked to see the paperwork at breakfast, not because he didn't trust Lucie, but because it seemed he should be taking an active role in the situation. And maybe there was some part of him that would need time to trust her fully again.

"No meds?" Dory asked.

"They say if she gets depressed or anxious, her doctor here can prescribe something. But she doesn't seem depressed or anxious. She seems kind of, well, fine."

"And does she have an appointment with the doctor?"

"Well, we just got here."

"Don't put it off. Don't let her put it off."

"Yeah, yeah. I know." Grady heard movement in the living room. "I better go. Let's talk more later, okay?"

"Call that doctor today. Even if Lucie won't."

Grady rolled his eyes. "Yes, ma'am."

"Fuck you," Dory said, then laughed. "Give Lucie a hug for me."

"And fuck you very much, too." He knew she wanted to help. "Don't worry, I can handle this. But thanks. You're the best."

After hanging up, Grady crept back toward the door, cracking it open to listen. He heard the squeak and give of his leather chair, the scrape of the ottoman on the wood floor. Lucie had always hated that chair, but had allowed the one concession when they moved in together. She always sat on the expensive Swedish couch when they relaxed in the living room in the evenings, folding one leg beneath her, posture nearly perfect. In fact, he didn't remember ever seeing her sit in his chair, and couldn't imagine it now.

Grady eased the door open enough to see her bare legs, sandals off now, stretched in front of her on the worn leather. She was very still. She couldn't see him. He wondered if she'd fallen asleep.

"Hello?" she said. Her legs slid off the ottoman.

"Yes?" Grady shook his head at his formality. "Hi," he said, walking into the living room to cover his spying. "I was just wondering how you're doing. Have you, are you . . . settled in?"

She shifted in his chair, tucking her leg beneath her like she always had, looking just like herself, and Grady felt his pulse quicken. She even looked at him with the narrowed eyes that meant something was bothering her. Was she coming back into herself? He waited for another sign.

"I was thinking," she said, in her old, more measured way, "that maybe, just for a while . . . well, I noticed there's a guest room."

"Oh," he said. "Of course." It wasn't her. This Lucie didn't want him sleeping anywhere near her. He'd missed her presence next to him in bed most of all, just the length of her against him in the night. "Sure, then, I'll take the guest room."

"No, I don't want to kick you out of—"

"But you should have—"

"Really, I mean, I'm like the guest here, anyway."

Grady must have looked as awful as he felt, because she said, "I'm sorry, but you should stay in your . . . our room, where you're comfortable." She shrugged. "It's just for a little while, right? Until, well . . ." She looked away.

The wedding was in two months. The venue was booked, the band hired, the invitations printed and sitting in sleek white boxes in the dining room waiting to be addressed. She'd insisted they be sent six weeks in advance, on the nose. Had she seen them? Would they still send them out to the one hundred and thirty guests they'd planned to in just two weeks, his family and her colleagues and their acquaintances? He'd almost thrown the boxes out when she left (had carried them to the recycling bin, in fact), but then returned them to their spot on the floor next to the buffet. He couldn't bear the thought of anything changing. He'd left everything in its place in the end. The only thing missing was Lucie.


FOR THE REST of the day they moved like careful, quiet ghosts through the house, their home, the place they'd been through so much in—laughing, fighting, screaming sometimes, horrible words. Making love. Grady felt embarrassed at how badly his body needed hers, at how much he wanted to bury his face in her naked shoulder, pull her muscular hips against him, and hear her call out in pleasure, just to feel whole and human and connected to something again. It had been tough when she was gone, but having her here-but-not-here was unbearable.

He called the office, put out fires, wondering how long he'd be able to get away with working from home. How was he ever going to be able to leave the house again, for any length of time, without worrying she'd disappear? The thought made him stop breathing, and he had to consciously suck air through his nose to come back to life.

Grady carried his laptop into the living room to sit and work, hoping to find her there, but the room was empty. Had she already left? He closed his eyes, trying to hear her. How long would it be this way, that he would imagine Lucie's departure at every turn? Grady sat in his chair, propped his legs on the ottoman, laptop on his thighs. His eyes burned from lack of sleep the night before. He let his head settle back into the soft leather, let his eyes close, just for a moment.

*   *   *

THE DAY BEFORE Lucie ran away had not been a good one. They'd been sniping at each other for weeks, for offenses so ridiculous it would have been laughable if it hadn't felt so sickening that they no longer got along. He'd stopped having opinions about the wedding because they were always shot down. Then she'd be mad that he wouldn't answer her question about which silver pattern would look best with the crystal, because really, didn't she just want him to choose the one she liked best? He'd have been happy with paper plates and plastic. And Lucie had accused him on two separate occasions of sabotaging the wedding by asking what, in the end, the final budget might be. He'd started to wonder why exactly they were getting married. Was it just so that Lucie could throw this lavish party? Did she even care who she was marrying? Each morning they woke at the far edges of the bed, where they'd fallen asleep the night before, the same void between them.

That morning, Lucie had gotten up and pulled on her running tights. He'd watched through slit eyes from his pillow, like he didn't care how lithe her body was, how luminous and silky her sun-protected skin. He felt embarrassed at his desire for her and rolled over to hide his arousal. She no longer seemed to desire him.

She finished dressing, went into the bathroom, then left the house having said nothing. He waited five long minutes before he realized she wasn't going to poke her head back in and say good-bye. He couldn't believe it. She always let him know she was leaving, even when they weren't getting along. She'd at least yell "Okay, bye" up the stairs, but that morning, nothing.

Even though they'd both been unusually hostile lately, this

was different. Something was changing in a way that felt un-bearable, and he got angry. *If she can be cold,* he reckoned, *so can I.*

After hastily showering and getting dressed, Grady tried to leave the house before she returned. He almost made it.

As he hurried down the front path to his car, he saw her running up the street toward home. She was a machine when she ran, legs and arms rhythmic and efficient, her gait per-fected over years of intense focus. She saw nothing and no one as she raced through the neighborhood, eyes shielded by polar-ized Bollés, a Nike cap pulled low on her brow. This accounted partly for her reputation with the neighbors as standoffish. Lucie turned completely inward to accomplish goals—everything from running a marathon to acquiring a new client—and saw only what she was aiming for. That's how it had been when they first fell in love: he was all she saw. Her attention had felt miraculous, undeserved but intoxicating. He'd hoped to drink from that well for the rest of his life.

Eventually of course, when they'd been together long enough to become comfortable, shinier objects—the house and its contents, her clothes and shoes and purses—stole her atten-tion. He'd sometimes wondered if she'd considered him a shiny object as well at first, an exotic pet with Native features; she loved his dark skin, his Geronimo hair.

And then, the wedding. She'd gotten so caught up in the details of the one day that he wondered if she'd forgotten about the reason for it all, the decision she'd made to spend her life with him.

Grady felt angrier by the second. He slinked into his partially rebuilt 1969 Volvo before she had the chance to reach him and shun him first, then sputtered away from the curb. He didn't call or text or e-mail her all day. That she didn't call or text either felt even more pointed than it might have on any other day. She'd started this silence, hadn't she? Why wasn't she calling to apologize or, at the very least, to break the heavy quiet bearing down between them? He was losing her, and it pissed him off so much at first he could ignore the despair beneath.

That evening, after working later than he needed to, he'd guilted two of his techs into going over to the pub to have a drink. He ordered Maker's Mark, not Manny's Pale Ale as usual. He consumed more than he could now recall. He didn't eat. He didn't remember driving home. He vaguely remembered checking his cell phone all night to no avail, and deciding to sleep on the uncomfortable Swedish couch. And, more painfully, his response to Lucie the next morning when she came in, all dressed up in her best suit, and sat next to his whiskey-breathed, hungover carcass on the sofa and said, testily, "Do you want out of this or what? Should I even go for my dress fitting today?"

He struggled up onto an elbow, still a little drunk, head throbbing. "Like you fucking care," he spat, glad for the hurt surprise that spread across her face. She didn't expect him to be mean, to fight back. It felt good. "You don't give a flying fuck what I think. And you know what?" He was snarling now, stabbing a finger at her for emphasis, as he lied, "I really don't give a fuck about you, either."

That was when she hit him. He saw the blow coming and

pulled his head back in surprise, and her knuckles glanced off his jaw and across his neck, her diamond slicing skin as it went. Instinctively, he covered his neck with his hands to protect himself—some monster had fallen upon him, an ugly fury of pummeling limbs and clawing hands. He tried to grab her arms, to calm her down, but his hands were wet, warm with blood, and her suit white, and his hands stopped midair.

They quit struggling as suddenly as they began, both staring at the blood. And then she let out a wail so inhuman and frightening he could have believed a wild animal was being flayed in the room with them; he'd never heard a sound like that, much less from Lucie. That was when she ran, bolting from the house like someone on fire. He didn't go after her, and he'd been trying to figure out why ever since. It was fear, of course, that froze him in place, but fear of what? The violence? The certain abandonment that was in progress? If he forgave himself at some point for the rest of it, he never would for just letting her go.

Grady was glad she'd lost her memory, glad she didn't have to replay that moment as he did, endure the animal emotions, the sounds, the sensations, the stupid, horrible mistakes, over and over. The one thing he could do for Lucie now was protect her from all of that. If they could start again, then . . . Well. They might have a chance.

# lucie

every surface in the house slicked cool and smooth
beneath her fingers, every piece of furniture and appli-
ance loomed sleek and expensive. The only exceptions
were the worn leather chair in the living room, which fit like a
comfortable old baseball mitt when she sat in it, and an upright
piano listing to one side in the unfinished basement. Did one
of them play?

Just as she'd had opinions about the decor in the hospital,
she had knowledge of these decorating choices as well: the ma-
terials, the finishes. This old bungalow had been remodeled
with a modernist's tastes, a granny dressed in haute couture.
Lucie wondered what had been there before, what warm woods
and quaint cabinetry and detail had been torn out and thrown
away. She wondered if former owners had remodeled it, or the
current ones. It wasn't that the house wasn't beautiful; it was.
She and Grady earned a lot of money—that was certain. How
would she do that now? Surely there was some expertise in-

volved in being a tech recruiter; could she just step back into it and pick up where she'd left off? Would it all come back to her eventually, as the doctor had suggested? Grady had said she was a sole proprietor, no employees. No one to remind her what she did all day every day. She'd been in the house for over an hour and . . . nothing. No matter how hard she tried, it all just felt like someone else's stuff, someone else's space. She hadn't gone into the bedroom. She knew she'd just find things that were personal to her once and now foreign. She didn't want them.

The guest bedroom was small but nicely decorated, a chocolate brown duvet and too many pillows on the bed. Lucie quietly closed the door, then lay across the covers, listening as Grady walked into the living room, looking for her, she supposed. What had he seen in her? she wondered. Why did he love her? Why did she love him?

Earlier in the day, when she'd decided to come to Seattle, she'd felt light and adventurous. Not quite brave but curious. Now she knew she'd made a serious mistake. This wasn't her house. This wasn't her life. She'd hoped for magic, bells, lights, cascading fireworks of recognition and memory. Instead, she was a guest in someone else's unfamiliar and not quite comfortable home.

She had to tell Grady, now, before they got too far into the charade. He was a nice man, and he must have loved the former Lucie Walker with all of his heart, but she was not that person. Not anymore, if she ever really had been. And yes, of course, the evidence was insurmountable. She was Lucie Walker. And she wasn't.

With a dry mouth and fluttering chest, she pulled herself upright, opened the door, and walked into the living room.

Grady sat in the leather chair, hands upon his laptop, eyes closed, mouth slightly agape. She wondered if he might be meditating or thinking, but his breathing had the legato of deep sleep.

*Legato.* Another musical term. Lucie felt a rush of something, a knowing, but she didn't know what it was she knew. Something teased from the edge of her consciousness, reaching out a small tentacle of understanding then withdrawing just as quickly.

She watched Grady breathe in, breathe out, and matched her respiration to his. The guy was exhausted after all she'd put him through. The fluttering in her chest subsided. The tenderness she'd felt when she first saw him returned. She might have walked over and stroked his unruly hair, in fact, kissed his forehead, but she left him there to sleep.


THE STEPS TO the basement creaked and groaned, and the air grew moist and fungal as she arrived at the concrete floor. There were so many things hidden away down here; Lucie felt like a detective, an archaeologist, trying to divine some kind of meaning from each item. A folding treadmill, dusty, unplugged. Hers? His? A garment rack filled with coats and clothing: a leather bomber jacket that was clearly Grady's size; various outdoorsy rainproof, windproof jackets; a red wool coat, stylish and long. She pulled it from the rack, held it up to her face, and breathed in. Slightly musty, but also a trace of lingering perfume. The coat was vintage, from the 1950s or '60s. She slipped her arms into the sleeves, wrapping it around her. It was a little too big, but she liked it.

At least twenty cardboard moving boxes lined one wall, up on wood pallets. The basement was damp, then; she'd suspected so from the smell. She pulled open the top of one and found old dishes, a teal and mauve pattern that suggested an era long past. It certainly didn't match the rest of the house, and Lucie knew instinctively what all these boxes were: remnants of life before the perfection that had been wrought upstairs. Again, she wondered: had they been Grady's? Hers? She pushed herself to remember: *where were these things before they were here?* She had to close her eyes at the resulting nausea, the panicky, hopeless feeling that rose from her gut to her throat. She backed away from the boxes, not wanting to look at them anymore. Maybe she'd ask Grady to come down with her sometime and talk her through each thing. Perhaps that would dislodge some shard of recognition, open a door.

Lucie looked around, then wandered over to the piano, still wearing the red coat over her T-shirt and short skirt. It was chilly in the basement, and the coat wrapped around her like a bathrobe.

The upright was old, the edges of the keys chipped, as if a rodent had been nibbling at them. The wood warped out in spots, and one foot in front was absent. Lucie looked around for something to prop it up with, then walked back to the boxes. Several contained books. A paperback wouldn't do; she dug beneath them, found a deeper layer of hardcovers, and pulled one out. *Man's Search for Meaning,* by Viktor Frankl. She took it over to the piano and tucked it under the broken foot, then rose and tried to wobble the piano. It stood solid now.

"There's your meaning," she said, sliding the piano bench out from under the keyboard. She sat, not knowing why, not knowing what she aimed to do, just sitting in front of the thing, trying to let her mind go blank. Was this something she used to do?

Lucie placed her hands on the keys and waited. *For what?* she wondered. *This is so stupid.*

Unguided by her conscious brain, her right thumb depressed a key. Middle C, she thought, not knowing how she knew this. She watched as her middle and pinkie fingers pressed the E and G keys. C major. She took her hands from the keys, let them rest on her legs, breath coming fast. Her fingers flexed against her thighs; perhaps it was just a twitch. She closed her eyes, blood pulsing in her ears.

*There are two pairs of hands on the keys,* she thought, *not just mine.*

Her eyes flew open at the empty, yawing sensation, the carving out of something in her chest. It was the same feeling she'd had at the hospital, deep sorrow at the loss of . . . of someone. Again she panicked, thinking, *Who have I misplaced? Who is missing?*

Lucie stood and reached down to scoot the bench beneath the piano, and saw carvings along the edge. Initials it seemed, or perhaps they were notes? D A . . . She squatted to examine more closely, rubbing her fingernail against grime packed into the lines, and found more: Y Y L U L U. Not notes, then. Lulu? Was that her? She stood, shivering, heart still pounding.

A child had scratched them. Whose hands had played along-side hers?

She waited a long moment for more, but her heart settled, her pulse quieted. She blew a long breath, glad to feel blank again. Should she ask Grady about it? Surely he'd have said something if she had children, right? She was acting flaky enough already. Yes, they needed to talk more, but there was time. Lucie suspected she wasn't the only one feeling unstable and out of sorts. She climbed back up the steps.

It had been bright midafternoon when they arrived home. Now the light was deepening toward gloaming, glancing off the stainless steel, warming the kitchen into a softer place. Lucie was famished, but the refrigerator held little other than a liter of sparkling water, a plastic-wrapped plate of something brown, a box of baking soda, and condiments in the door.

She pulled open the heavy freezer drawer at the bottom of the fridge, expecting frost-encrusted ice and not much else, and discovered a bonanza of Seal-a-Meal packets, each labeled and dated. There was goulash and chili, spaghetti sauce and chicken tetrazzini. Her body warmed inside the red coat, think-ing of homemade food like this. It was comforting to know she did indeed cook, and that she was this organized.

What sounded better, she wondered: goulash or te-trazzini? Another comforting thought: she knew what each was. Goulash, she decided, and pulled out a frozen slab to de-frost.

Something shifted behind her, and she turned, startled. Grady stood in the doorway with a strange expression.

"What are you doing?" he asked.

"I just thought we'd want something for dinner," she said, suddenly guilty, an intruder. "I hope you don't mind, I just pulled this out to defrost." She lifted the Seal-a-Meal goulash. "It sounded good. Did I make it?"

"My mom loaded me up last week." Grady squinted at her. "You hate her cooking." He paused, then asked, "Are you cold? It's like eighty degrees in here."

The coat. Of course it would be odd that she was wearing it.

"This isn't mine either, is it?"

"I don't know." Grady looked tense. "You've never said whose it is, but you've never worn it. I figured maybe it was your mom's or your aunt's or something."

"Maybe," she said, digging her hands into the pockets, pulling them in front of her so she was enveloped in the faded scent of something that had come before, something that had somehow, through blood or history or inheritance, been hers.

LUCIE THOUGHT GRADY might have been a little happier that she did, in fact, love his mother's goulash, but it only seemed to drive him deeper into his funk. He cleared the dining table, scraped and rinsed the plates, loaded them into the dishwasher silently, like a robot. She sat in the dining room, not knowing what to do next. The tall, straight chairs were not exactly comfortable.

She stood and surveyed the contents of a sleek cabinet, spying a wine rack with rows of dark bottles behind a lattice door. Grady came into the room to clear the rest of the table, and she turned. "Do you want some wine?" she asked.

He nodded. "We keep the stuff we drink in the kitchen," he said. "I'll get a bottle."

She frowned. "Why don't we drink this?"

He shrugged, seeming at a loss. "It's the good stuff? I don't know, Luce. It's not my rule. It's yours." His face was drawn; he looked ready to give up, on her, on them. On trying anymore.

Reaching into the cabinet, Lucie pulled out a bottle and held it up to him. "Open this one," she said. "If ever there was an occasion we needed a good bottle of wine, it would be now."

His eyes filled. He didn't move.

"Grady." She sighed. "I'm sorry I do everything wrong, that I choose all the wrong things and don't remember how to be her. I'm trying, but . . . I don't expect you to love me the way you loved her, really. I don't. Just . . ." Lucie closed her eyes, pushing back her own tears.

She felt him take the bottle. Slowly, she opened her eyes.

"I'll get us some glasses." Grady's expression had changed to concern. A look passed between them, a fleeting connection as when their hands had found their places together.

*Oh,* Lucie thought, *that may be worth every moment of despair.*

"Thank you," she said.

As he turned toward the kitchen, he said, "And I'll get the good ones."

How could she have left a man like this, Lucie wondered, a man who loved her this much?

"Want to watch TV?" she called after him, palming her eyes dry. Alcohol and television. What better numbing agents than those to get them through their first night?

It took a moment, a long moment, but then he called back, "Yeah, sure."

They settled into the living room, Lucie in the leather chair and Grady on the couch, his bare feet propped up on the ottoman. She tried not to stare, but his feet were as beautifully formed as his hands, long and elegant.

The wine was better than good. Châteauneuf-du-Pape, the pricey stuff, Lucie knew somehow. It warmed and mellowed even the hardest parts of the previous few days. By the time the eleven o'clock news came on, she and Grady had grown comfortably quiet and groggy together. Lucie felt ready for sleep, and hoped Grady wouldn't go back to looking hurt when she bid him good night and went to the guest room.

An older man and a youngish woman sat behind a news desk, smiling false smiles as graphics swirled and music blared.

"Up next," the male anchor said, "the amazing San Francisco reunion of a Wallingford man with his missing fiancée, right after this commercial break."

"No," Lucie said, dropping her feet to the floor. "They can't do that. I told them not to." She looked at Grady. "Can they?"

He shook his head, drained his glass. "Apparently they can."

"Everyone is going to see," Lucie said, heat creeping up from her chest, dampening her skin. "I mean, I guess people already know, huh?" The flyers. Maybe she'd already been on the local news in her absence. When people went missing, suddenly their photos were everywhere.

Grady winced. "I'm sorry," he said. "We just wanted to find

you." He picked up the bottle. It was empty. He set it back down. "We don't have to watch, if you don't want to."

She swallowed, felt her molars scrape against each other, her throat constrict. She sat forward in the chair, waiting. As much as she didn't want to, she had to see what would happen.

The last commercial faded and the silver-haired anchor came back on-screen. "And now, a heartwarming story for the Emerald City as a Seattle couple are reunited, from our sister station in San Francisco. Ann?"

The reporter from the day before stood in front of San Francisco General, big microphone to her face. "Today is a good day for Grady Goodall," she said, rather dramatically in Lucie's opinion. "The Seattle man has been searching tirelessly for his fiancée, who disappeared mysteriously over a week ago."

Lucie looked at Grady. He looked at his wineglass.

"Thirty-nine-year-old Lucie Walker went missing just two months before their wedding day," the reporter said. Now she sounded accusing, to Lucie's ear. "Whether a case of cold feet or foul play, no one knew."

"Jesus," Grady muttered.

"But it turns out that Walker had experienced a rare form of amnesia and wound up, somehow, in the frigid waters of the San Francisco Bay—"

"Only up to my knees," Lucie said. They made it sound like she'd thrown herself in.

"—admitted to San Francisco General, where yesterday the couple saw each other again for the first time, and we were there to bring their reunion to you."

And there it was, the footage of Grady walking toward her,

his face contorted in such a sad and private way, meant only for her, but everyone was seeing now what Lucie had put him through. She glanced over and saw that he, too, was entranced as they embraced on-screen.

"Amazing, Ann," said the anchor. "Who'd have thought this story would turn out so well?"

The footage lasted only a few seconds, and didn't include Lucie's admonishment or the nurses' efforts to shut the videographer down. Only the fairy-tale image of two people in love remained.

"I'm really sorry, Luce," Grady said, clicking off the TV. He leaned forward, elbows on knees, face in hands. "I should never have let my sisters contact the media."

"You were just trying to find me." It wouldn't have been that bad if not for the humiliation of losing her mind so publicly, of hurting someone so much by running away.

He sighed. "I just didn't know what to do. I should've known my sisters would overreact." He sounded angry now.

"But, you needed someone, you needed your family." She almost wished it had been her, in his shoes, surrounded by a family who cared so much.

Grady didn't answer. After a long moment he stood. "I'm beat. You must be, too."

Lucie nodded.

"You need anything from upstairs? All your stuff is in our . . . in the bathroom up there, if you'd like to go grab anything."

Lucie shook her head. "No, that's okay. I'm fine."

What did she want from him? Something, something more than this, even though she'd insisted she was just a guest in the house. Some sense of familiarity; one of those looks that meant they were okay. That they were connected at some level, even though she couldn't remember it.

"All right, then," he said. "See you in the morning." He started to walk away, then turned again. "Hey, we need to make sure to call that doctor tomorrow, get you an appointment." He nodded, said good night, and left her there.

Lucie sighed as he ascended the stairs. She didn't move until she'd heard him walk across the creaky floorboards and close a door.

Later, as she tried to relax into sleep, Lucie replayed the image of the two of them together on-screen, two people who loved each other. She remembered the way his back had felt beneath her hands, how she'd caressed him, breathed in his scent. A song filtered into her subconscious, a woman's voice singing: *The memory of all that, no, no, they can't take that away from me.*

Gershwin. She knew that. The realization jolted her awake. She lay there for a moment, heart pounding, then got out of bed. She pulled on the red coat and slipped into the dark hall-way, finding the basement steps. At the bottom, she switched on the light and walked to the piano, took a seat, and let her hands come to rest on top of the keys.

Her left hand made a chord, and then another. What was it? E flat something or other. What was next? Lucie shook her head. *Don't try so hard,* she thought. Softly, she hummed the melody: *The way you wear your hat . . .* Her hands moved uncertainly into position, pressing lightly, using the damper pedal to further soften the notes, her excitement increasing, knowing but not knowing how this song was being formed beneath her hands.

# helen

fter a dinner of one chicken drumstick, one buttered roll, and a small portion of deli coleslaw, Helen nursed her nightly tumbler of Canadian Club while looking through photo albums. She often turned to her old pictures—her entire life organized by date and occasion—for company in the evening. No longer connected by blood or relation to any living soul (that would have her, anyway), she preferred slipping into a whiskey-induced past over watching television, which no longer showed anything of value. Not like the old days, when even game shows were entertaining, and educational to boot. Helen sighed. She missed Betty White's husband—what was his name? She closed her eyes, struggling to recollect, then nodded. That's right. Allen Ludden. Nice crew cut, smart-looking glasses.

But even more, she missed her own husband, a better

looker than anyone on TV. His people were mostly Skykomish, and they'd lived on or near the reservation for generations. Edward's paternal grandfather had been part Flathead, though, from Montana, and had come west, the story went, with two mules, a blanket woven by his mother, and the name Ten Hands, accounting for the tireless work ethic of the family. Edward had certainly had it, always fixing things and helping neighbors with remodels while working full-time for the port all his life, right up until a few weeks before he passed. *Poor soul,* she thought, remembering the pain he'd suffered those last days as the cancer took him. But that had been over ten years ago.

Helen sighed, and turned to her favorite photo. There was Edward in his late twenties, putting in the rowboat on Silver Lake, back and shoulders strong, thick black hair ruffled in the bright breeze of the morning. She'd waded out and climbed aboard just after snapping the photo. They fished for kokanee and rainbow trout, spending long weekend days drinking Rainier from cans and eating bologna sandwiches, waiting for fish to pull their bobbers under, hoping for big ones. Edward was not one to talk much, but Helen had enough talking in her for the both of them. They'd been happy, then. They'd been happy for most of their years together.

But not after they took Lucie back in after her mother's death. What had once been a delightful child, full of laughter and love for her aunt and uncle, had turned into a silent wall of teenager. Yes, Lucie went to school, got straight A's, and never misbehaved—never even left the house much until she walked out for good upon graduation three years later. But she kept to herself, shunned their attempts to help her fit in back in Marysville. They knew she'd experienced more horror than anyone should have to, but if she'd given them even the smallest hint that she was hurting, or that she appreciated them or their efforts, it could have been different.

Helen had wanted so terribly to do right by her sister, to finish raising her niece to adulthood; what else could she do for poor Gloria? Her younger sister had always been so damn impulsive, running off with this man and that, making decisions like she was changing the channel on the TV. Helen knew their mother and father looked down and judged Gloria for her behavior and, worse, Helen for her inability to take better care of her sister. And for failing Lucie, no doubt, but Helen would have liked to see anyone deal with the girl when she came back from California. No one could've gotten through to her. She was ice and stone.

Edward ended up shunning this girl he'd loved as his own, after watching Helen get her feelings hurt so regularly. He quit trying altogether, and ignored their niece as coldly as she ignored them.

Helen couldn't hate her, though. The child had loved them once, almost like a child loves her real parents. Helen took a long, searing pull of whiskey. Even after all these years, from the time Lucie had left them when she was just eighteen, Helen still yearned to see her, to witness the girl's striking resemblance to Gloria, gone so long now, like everyone who'd ever mattered.

It was still dark when Helen startled awake in her recliner, sour-mouthed and headachy, the last photo album she'd been looking at splayed at an awkward angle on the brown carpet. Several pages were bent. Helen peered at her Timex in the near dark; it was after eleven. She'd nearly missed the Channel 5 news.

She clicked it on, hoping to see Lucie, and then there the girl was, almost like she'd been waiting till that moment for Helen to wake up. Only this was the living, breathing Lucie, not the photo they'd been showing of her every night, one of those posed things that no more looked like a person than a corpse did. This was the real Lucie, and Helen yearned for every gesture and expression.

And there was the fellow who claimed to be her fiancé, rushing into her arms. What right did he have? But she knew; a young woman could be swayed so easily by a good-looking man, and Lucie was her mother's daughter. Helen guessed he was about as tall as Edward, and there was a striking similarity, though he surely wasn't half the man her husband had been. This fellow had become some kind of local hero, as if losing someone you loved made you a celebrity.

"Hmph," she said, shaking her head. She should be the damn queen of England, then. She'd lost everyone.

Helen's nose dripped; tears fell. She wiped them on her sleeve. The authorities hadn't believed her, but they'd believed him, and look. The girl didn't have any feelings for him. Helen could have told them Lucie was just that way when she first came to them all those years ago. Helen had been calling and calling the police, trying to tell them the whole story as to why Lucie might not be right in the head, but they'd been patronizing at first, then skeptical as the story grew worse, and now just paid her lip service whenever she tried.

Goodall, his name was. Worked for Boeing. Lived in Wallingford. His number was unlisted, this Helen knew. Oh, she knew everything about him—well, as much as she could from watching the TV. Yes, he was as tall and handsome as Edward, and looked to be at least part Indian, and the girl was probably attracted to that at first. She'd loved her uncle like a father once upon a time. Edward was certainly the closest thing she'd ever had to one, even though she didn't come to the funeral. Helen had been almost glad about that, though. She didn't have to picture Edward rolling over in his narrow casket.

*Boeing,* the old woman thought, the sound of it a clear ringing bell in the fuzzy clockworks of her brain. *He works at Boeing.* Now *there* was a number that would not be unlisted. She would check out this Grady Goodall character, see what kind of man he was. See if maybe, through him, she couldn't find a way to Lucie. Helen coughed into her Kleenex, feeling the deep burn in her old lungs. It was now or never.

# twelve

# grady

h e dreamed of music, of a familiar song. The sound was far away, through door after door, and he couldn't reach it. He pulled open the last door only to trip on the threshold, jerking himself awake.

The music didn't stop. Grady fought the cobweb pull of his dream. He rolled over to find Lucie, to burrow his face into the nape of her neck and place his palm on her hip, until he remembered, as he did every night. Lucie wasn't there.

Only now, she was. She was playing the piano in the basement, something he'd never heard her do, even though he assumed she knew how. It was the song they'd chosen for their wedding, old-fashioned but they'd both loved it. When they'd practiced dancing to it in the living room, Grady had been worried what the neighbors might think if they saw them through the windows. If Lucie would dance with him now, he thought, he'd never care what anyone thought again.

He rolled from the bed and crept down the stairs to the

main floor, Lucie's playing growing louder and less tentative. Had she come to and this was her way of telling him? Should he run down into the basement, take her in his arms? *No,* he thought. If he went downstairs she might stop playing, or look at him with that vacant expression.

He stopped in the hallway. The guest room door was open. What if he went in, lay upon the bed and waited for her? *Creepy,* he thought. *That would just be creepy.*

He couldn't imagine Lucie having to go to a shrink, taking drugs. Old her would hate that, and frankly, new her seemed mellower than old her ever had. How important was it that she remember every little thing that ever happened to her? He barely remembered most of his childhood, just the moments that hurt the most.

Leaning back against the wall, he slid down to a sitting position, stretching his legs across the wood floor until his feet came to rest on the opposite wall. He closed his eyes to listen. This might mean something, this song, and he would wait to see what happened next.


THEIR FIRST YEAR together had blindsided Grady. He'd heard about that kind of love—the consuming infatuation that makes you see only your lover in a crowd, that makes you stay in bed together long past the time you should have been at work, that makes you promise everything you have to give until the day you die—but he'd never experienced it. Until he saw Lucie. Or to be truthful, until he saw the way Lucie saw him.

Even though he'd been under the watchful eyes of seven

females his entire life, Lucie's gaze was different. It said, "I see you as a man." It said, "I find you interesting/handsome/desirable." Any number of things that he felt pleasantly embarrassed about, and grateful for. No one had seen him that way before.

His family considered him a boy, still, the youngest and only son having a hard time coping with his father's death. They'd never noticed when he grew beyond that. He was the container for all things sad in the family, their urn of grief.

During their first year together, he'd found Lucie fascinating, too, and mysterious. That was her charm, her reluctance to talk about herself. "I don't know anything about you," he'd say, "except that you're smart and hot and—"

"That I adore you," she'd say, covering his mouth with hers, insinuating her body into the spaces his created. "You know that, right?"

He'd nod, groan with pleasure, and she'd say, "That's enough for now."

If he pressed for information, her face would lose expression. He hated that look; it took her away from him. But occasionally he would ask anyway, feeling that he really ought to know more about her family and her past. Their relationship was growing serious.

Somewhere near the end of their first year, he had pressed one too many times, and she got angry.

"Fine," she said, "you want to know? My parents are dead. My aunt and uncle had no choice but to take me in when I was fifteen, and we all hated it, and everyone was relieved the day I left for college. Okay? Is that enough to satisfy you? My family life sucked."

Grady regretted pushing her. "I'm sorry, I didn't realize," he said. "Why didn't you just tell me? I mean, Jesus, how did your mom and dad die?" Together, he wondered, or separately? Illness, car crash?

She closed her eyes and shook her head. Whatever she was remembering had to be bad.

"I'm sorry," he said, holding her. He'd let her tell him when she felt ready to.

That never happened over the next four years. He never learned another thing about Lucie's life as a kid, even when he gently prodded her. She mentioned her aunt occasionally, the only living relative she had left; her uncle had died, too, years after she'd moved away. The aunt had been smothering and invasive, constantly worrying and fretting over Lucie to the point of obsession. The uncle had told Lucie that if she couldn't get along with her aunt, she was not welcome in their home. She'd made a plan at sixteen with her high school counselor and got good enough grades to get scholarships and grants at the University of Washington when she graduated.

Grady knew these experiences—as awful as they sounded—made her the Lucie he loved: savvy, competent. A survivor. All the qualities he wished for himself, things that didn't come from being coddled by family. Still, they had wounded her, too, and he vowed to love her enough to make up for all of it.

She never did tell him how her parents died. Sometimes he wondered if she didn't know, or if she knew too much. He would trace the three circles at the top of her thigh, cigarette burns, he was sure of it, and ask her how she got them.

"They've just always been there," she'd say.

He'd worried that they were self-inflicted, although he
wasn't sure if Lucie had ever smoked. Still, she bore a few thin,
white scars near her ankles that were similar to those of his
cousin Ronnie Lynn, who'd been a cutter as a teenager. It was
all too sad and too difficult, and it became easier just to let it
rest there between them. Besides, any man in his shoes would
have jumped at the chance to love a woman like this, one who
had no need to talk through every moment of her past, who carried no baggage from old relationships to hurl at him, and who
didn't care if he didn't want to talk. She didn't want to talk, either, not about emotions or feelings or old hurts or scars.

Even so, the passion of the first year waned and the reality
of making a relationship work set in. Lucie was strong willed
and wanted things a certain way. Before the wedding planning
started, Grady had found he could live with most of it, as long
as it made Lucie happy. The things he couldn't live with, well,
he found a way to compress them, to miniaturize and remold
them in his mind until they fit into the tiny, locked compart-
ment of his brain where he stored the other bad stuff: his failures; his knowing that, somehow, he would never be enough for
Lucie; and thoughts of his dad, the salmon, swimming eternally
away from him.

IT WAS NO longer dark; daylight seeped into the windows.
Grady had fallen asleep sitting on the hard floor, head bent to
the right, neck muscles now in spasm. The guest room door was
closed. He covered his face with his hands and leaned back.

She'd seen him there, sleeping, snoring, no doubt. Jesus.

He needed to swim. He needed to go to work. He needed to do something normal. As odd as she was acting, Lucie seemed stable and content to be at home.

Grady groaned and got to his feet. A small piece of paper lay on the floor just outside the guest room. He walked quietly over to pick it up. "D A Y Y L U L U," it read. He shook his head. Maybe Lucie's mind still sparked like a frayed, live wire. He carried the note into the kitchen and laid it on the counter for her to find when she woke.

After putting on coffee to brew, he climbed the stairs to get dressed for work and pack his swim gear. He would leave Lucie a note, write down his cell number, because of course she no longer knew it.

Who knew what had happened to her cell phone? Her entire life was on that thing. He shook his head. He didn't know her password. He could try tracking down data through the service provider, but at this point, it seemed easier to let it go. Any messages that had been left for her were just ghosts, now, from another time.

An hour later at the office, Grady felt relief as the glass security door clicked into place behind him. He was safe. Problems that came up here he could solve. And sure enough, the day was filled with issues that had previously seemed dire and important. They seemed trivial now, and completely intoxicating. He could fill his mind with their pettiness and technicalities. People counted on him, and he felt the pull he always did to let work consume him.

Late in the afternoon, Grady sat in his cubicle, a rare break from meetings. He checked his cell phone—nothing from

Lucie—and had just stuck it back in its holster when his desk phone rang. No one at Boeing called each other on the land-lines anymore. His family always used his cell. Had Lucie called the main Boeing number to track him down? But he'd left her his number.

"Hello?" His heart beat a little faster, the way it used to when she'd call him just to say hi.

"Is this Grady Goodall?" An older woman's voice.

Not his mother, not Donna in accounting. "Uh, yes."

"Mr. Goodall, my name is Helen Ten Hands?"

Was she asking him or telling him? And did she say ten . . . hands? "Okay," he replied.

"Well, Mr. Goodall, now I know this is awkward and maybe I shouldn't even be calling you, but I think you should know that Lucie Walker is my niece. I used to be her legal guardian, in fact."

The aunt that Lucie hated. "Okay," he said again, both re-luctant and eager for information. He scrambled for paper and pen.

"I saw you on the news last night, and well, actually I've been following this whole ordeal. You know, it used to be that family kept things private, but, well. You're not exactly family, I suppose. Anyway, I tried calling that hospital where you found her, but they thought I was some kind of fruit basket."

"Oh," Grady said again. "But . . ."

"But you, they believed." She gave a little harrumph. "Obvi-ously not from your articulate nature, so I'm giving you the ben-efit of the doubt that you have proof, or else they wouldn't have let you take her. Is that right, Mr. Goodall?"

"Yeah, of course," he stammered. "But, how, how do I know you're really her aunt?"

"You two live together, I presume? Meaning, bed down together without the benefit of wedlock?"

Grady blushed. "Well, I, uh . . ." He sighed. "Yes, ma'am."

"Then you know about her scars as well as I do."

Grady inhaled so abruptly that he coughed, choking on spit he'd sucked into his windpipe.

"Are you all right, son? Is someone there who can clap you on the back?"

"No, no, I'm fine," he wheezed, then coughed again before he was able to speak. "I, well, I knew that was a scar. She always says it's a birthmark."

The woman clucked. "Why don't you describe it for me, just so I can be sure."

Grady closed his eyes. "Three circles, top of her right thigh. They're cigarette burns, aren't they? Oh, man, I knew it, but she always . . ."

She sniffed, and he heard the whispery sound of tissue.

"How?" he asked.

"All I know is she didn't leave here that way. It happened after they left. By the time I got her back, she had more than that wrong with her, I can tell you."

"When she got back from where? What happened with her, with her parents, and—"

"Well, I believe this is her business, and if she wanted to share it with you—"

"Well, the problem is she doesn't remember anything, Mrs. Ten . . ."

"Hands. And my number is— Do you have a pencil? She needs her family right now, Mr. Goodall."

He quickly jotted down the number she rattled off, trying to think of a way to convince her to tell him more. "I am her family. Trust me, no one is closer to Lucie than I am.

"Just tell her to call me, if you please."

The line went dead. As Lucie had said, the old lady was cranky and demanding, and more than a little weird. He slipped the piece of paper into his messenger bag and packed up his laptop, his hands jittery at the latches.

A good, long swim would calm him.

# lucie

Waking to muted gray instead of the hospital's bright white, Lucie looked for a clock, disoriented until she remembered: she was in Seattle. She was "home," whatever that meant.

She'd been up late, playing song after song as they returned to her, gifts unwrapping themselves: jazz and classical, rock, a Beatles tune, she thought, or was it another band? Something old, she knew.

And there had been no words with the melodies after that first line, no song titles, just the notes in glissando or staccato, the chord progressions and harmonies and refrains. Just as before, she felt the presence of someone else beside her on the bench, small hands on the keys with hers. Perhaps she was remembering something from childhood, her own hands as she learned to play, for surely she played well enough to have been at it for many years. The letters on the bench remained a mystery, but they felt connected, somehow, to everything. She had written them down so she could study them.

Exhausted finally, Lucie had crept back up the stairs—as though that sound would wake Grady instead of the music—and found him asleep in the hallway. He'd been listening, a thought so profound and moving that she felt a rush of love for him. She must have played for him all the time in their former life together, and this was how it had felt. She stood for a moment, watching him sleep. Why hadn't he come down to the basement when he heard her? If it had been before she disappeared, and she was still the woman he loved, would he have? Lucie had a feeling that he found this new Lucie too strange and disconcerting to act naturally. She sighed. Well, he must have found some comfort in the music, to have sat on the hard floor and listened until he fell asleep. She'd have brought out a pillow, but he was sitting. She'd have brought him a blanket, but it was warm. What could she do to be the Lucie he loved? That thought hurt too much to think, so she'd just gone to bed.

Now Lucie pulled her denim skirt back on, having slept in her T-shirt. When she ventured out into the house, Grady was gone. He'd left coffee in the thermal pot along with a note detailing where she might find everything she'd need for breakfast. It was a bit perfunctory until the end, which he signed, "Love, G." She smiled and turned the note over; it was the same paper she'd written the letters on the night before, and she wondered where he'd found it, what he'd thought it was. It might make more sense to her when she'd been home awhile, when her memories started to return, which they said was a ninety percent possibility. So why did they feel so far away?

Lucie ran her hand through her hair and sighed. Breakfast. Then shower. One step at a time.

Bypassing the oatmeal and ultra-fiber cereals Grady mentioned in his note, Lucie found a heel of twelve-grain bread lonely in its bag in the back of the fridge. She toasted it and spread it thick with jam. Maybe she'd walk around the neighborhood to find a grocery store later on; Grady had said they did all their shopping and errands just a few blocks away. First, though, she knew she had to go upstairs to the master bedroom, something she'd been steeling herself for since arriving home the day before. It would be the most personal space of the former Lucie's, and this Lucie still wasn't sure how well she wanted to get to know that one. Fresh clothes were definitely required, though, and a hot shower. Licking jam from her fingers, she stood. It was time.

She mounted the bare wood steps, and at the top she exhaled, relieved. Rather than the cool perfection of the rest of the house, the room glowed warm and golden, a little messy with Grady's clothes hanging over a chair, the bed made hurriedly with a cinnamon-colored spread. Light and a cool breeze spilled through south-facing windows, an impressionist view of the Seattle skyline in the distance through marine layer and tree leaves.

Which side of the bed was hers? She considered the items on top of the two bedside tables. Each had a lamp, a pile of books, and a framed photo of the two of them. She picked up the picture closest to her, the two of them a study in dark and light. They looked good together, with their opposite coloring, dressed formally at some kind of event. They both smiled rather maniacally. False smiles, that's what they were. The kind you smile at such a function when someone pulls out a camera and points it at you.

She crawled across the bed to grab the other photo, then lay on her back to compare the two, pleasantly aware of Grady's scent in the bedclothes. So, this was his side, and his picture was taken in a kitchen, blue flowered wallpaper in the background, as they sat behind mammoth slices of pie. Grady had his arm around her shoulders, drawing her to him. Lucie could see how much he cared for her. Well, for the Lucie in the photo. They were at ease and happy together, and she wondered if they ever would be again.

The pile of books confirmed it was Grady's side of the bed: *100 Years of Flight. Managing Aviation Projects from Concept to Completion*. He'd mentioned working at Boeing. Why hadn't she asked him more about his job? She would that evening.

Lucie sat up and studied the books on her side of the bed: *The Power of Self; Optimal Thinking; The 8th Habit: From Effectiveness to Greatness*. They seemed a little dry, if not desperate.

She pulled open the top drawer of her nightstand, finding a series of small organizing containers. One held a nail file, Burt's Bees lip balm and hand lotion, and a tube of K-Y gel. Lucie felt her cheeks color. The other containers held safety pins and assorted buttons, a small pad of paper and pen, miniature bottles of Tylenol PM and Tums. In the back of the drawer, a plain plastic box caught her attention. She pulled it out and opened it, revealing an oddly shaped sex toy. It was of the vibrating variety, a deep raspberry color, with various unusual protrusions.

So, Lucie thought, feeling light-headed; she was a prim neatnik with a wild side. Her face flushed hot. This was how intimate she had been with Grady, for five long years. Of course she had been! Why was she so embarrassed? How would she look at him when he came home later without thinking about what he knew about her but she didn't know about him? He knew what she looked like naked, probably from every angle imaginable. He knew every square centimeter of her, in fact, how she . . . well, how she *was,* that way. Sexually. Something she didn't even know about herself. Should she cry or laugh or pack her meager things and leave? It was all too crazy—she was crazy, she had to be, not to remember even such a thing as that.

Lucie lay back on the bed, hands over her face, panic at the back of her throat. How could she not know anything, not one stupid thing, about herself? What god was this cruel? Did she believe in God? She paused for a moment, realizing she didn't even know that. Tears rushed up, but she wouldn't cry. No. No damn crying. But then she was—like it or not—sobbing, her abdomen convulsing. She'd been alive thirty-nine years and only remembered four days of it. Where had she been between going missing and coming to? How had she traveled so far? What had happened along the way?

And why couldn't she shake the feeling that she'd left someone behind, somewhere, someone who depended on her? She supposed it could be this aunt of hers, but they weren't close, Grady said. He seemed to be the only person in her life now, but it wasn't him. As much as he loved her and had missed her, she knew this.

And how on earth could an argument with Grady be so

traumatic that she'd completely freak out and lose her mind, lose her self? She sat up. It had to be a pretty big damn argument, didn't it?

The crying stopped as suddenly as it had started. What was Grady not telling her? There had to be more to the story. Prewedding jitters did not make normal, sane people lose their memories. Either she was not normal, or something really bad had happened between her and Grady. Was he safe to be with? *Yes,* she knew, even as little as she knew him, but one thing was for sure. She needed more information, and not from another shrink who knew nothing about her. The things Lucie needed to know were all around her, in this house, in the drawers and cabinets and files. And in Grady.

Lucie wiped her face with her T-shirt, then pulled it off over her head. She would shower. She would find clean clothes. And then she would find out what the hell happened on the day she ran.

COSMETIC PRODUCTS BULGED from every drawer, shelf, and cupboard in the bathroom. The shower organizer was crowded with shampoos and body scrubs and conditioners and foot treatments. And she'd thought the contents of her purse were over the top. Did she really use all this stuff? Aside from shaving cream, deodorant, and toothpaste, it didn't seem like much of it was Grady's. The products were all of the insecure female variety: elbow softeners, eyelid tighteners, age spot bleachers, wrinkle reducers. One drawer held all of the same makeup items she'd found in the purse, exact duplicates. And in the cabinet below there were tons of hairstyling products: balms and mousses and crèmes and gels and sprays. Could any of this be Grady's, for those wild, gorgeous locks? She had so little hair, what on earth would she do with any of this stuff?

After a quick shower, Lucie found a lotion she liked the smell of and applied it to her face and body, stroked on the more feminine deodorant in the medicine chest, then combed her fingers through her hair. She stood looking at her plain face in the mirror. She was beginning to look familiar. Lucie turned her head to the left, to the right, tipped it back, then forward, looking up into her own reflected eyes. They were an interesting shade of green. Did Grady like her eyes? She sighed and went to find clean underwear.

Guessing the larger chest of drawers was hers, she slid open the top drawer to reveal neatly folded stacks of undergarments in muted silks. At the back was a pile of cotton-blend briefs, an athletic brand, and she pulled out a pair. The bras all looked too structural and uncomfortable, and she wasn't all that big in the first place; she closed the drawer. Each of the subsequent drawers was filled to the top, all too neat and orderly, made even more so by the limited color palette of beige, gray, taupe, and a few black and white pieces mixed in. Before she closed each drawer she rummaged her hands through the clothes, untidying them just enough to feel comfortable. The bottom drawer held athletic gear—tights and yoga pants; long, fitted T-shirts; and hoodies. Lucie relaxed, choosing black tights and a white T-shirt, a gray hoodie. The morning chill had not yet burned off outside.

The closet was as stuffed as the drawers had been. She'd

come in to find shoes, but the array of items was fascinating. In addition to the rows of women's suits and business attire, there was a short rack of evening dresses, several black coats, and stacks and stacks of shoe boxes. Inside each was a pair of something expensive: strappy silver sandals, jeweled flats, basic black pumps in three heel heights, and then red, and then bone. Along one wall was an array of athletic shoes. She became aware that not all of the items had been worn; some of the hanging clothes still had tags, plastic bags covering them. Behind the clothes were stacks of packages, some opened, some not. The mailing labels were from Saks and Zappos, Designer Discount and Sephora. It was like she'd been on a mission to procure as much as possible without regard to what she actually needed. *"Eesh,"* Lucie whispered. What drove a person to do that?

She picked the most worn looking pair of athletic shoes and slipped into them, sighing at how they molded to her feet. She must have worn them a lot, a comforting thought. She hadn't only worn heels.

Lucie was more than curious now. The other room she'd been avoiding was the office. Was it hers or Grady's? Or both of theirs? She headed downstairs.

Crossing the living room, she remembered the night before, how the two of them had become almost comfortable together, watching TV, sharing a bottle of wine. If it hadn't been for the news report, they might have made progress. She rounded the corner to the office and stood in the doorway.

There were two work spaces in opposite corners, sleek tabletop desks with minimalist cabinetry. Here, their spaces were easy to tell apart. His was casually strewn with mementos of his life: framed photos of people who must be his family with their earthen complexions; paper airplanes; a pair of broken goggles (the kind for swimming, it appeared). The other desk was neat. Nothing on it but a thin silver laptop computer. Lucie didn't know whether to open it or not. She opened drawers instead, finding crisp file folders with labels neatly affixed: Josh Clark, Indu Parekh, Buppha Srisai, and company names like Google, CompuCom, InterStat, Microsoft, and yes, Boeing. She looked for a file on Grady but found none.

Disappointed, she pulled open more drawers, wondering if she'd find personal notes, letters, an address book, or something to tell her who she knew. Instead she found the same organizers used in the drawers upstairs, holding paper clips and rubber bands, pens, pencils, more nail files and hand lotion. And behind everything, much like the sex toy had been, a rubber-banded stack of brochures. Another secret, Lucie guessed. She pulled them out and thumbed through them. Beauty spas, aestheticians promising skin renewal, dentists specializing in brilliant smiles. And yes, plastic surgeons. Some in Seattle, and some elsewhere: Los Angeles, the Bahamas, even. Lucie replaced the rubber band and put the bundle back into the drawer. Was she really this vain? Did Grady want her to do these things? She tried to remember why the brochures had felt worth saving, but the effort left her feeling empty and hopeless. She'd never know what she'd been thinking then, or at any time, it seemed.

Lucie looked at the laptop and sighed. Should she open it or not? What had she not done while she'd been gone that she was supposed to do? Who had she disappointed? What havoc had she wreaked in people's lives?

Drawing a deep breath, Lucie closed her eyes. Did it matter? She had no way of helping them now, a thought both painful and relieving. She didn't seem to have a cell phone—not anymore, anyway. No doubt she'd lost it or discarded it while she was gone. No doubt she had phone messages piled high somewhere in the ether, messages she'd never retrieve, people who'd never get answers.

Lucie opened her eyes. She slid the laptop toward her and lifted the lid. She knew how to do this. She knew the icons that appeared on the screen, which was for e-mail, which for browsing online. She knew the sounds that accompanied the functions. But when she opened her e-mail program and scanned the list of incoming messages, she didn't know any of the names. Many were clearly junk mail from online retailers and discount coupon companies. There were messages from people as well, of course, most with tech company names for addresses. Some with Gmail accounts or Yahoo. She recognized none of them, so she studied the subject lines to see which she should open. Who was worried about her? Who had checked in while she was gone to say they were concerned, or praying for her safe return? Her disappearance had been on the news, on telephone poles. Of the hundreds of new messages, who was actually e-mailing Lucie the person and not Lucie the consumer or job recruiter?

"Available July 1." "Resume attached." "Any opportunities yet for software developer?" They were from people in need of something from her. There were a few "Thank yous!" and a "Resubmitting Your Invoice." Presumably someone hadn't paid her.

Next, Lucie looked at the dates. Aside from the automatic junk deliveries, nothing was more recent than June twenty-eighth. No one had tried to reach her in the past ten days. They'd given up, moved on.

Sighing, she closed the computer and left the office. She needed a walk. And some real food. The world outside felt far more promising than this one.

# grady

t he home phone rang unanswered at noon, as it had before Grady left the office. Now in the locker room at Sound Fitness, he felt on the verge of panic. He was trying so hard not to worry, not to obsess, to just let Lucie be. Maybe she didn't answer the phone because she thought of it as someone else's. Or maybe she'd gone out, but how would she even know where to go? Would she get lost? He wouldn't let himself think the other thing, the thing about her leaving again.

He already had on his Speedo, his hair tucked and flattened inside his cap, goggles ready to pull into position. Should he just get dressed and go home? If he hadn't been so stubborn the day before she left, they might have avoided this whole mess. He turned toward his locker. He should go home.

Opening his locker door, he shook his head. If he went home now, he'd be edgy and moody. Lucie knew how to operate a phone, she had his number. She'd survived, somehow, for a week alone in San Francisco. She would survive her first half day at home alone. His insides juddered, but he couldn't stand guard over her night and day. He remembered something his mother had said after his dad didn't return from the last fishing trip and the sisters were hysterical: "Girls, it wasn't our fault. It wasn't our job to keep him alive."

But Grady, the boy, held himself responsible postmortem, as irrational as he now realized it was. He should have been a better son. He should have paid more attention when his dad tried to teach him words from the old language (which embarrassed Grady in front of the neighbor kids). He should have watched more closely when his dad showed him how to spool line on a reel so that it didn't get tangled when casting. But Grady hadn't wanted to know about fishing line. He'd wanted his dad to teach him how to throw a Frisbee or pop a wheelie on the one decrepit bike he shared with his sisters. Even when his father tried, though, it was clear that these were not his strengths. Grady inevitably landed on his ass in the driveway, bike skidding out from under him, or threw the Frisbee high and wide, then chased it into the street. The kids all laughed from behind their own fences, inside their own safe squares of patchy lawn. Grady knew even then that these were not his father's failures; they were his own. He could still feel the sting in his eyes, the look on his dad's face when he turned to go inside the house.

Grady closed the locker harder than he meant to, spun the lock dial, and walked barefoot across the blue tile floor that led to the pool.

Most of the regular lunchtime swimmers were already in the pool, the older guy with the pierced ear and silver BMW sharing a lane with the youngish, bottom-heavy woman that always said hello when they passed on the pool deck. Three young and cocky Boeing field reps had a lane each, which always pissed Grady off. They swam at approximately the same skill level and speed as each other, yet never shared lanes. People shared lanes all the time, especially when it was busy. The regulars were all so used to each other they never even asked anymore, just timed their entrances carefully. Grady had tried getting in the lanes with these guys before, but they swam too fast, lapping him, making him feel old and ridiculous.

The outside lane farthest from the entrance had a lone swimmer, one Grady didn't recognize. He walked over, windmilling his arms as he waited for the swimmer to get close to the opposite wall. At the optimal moment, Grady dove efficiently, the relief of submersion immediate. This was good; it was good he'd decided to stay and swim.

Just as he and the other swimmer were about to pass, Grady realized the man wasn't giving way. Grady's forearm scraped the pool wall as he pulled right to accommodate him, chlorine immediately stinging raw skin. There was no chance the guy hadn't seen him, but maybe he'd never shared a lane before. He wasn't the worst swimmer Grady had ever seen, but his form was sloppy.

At the end of the lane, Grady prepped for his kick turn, executing decently. Maybe the day off had been good for him; he was swimming well. As he approached midlane, the guy, once again, wasn't budging from the center, so Grady pulled up, motioned with his hand for the swimmer to pass on the left.

Instead, the swimmer nearly swam over Grady, wheezing

out, "Fuck you, Tonto, get out of my lane," before he turned his head back underwater.

Stunned, Grady reached forward again to begin his stroke, but he felt shaky, his arm not pulling the way he wanted it to. His rhythm was off, his limbs rubbery, and his breathing shallow because he was so damn pissed off. Who the hell did this guy think he was?

Setting up for his turn at the wall, Grady realized too late he was out of position and threw his feet up and over as hard as he could to correct. In the next instant, his heels slammed like two fleshy sledgehammers against the concrete deck.

The intensity of the pain staggered Grady more than the rude swimmer, more than the fact that he'd messed up and turned too late and, *holy shit,* how would he get to the surface in this agony? There were no words for the pain, only the emergency feeling that he'd really gone and done it this time because his body was flailing, and he would drown if he didn't pull himself together and fast, and get the hell out of the water.

Surfacing, he gasped for air, clawed doggy-paddle style to the side, his useless feet trailing behind him. If he tried to kick, pain raced up his legs like searing knives. What had he done? Could you break your heels? Grady had never heard of such a thing.

As he struggled to hold on to the pool edge, the other swimmer passed, smiling when he turned his head to breathe and flashing his middle finger before disappearing beneath the water.

"No," Grady said. "No you goddamn don't."

The man performed an ugly, graceless turn at the end of

the lane and headed back. Grady's blood surged through his veins, thick and roiling.

Why didn't he ever fucking fight back? Look where it had gotten him all his life: crippled and feeling like a loser.

He let go of the side and swam straight for the rude swimmer, high on adrenaline now, each yard torture for his feet, finally colliding shoulders-on with a hard, satisfying, wet thud. Grady railed at the man, arms pounding like industrial fan blades against his slick back and shoulders, as if he were trying to swim right through him.

The man recoiled, sinking, then fought through Grady's thrashing arms to get back to the surface. Head popping out, goggles knocked askew, he yelled, "What the fuck? What the fuck, man?" and everyone in the pool stopped swimming to look.

"You're supposed to fucking share!" Grady knew he sounded like a sniveling kid, but those were the rules. How could this idiot just break them and get away with it? "You fucking asshole!"

"Everyone okay over there?" the nice woman swimmer called, and Grady felt suddenly sick. He submerged, using only his arms to flounder to the far end of the lane, where he stayed under, hoping everyone would go back to swimming, but when he came up to breathe, the whole place was in disarray, the other swimmers all talking and pointing. The rude swimmer was out of the pool now, talking to one of the girls from the front desk. They started walking toward Grady, and he sank back under, heels throbbing like hot coals.

Looking up through his goggles, he could see them standing over him now, bodies wiggling and quavering in the blue turbulence. It was the cute blonde who always gave Grady an extra towel, even when he didn't ask. And he'd watched to see if she did it with everyone. She didn't.

He closed his eyes. He had the capacity to stay under for a very long time, like a salmon. Like his father, who'd been under now for thirty-four long years. Why didn't anyone follow the rules in life, like stay alive until your offspring reach adulthood? Like, don't just completely forget the person you love and become a stranger. Like, share the fucking pool lanes, for god's sake.


ON THE LAST morning of Grady's childhood, the summer sun had been casting diamonds across the South Puget Sound as he and his three eldest sisters swam and splashed near the Dash Point State Park dock. His mother had taken the three younger girls to ballet lessons and would return at noon to pick up the others. Even though Grady was just eight years old, his parents trusted him in the water. He was *pish pish,* his father had said, "little fish" in Chinook. Grady felt proud of his abilities, but most especially of the fact that his dad had noticed. Harry Goodall was a taciturn man who spoke mostly of his work at sea and family finances, and he was always exhausted during his brief times at home. Fishing was the hardest work of all, Grady and his sisters knew, even though their friends acted like their dad was out on a cruise ship all the time because he wasn't like their dads, working in the mill or at a trade or in the service.

That day, Grady had been practicing staying under the

water for increasingly longer increments of time, asking his sisters to count while he was submerged. He couldn't wait to report in to his dad the next time they got a phone call from him.

"Eunie!" he shouted to shore, where the girls now lounged on beach towels. "I'm going under! Start counting."

She nodded, and he took the deepest breath he could, folded his legs Indian style, and let himself sink slowly toward the dirt bottom. It wasn't wise to keep your eyes open underwater, but he slit them every now and again to have a look around at the murky plant life and smelt and occasional rockfish. His lungs were beginning to burn, but he wanted to break his record. Muffled voices overhead drew his attention. He looked up through the gray-green water with his squinting eyes and saw people on the dock. They were waving at him, it seemed, so he waved back. He was breaking his record, that was it, and Eunie had run out to the dock to congratulate him when he surfaced. Then Grady noticed that it wasn't just the three figures, but more people, all acting frantic.

Something was wrong. He pushed his feet into the spongy bottom and launched upward. Too much time was passing, though, as he tried to reach the top. Would he make it or would he run out of breath? Why had he stayed under so long? His lungs were on fire now, and he had a bad feeling, like he'd really gone and done it this time. He hadn't thought about leaving enough air to swim up, and now he might die.

As Grady broke the surface, gasping for air, he saw all of his sisters crying, hanging on to each other and to their mother, steadfast and pale beneath her gardening hat.

"Get out, now, Son. We have to go home," she said calmly,

but something in her voice made Grady understand that she had been crying, too.

"Why, what's wrong?" he sputtered, still out of breath, treading water with his feet and hands. He didn't really want to know, but why were all the girls so upset?

"Dammit, Grady, just mind," his mother said and turned to walk back to the car. She rarely cursed; this was serious.

"There was an accident on the boat! Daddy's dead!" blurted one of the girls, Grady didn't even know which one, and they all started to wail and grab for each other's hands as they followed their mother.

*I am pish pish,* Grady thought, *not a boy, not a brother, not a son.* He sucked in the largest breath ever, lungs filling his rib cage to splitting. Leaving his eyes open as he descended, he studied the watery world around him. It was the only world he wanted, this hazy, quiet place. He might have stayed under forever, there in the deep with his father, but from out of nowhere a body sliced through the water toward him. It was only when she was right upon him that Grady could see the wide blue eyes and swirling black hair of his mother.

fifteen

# lucie

~~~~~~

She lived on a street called Meridian, a name that pleased Lucie as she walked, studying the cottages and bungalows, their gardens and big trees. The sun warmed her head and back, and she ambled along, stopping occasionally to look at a half-bloomed hydrangea up close, or to rub lavender into her palms. She picked a sprig and tucked it into her little bag, next to a folded wad of cash Grady had left for her in case she needed anything.

In one particularly striking garden, an older woman in a straw hat pruned a laceleaf maple.

"That's lovely," Lucie called to her, and the woman, Asian and pretty at her age, looked up, startled. "The way you're shaping that, I mean," Lucie explained. "So feathery and open."

"So, you've been found," the woman said but kept working.

Lucie's skin went clammy. Of course. The flyers, the news reports. She started to walk again, but stopped at the woman's property line and turned back.

"Do you know me?"

The woman straightened to look at Lucie, fists in the small of her back as she stretched. "Not really," she said. "No one does. Isn't that the way you want it?"

"No," Lucie said. "Why would I want that?"

"You've lived here four, five years, and this is the first time you've even spoken a word to me. I suppose it's that amnesia thing, hmm?"

Lucie backed up a step. "I . . . I just thought your garden was so beautiful, and, well . . ."

The woman bent back over her work.

Lucie wanted to turn and run, but here was someone who had known her, in a way, and seemed comfortable telling the truth, something she suspected Grady wasn't. Lucie walked closer. "Was I a horrible person?"

The woman looked up through the branches, her eyes a surprising light gray. "Is this for real?"

Lucie shrugged, not knowing what she was being asked. Was she for real? Was her question for real?

The woman sighed and removed her hat, came out from behind the maple. Her silver hair glinted in the sunlight. "God," she said and sighed. "Would you like to come inside for some tea?"

Lucie nodded. As surly as this woman was, Lucie wanted to know more about herself, about this woman's perceptions of her. "That would be nice. Thank you."

The interior of the small cottage was as artfully arranged as the garden, and smelled of lemon oil, which, Lucie thought, probably coated the teak table and chairs that made a dining room out of half the living room.

"Have a seat and I'll pour us some tea." The woman smiled for the first time. "I doubt you know my name. I'm Susan."

"Lucie."

The woman nodded. "Oh, yeah," she said, "I know," and went through a push door into the kitchen.

An old built-in hutch filled the wall across from Lucie, displaying souvenirs of a life and family: baby cups, wedding goblets, small vases and old jars, a tarnished silver sugar bowl and creamer. Susan pushed back through the door with a tray holding mismatched glasses of iced tea and a plate of sugar cookies.

Sweets. Lucie smiled. "Wow, thank you."

Susan took a seat across from her and sipped from a glass. "So, amnesia, huh? What's that like?"

Lucie's eyes filled. "It's . . . It's terrible."

"God, I'm sorry," the other woman said, wincing. "I do this bitch thing when I'm nervous. It's just so awkward, this whole thing."

"It's okay." Lucie slid a cookie from the plate.

"Not really," Susan said. "I'm horrible at this. Are you okay? I mean . . ."

Lucie shook her head. "I don't know. I'm just . . ." She shrugged. "Empty."

Susan squinted. "How about I just fill you in on neighborhood gossip?"

Lucie nodded. What she really wanted to know about was

herself, but this seemed safer. She took a bite of cookie, letting it rest on her tongue to savor it.

"We have a few interesting characters around here, like the death metal band that rents the house around the corner. They're actually nice kids and practice in their basement only until ten o'clock, which is good of them, and they play at our annual block party, which, by the way, you've never made it to."

Lucie looked into her lap.

"Shit!" Susan said. "Shit shit shit. I'm sorry. Slap me next time."

Lucie smiled. "Okay," she said, looking up.

Susan winked and continued. "We also have a local sports anchor who lives with his partner in that yellow house on the corner, although he calls him his 'roommate' and pretends he has a long-distance girlfriend in San Diego. Both nice guys, and always ready to help out if you need to move something heavy. And then there's old Don Donaldson, your neighbor actually. Lives on the left as you face your house from the street. All the neighborhood kids are scared to death of him."

"The big gray house? It does look kind of haunted."

Susan nodded. "Don is, shall we say, eccentric, but I don't think he'd hurt a bug. You never used to hear much from him until his wife died, but now he's outside all the time, all summer, all winter, yelling at the kids to keep their bikes off his lawn, so they won't even ride by there anymore. I think he's just trying to keep up that big place so that it's perfect, the way his wife did. She was quite the gardener; she gave me most of my plant starts. Unfortunately, perfect to Don means cleared free of all plant life except for grass and those ugly old shrubs along his property lines."

"Do I know him?" Lucie asked, an odd question, she realized, but Susan nodded.

"Oh, yeah. You two famously don't get along. Your landscaping drives him crazy because, you know, plants don't know property lines. Sometimes things reseed on his side, or spread over. He tried to get you to cut down an old birch a couple of years ago because it dropped leaves on his side in the fall, which is ridiculous. I mean, this is a city of trees and leaves, right? So, when you wouldn't, he went out there early one morning and started sawing limbs off on his side."

"Oh my god," Lucie said. "What happened?"

"You and your boyfriend came running out screaming at him. Well, you were screaming. I think your boyfriend was just there for moral support." Susan smiled, as if it were a pleasant memory. "A little excitement for the whole neighborhood."

"But we were right. The tree was on our side of the property line, you said."

Susan nodded. "Technically, yes, although your boyfriend did tell another neighbor across the street that you two didn't really want that tree anyway. You were just determined not to let him cut it down."

Lucie wrinkled her nose, set the cookie in front of her. "Well, that's kind of mean."

Susan shrugged. "Don's just a lonely old man without any friends. I don't know how he makes it without his wife. He counted on her for everything. Sometimes I take him a coffee cake or something just to pop in and see how he's holding up."

"He hates me."

"Probably so."

"And do you? Does everyone?"

The older woman paused, considering her answer. "No, not hate. You've never given us much of anything to either like or dislike. You . . . well. For example. You're a runner, right?"

Ah, the athletic clothes. Lucie looked down at her tights and shoes. "I guess so."

"So, okay, you come out every morning, dressed much like that, but you have on these dark glasses that wrap around your face, even when it's raining, and a hat pulled down so low it's amazing you can even see. And you run through the neighborhood never acknowledging anyone, never saying hi, or smiling, or even waving or nodding like the rest of us do. I mean, we're not all best friends or anything, but you know. We acknowledge each other. Like you did today. Just neighborly."

No one liked her. She was an unlikable person. Did she have any friends?

They sat silently for a moment. Lucie sighed. "Well, I really should get going."

Susan frowned. "You did want to know, right?"

"I did." Lucie shrugged. "I did." She nodded and stood, walked toward the door.

"If you need anything . . ." Susan gestured with open hands. "I'm right here. Neighbor."

Lucie stopped and turned. "Well, actually, there is something. Can you tell me how to get to the grocery store?"

Susan smiled. "I'll tell you what. I need a few things, too. Why don't I walk with you?"

ONCE BACK HOME, Lucie sliced sharp cheddar and buttered bread to make a grilled cheese sandwich. The market Susan had taken her to was an explosion of colorful produce and fresh baked goods, with an entire display of fancy chocolates, coffee beans waiting to be ground, and a well-stocked fish and meat counter. Lucie bought enough to make the kitchen look lived in. Once she'd eaten, she would go back to the basement, dig into some of the boxes. She'd study the letters carved into the piano bench, look it over for more clues. Maybe she'd play the piano and see what happened. Memories seemed closest when she was playing; she could almost feel the presence of someone there with her, someone important, someone—

The trill of a phone startled her. Where was it? She traced the sound to a shelf between the dining room and kitchen. Wiping her hands clean of butter and crumbs, she walked over and answered, feeling as if she were answering the phone at a friend's. "Hello?"

"Hey."

Lucie paused. A man, familiar . . .

"It's Grady."

"Of course, I know. Hi."

"I kind of have a problem."

"Are you okay?" There was something different in his voice.

"Well, actually, I'm at the emergency room. I, uh . . . I can't drive."

"Oh my god, what happened? Are you all right?"

He didn't say anything, but she could hear him breathing. She waited for him to speak again.

"I'm actually not doing too good, Luce," he finally said. "I was at the pool and I hurt my feet. Broke one and bruised the other. I can't drive. Not even sure how I'm going to walk. I can't believe I did this."

"How did it happen? I mean, like, jumping in, or . . . ?" She pictured him at a pool in swim trunks, but couldn't picture what his chest would look like. Did he have body hair? Or did he wear the bikini kind of bathing suit, like the man who'd led her from the water?

"Can I tell you later? I just really lost it today."

"You lost—"

"Do you remember how to drive?"

"Oh." Lucie considered this. *Sure,* she thought, feeling her hands on the wheel, her foot on the accelerator, the sensation of turning to look over her shoulder. Driving was like, what? Walking. Taking a shower. Buttering bread. A mechanical thing. Muscle memory. "Yeah, yeah, I do."

"There's an extra key to your car in the bowl next to the phone. The key ring has a big silver *L* on it. See it?"

"Yep." Lucie picked it up. "Which one's my car?"

"Black Acura, parked in front of where I parked yesterday, at the curb."

"Oh, yeah." She'd admired it the day before. "But how do I find you?" Lucie looked around for paper to write on.

"Just enter this address into the navigation system." Grady gave her the hospital address, sounding a little better now.

Before they hung up she said, "Is life always this interesting around here?"

He laughed, a real, honest laugh, inducing a feeling in her that she liked very much. She would try to do that again some-time soon.

# grady

O f course his mother would pick now to call, Grady thought, sitting near the window in the ER waiting room so he'd see when Lucie pulled up. He clicked the answer button on, then off, hoping his mom would think he was in a bad reception area and try later. He couldn't handle talking to his family right now. His phone had been buzzing with calls from Dory while the doctor and nurses were working on his feet. He blew a long sigh. His youngest sister had some kind of internal tracking device when it came to him.

The summer before fourth grade, a full year after his father had died, Grady had taken up thievery. Nothing too illicit, just some light shoplifting at the corner store, hard candies and baseball cards—the kind with a thin sheet of pink bubble gum inside. Then he'd moved on to neighborhood targets. The Shimleys' plums and figs, a yellow squirt gun left carelessly in the front yard at the Chens' house. It was when Mrs. Helgason came running out of her back door, yelling at Grady to get his sticky hands off of her underwear on the clothesline (when all he'd been after were the clothespins) that he realized what a bad idea stealing was.

He ran like dogs were chasing him, and hid out in the timber playground structure in the park. He sat there for hours, or so it felt, knowing it wouldn't take much for Mrs. Helgason to figure out which neighborhood boy he was, with his dark skin. Had she called his house yet? Of course, his mom wouldn't be home from work until after six, but depending on which sister answered, he could be in just as much trouble.

The neighborhood gang of kids wandered into the playground, congregating above him on the higher timbers. They didn't see him hiding below, heart pounding; he decided to wait them out. Otherwise, he'd risk getting called "squaw," or worse, jumped on.

And then he heard a familiar voice call, "Hey! Have you seen my brother?" It was Dory, out looking for him, which was no surprise. Whenever Grady was in trouble, Dory knew.

"You mean your retarded pussy brother?" a male voice said.

*Ugh,* Grady thought. Definitely worse than "squaw."

"You suck," Dory said, and Grady could tell she was coming closer. Somehow, she thought she could get away with saying things like that to other kids. Sure, she was twelve and going into junior high, but Grady knew better than to try it. Even though his father's people had lived on this land longer than anyone, the Goodalls were the minority in their neighborhood now.

"I suck, huh? Well, suck this," the boy said to Dory, followed by nervous laughter from some of the others.

"Like I'd want to taste your nasty, disgusting thing. Hell, it's probably too little to even find in all that flub." Meaning it was Derek, the biggest and meanest sixth grader.

"Jeez, Dory," Grady muttered under his breath. If only she'd just walked on, but now she was in more trouble than he was. He crawled out from under the structure.

Dory stood a few yards from the other kids, hands on her straight hips, locked in a stare war with Derek, who glowered down at her from his perch. It would take him a while to climb off the structure, he was so fat, and Dory could run like a small deer. Grady called out, "Only pussy retards hit girls, Derek. Leave her alone."

The boy's jowly stare turned in Grady's direction. Grady knew in that moment that he would be obliterated, and that it would hurt. A lot.

"Run, Dory!" he yelled, as Derek and the rest of them scrambled down to where Grady stood, surrounding him.

Dory came running into the crowd instead. "Stop it!" she demanded. "Leave my little brother alone."

Grady knew she was trying to protect him, but she just kept making it worse. Now they knew that even his sister thought he was a wimp. "Get out of here, Dory," he said in his meanest voice. "Now."

The next thing he knew he had a mouth and nose full of dirt and someone was on his back, pounding on him while many other feet and hands struck him. He covered his face and scrunched into a ball, waiting for it to be over.

And then he thought maybe he was hallucinating from a kick to the head, because he heard a wild sound, like a flock of screaming eagles, coming closer and closer. The other kids heard it, too, and stopped all at once, staring in the same direction. Grady looked out through his one operable eye and saw them, his sisters, shrieking like banshees toward them, all angry faces and raised arms.

"What the hell?" said Derek.

"It's them wild Indian kids," a girl said. "Run!"

"They're just girls," Derek said, but as his troops abandoned him, he gave Grady one last kick in the kidneys and took off.

The Goodall girls, all six of them, came running up to Grady, Floss falling to her knees beside him. "Are you all right? Grady, are you okay?"

"Let's go get those asswipes," he heard Dory say.

"No," he mumbled through swollen lips, but it didn't matter that Dory couldn't hear him. The other sisters held her by the arms until she'd calmed down, and then they stood him up and brushed him off, trying to make him feel better by saying things like "Those kids are just losers" and "Boy, are you going to have a shiner."

He knew what was going on and he hated it, hated their protectiveness, their cavalry-style rescues. But ever since the day he wouldn't come out of the water, the day his father had died, his sisters had been acting like they thought they were his guardian angels. They thought he couldn't take care of himself. Worse, they thought he might hurt himself and, in so doing, hurt their mother even more.

Like it or not, forevermore they would fly to his side when anything went wrong and try to fix the situation. Even if he was disappointed about something he had every right to be disappointed about, they'd flurry around in nervous, false cheerfulness until he wanted to close his eyes and slap his hands over his ears.

"Girls, don't worry so much over Grady," their mother would say. "He's just sensitive." She said it like it was a normal thing, but he hated that word. Just because he'd wanted to stay under the water that one damn day, they would always see him as too weak to survive on his own. They didn't understand at all. They didn't know how strong you had to be to stay down there in the deep.

IT WAS ALMOST laughable, now, sitting in hospital number two in three days. He'd wanted to stay under forever in the pool, too. Now he was banned, his gym membership suspended. The gym owner said Grady was lucky they'd offered the rude swimmer a free year so he wouldn't press charges against either of them. But to tell the truth, beating the crap out of the guy had felt so good that Grady wasn't sorry, and he wished he'd known that when he was a kid. If only he'd known to throw the first punch and keep on going. There was advantage in that, he realized now.

Even the pain was worth it. He'd broken his right calcaneus, the heel bone, and bruised the left. The right was booted in a midcalf-level plastic contraption, and he was not to bear weight on it for four weeks. Grady had no idea how he could avoid it, even with the crutches they'd supplied. One thing was for sure, though: the drugs were good. The pain had gone from emergency threat level to dull, aching presence.

Grady's phone rang again; his mother was persistent. He grimaced and answered. "Hi, Mom."

"Honey, Dory called and told me all about this awful thing Lucie has, and I just want you both to know that I'm here to help, however I can. I just wish you'd have called me yourself."

"Yeah, yeah, I know." Grady tried to think of what to say. Usually the sister daisy chain got him out of talking with everyone, but yes, he should have called his mother. He was not ready, however, to confess about his fighting and injuries. "I'm sorry I didn't call."

"So, how is she? How are you? I have nothing but time on my hands, you know that. I could come up and help."

"No, no. No, we're fine." Grady knew that sounded wrong. "It's just that . . ." He contemplated what to say next, watching an enormously pregnant woman a few chairs over struggling to pick up her toddler's toys from the floor. As soon as she placed a retrieved toy in the diaper bag, the youngster would dig it out and throw it back to the carpet. The young mother would smile at the child as if it were a genius and then struggle over all that belly again to pick up the toy.

"It's just been more than enough," he finally said, "trying to get Lucie home and settled and life back to normal." He closed his eyes at the word.

"Oh, honey, I'm sorry. I'm just worried about you, about the both of you."

"Well, I can't really talk right now, but basically we're fine. Lucie's fine. A little thin but eating like a horse, so that shouldn't last too long." He forced a false chuckle, puzzling at the thought of a chubby Lucie, something he couldn't imagine. "I'm actually back at work already."

"So soon? Shouldn't you be with her?"

"Mom, she's fine. She doesn't remember things, but she's actually, well . . . I don't know. It's kind of weird how well she seems to be taking it all." *Better than I am,* he didn't say.

"Is she going to go to the psychiatrist? Dory told me that's an important part of the healing process. You don't want to mess around with this without professional help, Son. And Dory said we should all try to think of ways to help her remember things, like pictures and stories, and places. Why don't you bring her here to the house this weekend? Surely she'd remember all the good times we've had."

"Well, I don't think she's quite up for that."

"As soon as you think she's ready, I mean."

"Right, yes. Of course." At this moment, there was nothing Grady wanted less than to subject Lucie to the lot of them. To any of them. They made the tension between Lucie and Grady unbearable at the best of times. "We'll see how it goes for a little while, you know? Let her settle back into life, her routines and stuff."

"Has she gone back to work, too, then?"

"Not yet." How could he tell his mother that Lucie's business, and her reputation, were already too decimated to recover? His mom was an old-fashioned woman with no understanding of modern business, the speed at which it was transacted. She didn't know how quickly everything could implode.

The Acura appeared in the circular drive outside.

"Sorry, Mom. I've got to go. You're okay? Everything's all right?"

"Oh yes, I'm fine. Picking blueberries with little Sam this afternoon." Three-year-old Sam was the first great-grandchild in the family, Eunie's grandson, and Grady's mother loved her once-weekly afternoons with him. "You give Lucie a big fat hug from me, now, will you? And tell her we want to see her!"

"Yes, ma'am," he said, though he knew he wouldn't tell Lucie any of it. Not yet. He stood, swung his messenger bag over his shoulder, and hobbled toward the door on one foot and two crutches.

Lucie was already out of the car with the passenger side open. She was so much her old self when in action: her posture, her athletic gait and movements. She wore her running tights and a T-shirt, her face moist in the heat, and he had to admit he liked her unmade-up. Her freckles had always been the bane of her existence—well, one of many banes—and seeing them scattered like so many stars across her cheeks and nose was like seeing a whole new Lucie. Which of course, she was. And, god help him, she was not wearing a bra. Had Grady not been on crutches, he might have fallen over at his surprise and sudden desire for her.

"Hi," he said, feeling as shy as he had the first day he met her. "So you *can* drive."

She shrugged. "So far, so good."

He chuckled and she smiled, then took his bag and crutches and slid them into the back. "Can you, um, manage, there?" she asked, hovering and watching as he ducked down on one leg, the other sticking out, trying to fit inside the car.

All he could see were her breasts moving against the thin fabric of her shirt like warm coddled eggs, dampness glistening in the hollow at her throat. How could he get an erection now, of all times? He mumbled that he was fine, hoping she'd go to the driver's side and get in so he could arrange himself decently.

As he struggled to pull his booted leg into the car, she knelt down on the pavement to help. "Please, don't," he said, and she looked up, her eyes the palest jade in the bright daylight.

"What? Am I hurting you?"

"No, no, I'm fine. Really. I've got it."

She looked dismayed, but stood and walked around the car to get in. Grady struggled with his foot a moment longer, grateful for the drugs so that he could finally just shove it in and feel only mildly nauseated. The heat had been building throughout the day, and now he sat in a black car on black asphalt, his shirt soaked through in just the short time he'd been outside.

Lucie sat silently in the driver's seat without starting the car.

*Please,* he thought. *Just turn on the air-conditioning and get me home.*

She turned to look at him. "Are you going to tell me what happened?"

"Later," he snapped, knowing how it sounded, but he really needed to get home before he puked or passed out. "I just mean—"

"Got it," Lucie said. She sounded mad. "How do I get home?"

"First you have to start the car," he said, feeling entitled to the sarcasm. "Then select Home on the navigator."

She sighed and turned the key, cool air pouring from the vents. Grady leaned back and closed his eyes as she pulled out of the parking lot. He didn't think he'd fallen asleep, but suddenly they were in front of their house, Lucie outside his door.

She already had his bag strapped around her, and she watched as he extricated himself from the car, then handed him his crutches. He knew he was lucky she hadn't just stormed up the sidewalk, leaving him to fend for himself as she would have in their previous life.

"I'm sorry," he said, meaning it in some new, unfamiliar way. Before, it had always been an automatic response, but now he did feel sorry for his behavior. "I don't mean to be a jerk."

She squinted at him, then shrugged. "Then don't be?"

"Okay," he said. She didn't seem mad, exactly, and walked behind him as he struggled up the walkway, then took his house key and opened the door. She was now the one in full control, but not in the old way. Not controlling, but taking care of him. Taking care of herself, even in such difficult circumstances.

Grady thrust his crutches over the threshold, pitching his body inside. He'd been too pissed off to pay attention when they told him how to use the crutches, and now he kept putting pressure on the broken foot by mistake. If he didn't get off his feet soon, he thought he might faint.

"Could you help me get to my chair?" he asked, driblets of sweat along his lip.

She settled his bag on the floor, took the crutch from his

bad side, and slid her arm around his waist. His arm went around her shoulders, and she was strong enough to hold him steady as he hobbled over, then lowered himself into the leather chair. Again, she knelt in front of him, and he drew a quick breath. She was simply lifting his feet to the ottoman, gently.

"Did I hurt you?" she asked, and he shook his head.

"You need to tell me things," she said. "Lots of things. Everything."

If only he could, Grady thought. If only he could say, "It's just that the sight of you, looking up at me like that, undoes me." He couldn't, not to this person who may or may not grow to love him again. It hadn't occurred to him when they found her that their courtship would have to start over again, at day one, as complete strangers. His eyelids grew heavy, his mind fuzzing over.

"Like, for instance, you could have told me this was your chair last night," she said. "I hogged it all night."

His eyes closed, even though he wanted to gaze at her still. "You looked good in it," he mumbled, slipping into a heavy, empty place. He thought he heard her smiling.

# lucie

~~~~~~~~~~~

Vestigial chlorine smell seeped from Grady, and his hair had dried funny and flat on top of his head. Lucie sat on the ottoman, studying him as the pain medication pulled him under. Whatever had happened at the pool had been worse than simply having an accident and breaking his foot, she was sure of it. He seemed beaten by something, maybe by everything that had happened.

Was she even good for him? If she were this person she was beginning to understand herself to be, why would he have wanted to marry her? Her head hurt thinking about all of the merchandise stacked up in the closet, unused, unneeded, unreturned. She felt nauseated at Susan's description of her running through the neighborhood, not seeing or acknowledging anyone. And knowing the old leather chair was Grady's confirmed her worst fear. She'd been the one who'd chosen how the house was decorated. Most of the things in the basement were Grady's. He'd said the coat might be her aunt's or mother's. But the piano, well, it had to be hers. It felt as though she had been playing it her whole life. The rest of the remnants were his life previous to her, all packed away and forgotten, and Lucie wondered why he even liked her.

She leaned forward, pressed a hand on Grady's left thigh, which was all muscle. His breathing didn't change, even when she increased the pressure. He was out. He looked peaceful now, no longer in pain, no longer worrying about whatever it was he worried about so much.

He had a history, a family. He had a son. Did he feel sad at not being with him? She thought again of the small hands, wondering if maybe the boy had come to visit.

She grew calm, looking at Grady. She wondered if she had fallen first for his looks, or had she appreciated his kindness then as much as she did now? But his beauty was inescapable. Tawny skin stretched smooth over the architecture of firm cheekbones, long nose, and high forehead. His lips were a darker shade of wood, the bottom one full and muscular. She had kissed those lips, that face. She wished she could remember it. Her hands had caressed his wide shoulders, and probably tangled themselves in his hair at the kinds of moments she almost ached to think about now that she'd had her realization that morning. They were lovers and, if she stayed, would be again.

Scooting a little closer, Lucie reached to undo the first button of his shirt, a marine blue variant of the white one he'd worn the day before. He didn't stir, so she unbuttoned the next, her heart pounding. It would take one more button to find what she was after, and on this one he stirred, but not to the point of waking. And then she could see: his chest was specked in dark hair, a sparse enough cover that his skin was more prominent than hair. Where she hadn't been able to imagine him naked earlier, she could now deduce the rest. *Well,* she thought, *most of the rest.* She wasn't that bold, even though it seemed unfair that he knew her body so well.

The scratch across his neck was thin at the jawbone, mostly pink scar, then scabbed the farther it went into the soft skin of his neck. It had bled a lot when it happened, but was well on its way to healing now. Again, she shuddered, seeing it. How had it happened? she wondered, wanting to touch it, to heal it.

Lucie knew she should close his shirt, but she eased the right side farther open to expose a well-formed pectoral muscle and perfect dark nipple. She swallowed and nodded. *Okay, that's enough,* she thought, but she let her fingers graze his nipple as she pulled the shirt closed, pleased at how it hardened at her touch.

STANDING IN GRADY'S—their—bedroom, Lucie wondered if it was wrong to snoop so much. She'd felt like an anthropologist looking through her own things, but now that she'd turned her attention to Grady, she might be edging into voyeur territory. But she needed, suddenly, to know everything about him. The clothes in his small dresser were all of the relaxed cotton variety he'd been wearing so far, loose and comfortable but not shabby, in shades of blue and green, tan and brown: a palette of water and earth she liked very much. After hesitating, she pulled his underwear drawer open, knowing it was juvenile, but she had the same feeling she'd had earlier, that she needed to catch up, somehow, on what was intimate between them.

Lying in a messy jumble, his stretchy boxer briefs looked soft and comfortable. She extracted a blue pair and slipped off her tights and underwear, then stepped into them. Though he was taller, his hips were slim. The briefs snugged her own hips and were loose and comfortable against her upper thighs. Would Grady miss them if she didn't return them to the drawer? There were easily fifteen pair in there; she didn't think so. After easing the drawer closed, she tossed her clothes into a laundry basket against the wall, where they mingled with things of Grady's: his shirt from the day before, black underwear, an oversize and well-worn T-shirt with holes along the seams. Something he slept in, perhaps? She picked up the T-shirt and pressed it to her face, breathed in his smell, then dropped it back in the basket. Sprawling across each other, their worn clothes looked content together.

Inside the closet, she pulled a linen shift from its hanger to wear, then studied the three walls of clothes more carefully. Grady did, indeed, have one short rack for his button-down shirts and trousers and two suits. He was a minimalist. By necessity? she wondered. The old Lucie had made so little room for him in this house.

She crept back down the stairs, wanting to be quiet for Grady, wanting to let him fill in the spaces she had occupied before. Something was happening inside her that she didn't quite understand. Was she falling in love with a stranger for the first time or remembering her feelings from before? Or was she just desperate for connection and he was her only option?

Grady hadn't moved. Lucie leaned in to listen for his breathing, to make sure he hadn't overdosed on the pain pills. He sighed and shifted in the chair, his hands swimming through space until he resettled, head leaning toward her. Lucie stood, backing away so that she would not be tempted to touch him again.

His messenger bag still slouched by the front door. Lucie retrieved and carried it to Grady's desk in the office. To look inside or not? She sighed and unlatched the flap, folded it back. *No,* she thought, it wasn't right.

Instead, she studied the photos pinned to the bulletin board. One was similar to the picture of the two of them eating pie, but showed a large group of middle-aged women around the table, all laughing or talking. His sisters, she guessed. Dark like Grady, they seemed to be decidedly less fit than he was— more round and, well, happy. A much smaller older woman stood in the background, a knot of white hair on top of her head. His mother. From the way he'd spoken of her, Lucie would have guessed she was tall and strong, a younger woman of, say, sixty-five or so. But Grady was the youngest of seven. Of course she would be older. And she was fair skinned. Irish American, Grady had said.

Lucie wanted to know these people. They looked fun to be with, but even more intriguing, they looked cohesive; they were a family. She removed the thumbtack that held the photo in place, deciding to keep the picture in her little bag of clues, things she could pull out and study. She was trying to build a road map for her brain, a path from person to thing to feeling to memory. She didn't know what else to do at this point. She had no desire to go see a psychiatrist—that was for sure. She hoped she never had to visit a hospital or doctor again, and cringed at the thought of it.

Lucie had only been home two days, but even so, she wondered why Grady hadn't mentioned anyone wanting to see or talk with her. Could it be she really didn't have friends? Acquaintances? If she'd been a part of Grady's big clan, which he said she was, why wouldn't they all have been there to welcome her home? And even if she hated her aunt, surely she'd be happy to know Lucie was all right, wouldn't she? Or had she even been aware that Lucie went missing?

Her questions were mounting, including how Grady had managed to break his foot while swimming. If she could just figure out how to talk with him in a way that would help him relax and tell her the things she needed to know, then maybe she would start to remember on her own. She knew she shouldn't spy, but it seemed more fruitful than waiting for answers at this point.

Lucie looked behind her at the open door, then pulled his laptop from the bag. It was a hulking piece of equipment compared to the sleek machine on her desk. His looked battle worn and roadworthy. Did he travel a lot? Did they spend a lot of time apart? Had that been the problem?

She eased the lid open. At the loud chime, she quickly closed it. She wouldn't even know what she was looking for on his computer.

The bag was otherwise filled with bent manila folders holding haphazard bunches of paper, various notes and scraps, pens with chewed ends. Lucie watched her hand enter the bag, then extract random pieces of papers: Boeing notepaper with a list of tasks written in engineerese. A receipt from the Dog & Pony Alehouse for sixty-four dollars. A blue sticky note that read, in the same handwriting as the to-do list: "Helen 10?" and a phone number.

Lucie's heart knocked hard in her chest, and hair rose on her scalp and the back of her neck. This was something bad, she could feel it, but what? Surely he wasn't seeing another woman; that didn't seem like this man at all. Her hands trembled as she shoved the pieces of paper back into the bag. What was she looking for anyway? Proof they'd had problems?

A phone rang from somewhere else in the house. Lucie sprinted out to find it before it woke Grady. It was his cell phone, sitting on the entry table. She picked it up to try to figure out how to turn off the ringer and saw "MF Goodall" on the display.

It had to be one of the sisters, but she couldn't remember their names for the life of her. There were no simple Megans or Mollys, she knew that much. Their names were unusual—not quite exotic, but wholly unexpected. *MF,* she pondered, *MF.* Motherfucker Goodall, perhaps? Lucie snorted, slightly ashamed, and found the correct button to quiet the phone.

AT DINNERTIME SHE finally woke him. Grady startled into consciousness, his eyes searching the room.

"I made some soup," Lucie said. "Are you hungry?"

"You know how to make soup?" He yawned.

"From a can, yes. Shall I bring it to you out here?"

"Wow. Sure." He shifted in his chair, moving the booted foot to a new position.

"Need a pillow? More painkillers?" Lucie started toward the kitchen.

"That would be . . . great." His voice was odd; she turned.

"What?" she asked.

"You don't have to take care of me. I mean, if you don't want to."

"Would you rather I—?"

"No! No, I mean—"

"It's just a can of soup. I just thought—"

Grady put his hands over his eyes. "I mean, thank you for cooking for me. Thank you for coming to get me today. Thank you for being . . ." He sighed and uncovered his eyes. "Thank you for being here. That's all I'm trying to tell you."

"You're welcome." Why did she feel so shy?

"I'm really sorry I was such a jerk earlier."

"It's okay. You'd been through a lot, right?" She shrugged and went to fetch dinner. "Someone called on your cell while you were asleep," she called over her shoulder.

"Tomorrow," he said. "I'll check tomorrow."

They spent the evening similarly to the first night, sitting in front of the television, quiet, but with no wine, as Grady's drugs had him fighting to stay awake through sitcom after sitcom.

When he had to use the restroom, he struggled to get out of the chair, and Lucie, now on the couch, stood beside him to try to help. It became apparent, to Lucie anyway, that there was no way he'd be getting up the stairs to the bedroom that night. What if he decided to sleep in the guest room? With her? Warmth surged into her face; she was wearing his underwear beneath her dress. Maybe she'd take the upstairs bedroom.

At ten o'clock, Grady sighed. "I need to go to bed. I'm beat."

"Okay," Lucie said, standing to help him. "I'm a little worried about you and those stairs."

"I'll be fine," he said. "I'll just take it slow."

She pushed the ottoman out of the way so he could navigate through the room and to the staircase. He stood at the bottom and looked up. Narrow and steep, the wooden steps shone in the half-light with glossy varnish.

"Shit," he said, shoulders slumping over the crutches.

"You can sleep in the guest room," Lucie said. "It will be so much easier, don't you think? For now?"

"I guess," he said. "Would you be up in our—the bedroom, then?"

"Well, sure. I can sleep anywhere." He hadn't even considered sleeping with her. Not that she wanted him to, but . . . Well. It would be nice if he wanted to.

"All right, then. Good night." He pointed his crutches down the hall and began a slow step-crutch-swing toward the guest room.

"Do you need any help?" *Please,* Lucie thought.

"I've got it," he said. "Thanks for everything today."

"Okay." What did she want?

He stopped and struggled his crutches around to look at her. "What?"

"Could you just tell me what happened?"

"What hap—"

"Your foot." He looked so overwhelmed she wished she'd just left it alone.

"Oh, I was trying to do a flip turn. You know, where you go kind of upside down and over?"

Lucie shrugged. She had no idea.

"Anyway, I messed up my timing. Bad. Slammed my heels into the edge of the pool." He winced, saying it. He'd said it was a really bad day and she knew there was much more to the story, but she nodded.

"Thanks," she said. "I just wanted to know."

Once in their bed upstairs, Lucie lay awake for a long while, fingers tracing the waistband of Grady's boxers around her hips. She'd wanted to talk more with him, but he'd been in no shape for it, between the pain, the drugs, the trauma of the day. She'd wanted to ask, *Why won't you tell me anything? Why is your family staying away? Where are my friends? Does everyone hate me? Do you hate me, too, but you feel obligated now?*

She rolled over, scooting herself to Grady's side of the bed. His pillow was softer and more comfortable. And it smelled like him. Lucie sighed. Should she call this Motherfucker Goodall? Or would that be really weird, without Grady knowing? She'd nearly bored herself to sleep with questions when a fresh one startled her awake: *Who is Helen?* The name was almost familiar. A co-worker of his? Someone they both knew? The reason she ran, perhaps? She sighed in exasperation. Would that really have been a cause for amnesia?

She groaned, determined to quit thinking about it. Grady had come to get her, after all. He must have wanted her back. She bunched his pillow under her cheek, reached an arm across to the edge, as she might have if she'd been lying next to him, to make contact before sleeping, and waited.

# grady

~

days passed, then a week, then another. A rhythm developed. Grady would wake in the guest room to the sound of Lucie in the kitchen, making coffee, getting out cereal bowls. This Lucie seemed so domestic, arranging fresh flowers from her new friend Susan's garden, wanting to cook all the time, even though she was no better at it now than she'd been before. This surprised Grady—so much about her had changed he'd thought maybe this would, too. And the questions! She asked question after question, about their past, about him, about her, but safe, surface questions, like she was dancing around something. Did she know, somehow, deep down inside her, that they'd been on the verge of falling apart before she ran?

He sometimes woke to her piano playing in the middle of the night, but never again did she play their wedding song. The invitations still sat in boxes in the dining room, and it was now officially past mailing day. Thank god they hadn't sent them before she ran away, Grady thought, but they weighed heavy, sit-

ting there. Would they send them before it was too late? The
wedding was less than six weeks away and they hadn't yet discussed it. He didn't even know how to bring it up.

The other thing he didn't know how to bring up was the
shrink Lucie wasn't calling. He knew he should insist, but she
seemed to be doing so well—why make her unhappy again?
Why encourage her to remember the things that had broken
her so badly? Same with the aunt. As much as Grady knew
Lucie wanted to find out about her family, he hated to subject
her to anything that would remind her of the past right now.
There'd be time for the aunt, time for the shrink, later. After
she'd settled and adjusted to this new life.

Grady checked the home phone messages regularly, field-
ing the now dwindling calls from reporters, including the persistent Ann Howe in San Francisco. Determined to document
their reunion at every step, she left message after message asking when the wedding would be. She wanted to continue the
fairy tale, but Grady knew the last thing they needed, he and
Lucie, was the pressure, so he told Lucie that they never actually answered the phone, just let it ring, because it was always
someone selling something, which was mostly true. Everyone
used their cell phones now. Lucie found this to be reasonable
and only answered when it was his number in the caller ID
display.

He was surprised that of all the connections Lucie had
made, of all the people she had helped land jobs or find good
employees, no one had called to send her their best wishes. Of
course, they probably only knew her cell phone number.

Fifteen days had passed since he last went swimming.

Grady couldn't remember when he'd spent so much time on dry land with no escape. *A fish out of water,* he thought, with a new appreciation for the phrase.

He worked at home now in the office, a room Lucie had no interest in occupying anymore; before, it had been her primary work space. He'd had a hard time getting her out of there, in fact, even to come eat the Thai takeout that was her favorite, or to venture out of the house on nice weekend days. She was the sole proprietor and had worried over the business as if it were her baby.

Lucie no longer went running every morning, but she took long walks around the neighborhood, meeting someone new, it seemed, at every turn. One day it would be the barista at Zoka on Fifty-Sixth, the next it was the florist up on Forty-Fifth. She'd have long chats, finding out the most personal things about them, which she'd then relay to Grady over dinner. She collected personal details, having none of her own. She was like a detective, almost, in everything she did, keeping her notes and scraps of paper in the colorful little bag she'd brought home from the hospital. Her own "wanted" poster was probably still in there.

And always, always, he sensed she wanted something more from him, but not like before. She didn't want him to dress or act a certain way. She wanted information; she wanted *his* personal details, but he wasn't able to satisfy her craving. There was nothing about him as interesting or fascinating as the barista's tragic love life or the florist's previous career as a corporate executive before the economic crash. Grady wanted to tell Lucie: *I am boring and I was nothing before I met you, and I will*

*never understand what you saw in me five years ago.* The mystery
would never be solved now, and Grady still found it hard to
fathom that she was staying in this life after escaping it so completely.

One evening, as they ate chewy chicken breasts and over-
salted mashed potatoes in front of the TV, Lucie said, "Do you
miss your dad?"

Grady could only blink at her, and chew. He swallowed,
then said, "Of course." It was a given that if someone had died,
especially your father, you missed him, right? "What do you
mean, like every day?"

She shrugged and bit her lip. "Should I not ask?"

"No, of course you can ask," he said and took a long pull of
wine. Other than with his sisters and mom, he'd never really
talked about his dad.

"How did he die?" She was leaning her head at him in that
way she did now, forthright and innocent at the same time.
He'd asked her that question so many times about her own parents, but she'd never once asked him before for his details. She
wanted to know, this Lucie.

Grady nodded, gathering his thoughts. "Every July he'd sign
on with a commercial fleet going to Alaska. Big king salmon run
up there, and a lot of money to be made, and you know—he
had seven kids. Lots of mouths to feed. He'd be gone the whole
month." Grady paused, sighing. "It was the week he was supposed to come back, but, well, they hit debris or something and
lost the rudder. They started taking on water. I guess the boat
sank in something like ten or fifteen minutes. It was in all the
papers. Thirty-one guys survived. Ten didn't. They never found

my dad." That was the part that always got him, for some reason, that his dad was alone down there. That it was so cold.

Lucie shook her head, reached for his hand. "I'm so sorry."

That could have been the end of it, but he was on a roll now; he was seeing that day: the swimming dock, the girls on the beach, sunning. The way he'd felt before finding out. The way he'd felt after.

"I was swimming with my sisters that day, and I wouldn't come out of the water." He paused, then said, "You know at the pool, when I broke my foot?"

Lucie nodded. Why was he telling her this part? She'd never have asked.

"It was the same thing. I was trying to hide or something, staying under the water."

"Hide from what?" she asked. "I mean, at the pool."

"I fucked up, Luce." He pressed his lips together, then continued. "I got into a fight with this asshole in the pool."

Her eyebrows rose. "You—"

"Got into a fight. Yeah. I started a fight with this guy who was being a jerk, and I just lost it, I . . ." He shook his head.

She leaned in. "I'd only just gotten home, Grady. You were so stressed out."

He shrugged. He hadn't really considered that.

"Why did you come out, finally?" she asked. "Of the pool."

"Because I had to breathe?" He shook his head and laughed, and she laughed with him.

"Good idea," she said. Then she cocked her head again. "Why'd you come out of the water after your dad died?"

Tears came to his eyes. "My mom. She jumped in and

pulled me out. Otherwise, I don't know if I would have." How could he have done that to his mother? How could he have been so selfish?

"She needed you," Lucie said, squeezing his hand, then standing. "She couldn't lose both of you on the same day."

Grady watched as she cleared the dishes. Was she speaking from experience, from memory? She'd lost both her parents— was that what she was talking about? But she didn't show any signs of being upset. Just this unending curiosity.

"How about your son?" she asked, returning to her seat. "Do you miss him?"

Grady squirmed in his leather chair. He'd thought that might be the end of it, after having revealed so much, but maybe it was good, to get it all out at once. "Well, sure. Yeah, I do."

"Do you ever see him? I mean, have you?"

"When he was born, at the hospital."

Grady remembered all those years ago, peering in the nursery window, worrying that the very angry (and white) Vountclaires would find him there and have him thrown out. He'd had to wipe the window where he'd fogged it with his breath, and there the baby was: a bundle, a thatch of wild black hair, an angry, red face. The kid knew Grady was abandoning him. Over the years Grady thought he'd caught glimpses of the boy, at two, at five, at eleven. (*Jesus*, he thought. He'd be twenty-four now. Did he look like Grady had at that age—tall and too skinny, but growing into his man's body?)

Always, he told Lucie, he rationalized those "glimpses" as wishful thinking, as he did the moments he thought he could feel the boy's yearning for him. But he'd agreed to stay away to appease his crazy ex-wife and her family, even though he knew he shouldn't, even though he knew the pain of growing up without a dad.

"I kind of think that someday he'll come look me up, when he's ready, and maybe we can start over then." The chance he'd never have with his own dad.

She waited a beat before asking, "Would you like to try to find him?"

He could only shrug. How could he tell her how awful it would feel to find his son only to discover he didn't want to be found?

Lucie must have noticed this made him sad. "Thank you for telling me about your dad, and your son."

He nodded.

"Um, I was hoping I could meet your family soon." She flushed, and Grady guessed she was scared to death of this huge herd of sisters-in-law and just waiting for the onslaught. "It's been a couple of weeks now, and, well . . ."

"You don't have to, you know," he said. "Not yet."

"Don't they want to see me?"

If only she knew, Grady thought. His mother and sisters had been taking turns haranguing him by e-mail, text message, voice mail, inviting them to dinners, lunches, out to the old house. His broken foot had been a pretty good excuse so far, but it was beginning to wear thin, and what would happen when he'd healed?

"Oh, they want to see you, but I figured we weren't ready yet."

"We aren't?"

"Okay," he said, leaning to rearrange his booted foot on the ottoman. "I'm not."

"Oh." She looked at him with so much concern he nearly turned to mush. This was how she did it with the florist and the neighbors. This was how she extracted the private hurts and longings, the tortured histories and details. The old Lucie knew exactly why he avoided talking about all this stuff, why he kept his family at arm's length, but now he had to—no, he wanted to—tell her everything.

"They're too much," he said. "They're just too damn much, and they always get between us, and they drive you crazy. And we always fight after we've been with my family."

"Oh, no. Why?"

"My sisters are overbearing. They try to tell me how to live my life. After my dad died it's like they took over. They're always telling me some new way that I can be a better person. And they're so loud."

"And they laugh a lot?" Lucie said.

"Yeah, always laughing, always with the jokes. How do you know that?"

"From the pictures."

Grady shook his head. They were a funny bunch, true, but too often at his expense.

"And your mom? Is she the same way?"

"Well, she wants what's best for me too, but she's a little more subtle about it. She accepts who I am, for the most part." He'd never thought of it that way, but it was true. She might make suggestions, but she knew when to back off, and she never made him feel like a fuckup. Even after his first marriage, the baby, all of it.

Lucie leaned her head to the side. "What if I just went to see them, without you?"

"What? No. I would never let you subject yourself to that. If you want to meet them, we'll go together."

At this Lucie smiled. Grady wished he could convince her it was a mistake, but she looked so pleased. She thought she was going to have family, a big storybook family. It had to be hard not remembering anyone. And not having anyone to remember.

"So, can we invite your family here next weekend? Maybe for a barbecue or something?"

"Let's start down at Mom's," he said. "That way we can escape if we need to. I'll call her tomorrow."

Lucie needed more than just him in her life, a realization that twisted his insides like a wet towel. He had to tell her about her aunt. He'd been ignoring phone calls from her at the office. He hadn't even listened to the messages.

*Next week,* he decided. He would tell Lucie about Helen Ten Hands next week. He had to, or she'd realize he'd been holding out on her when the aunt did eventually track her down. Lucie was just so newly formed and delighted at every single thing she discovered, and Grady couldn't let anything negative into her world, not yet. It seemed the only good in Lucie's life had been things she'd accomplished on her own, through sheer strength and force of will, and while she seemed to be doing it differently this time around, he liked recognizing that part of her. The tenacious Lucie. The same spirit in her that had always made him feel more confident and authentic as a human, just being in her presence.

Later that night, as he lay awake in the guest room, he heard Lucie playing a song she hadn't before. He strained to make it out—it was familiar in some way. Kind of bouncy and light, not like the jazz standards and old songs she'd been playing. And then he began to recognize it, something from the eighties, he thought. "Walk like an Egyptian," he sang under his breath, shaking his head. He chuckled and rolled over to sleep.

THE NEXT MORNING he woke earlier than usual and got up well before Lucie to make coffee. Over the past two weeks, he'd mastered mobility on the crutches, and truth be told, he liked being at home, tucked away in the office that had become his, hearing Lucie puttering around, humming, and then coming out at lunchtime to find she'd made something for them to eat. Even though it might not taste all that good, or might cause indigestion for the rest of the afternoon, she seemed so determined to cook for him.

She loved shopping at the organic market nearby, and always came home marveling about the plumpness of the blueberries from the Skagit Valley, or the creaminess of an Oregon goat cheese she'd purchased. He'd have worried about the expense of the upscale groceries, but they had to have cost less than all the take-out and restaurant meals they'd consumed before. True, Lucie's income was almost defunct. A couple of commission checks had come in, and when she seemed ready, he'd help her look through her accounts to see if there were any more outstanding, but soon they would be living solely on his paycheck.

Lucie was no longer online shopping, though, something that most of her income had always gone to anyway. He'd never understood it, but she'd had such a need for things. It was as though she filled herself by acquiring them, much as he swam to recharge. He'd never faulted her for it. When he'd first made good money, he'd gone out and bought all kinds of things: a new computer, electronic gadgets, a huge TV and surround-sound system. The typical bachelor-pad leather furniture that they'd sold when Lucie moved in, all except for his chair. Her taste had always been so much better than his. She'd made the house elegant and understated, gender neutral, which he appreciated. His sisters' houses were all flowers and frills. How their husbands felt like men in those houses, he did not know.

"Morning," Lucie said, behind him. "You're up early."

He swiveled on his good foot, crutches leaned against the counter. "Good morning to you," he said. Her eyes still looked sleepy, and her hair stuck up in places. The short spikes had grown out into a shaggy cap, the odd colors still present but her natural brown growing in.

"Thank you for the talk last night," she said. "I mean, I know it must be weird."

"No, it's fine." He wanted to hug her, he wanted her to hug him, but they'd not yet bridged the void of physical affection. How would they get beyond this new roomie status they'd developed?

There were so many things he'd like to say to her. Instead he asked, "Coffee?"

"Absolutely." She scratched her arm. "I'm exhausted this morning."

"You played pretty late," he said, turning to pull a cup from the cabinet. "I loved that one song, the one that goes, da na na, na na na . . ."

"Which one?"

He poured coffee into the cup. *"Walk like an Egyptian,"* he sang, embarrassed at how off-key it sounded.

"I don't think I know that one," she said, taking the cup from him.

"Yeah, you do. That old eighties song by that girl group. The Go-Go's, maybe? The Spangles? Something like that."

She shook her head, smiling. "I have no idea what you're talking about."

"Well, you played it."

"Did not."

"Did so."

She laughed. "I like this side of you, funny guy." She turned to the fridge to retrieve breakfast things, and Grady could only smile and watch. He was smitten, all over again. He thought about the wedding invitations. It was just five weeks before September fourth, but they could still send them. They hadn't canceled the venue, the officiant, none of it. They could still get married, on schedule, maybe without all the fancy stuff that had gotten in the way before Lucie ran. Grady was liking this new thought, this new hope, so when Lucie turned back toward him with a carton of yogurt in her hand, he stepped forward, leaned over, and kissed her on the lips.

She froze, and he pulled away.

"God, Luce, I'm sorry. I . . . I don't know why I did that." Heat burned in his cheeks.

"You don't?" She still looked dazed, standing in the same position, arm extended with yogurt in hand, like they'd been playing statues.

"Well, you know. I mean now, right this moment. We were having fun and I just kind of . . ." *Oh Jesus,* he thought. *What is wrong with me?*

"Try it again," she said, finally moving, putting the yogurt on the counter. She stood, ready, but not moving toward him.

Slowly, he reached to touch her shoulder, then let his hand slide down her arm, pulling so that she stepped into him. She smelled like her old sleepy self, like clean laundry and last night's soap. His chest filled with warmth; his limbs tingled. Cupping the back of her head with his other hand, he looked into her eyes. They were wide, and he couldn't tell if she was afraid, excited, or just curious. "Hi," he said, body sparking, pulse thudding.

"Kiss me," she said. "I mean, if you want t—"

He pressed his lips into hers. She made no move to kiss him back, just let him kiss her, as though she were a scientist studying the mating rituals of strangers. He was about to back off, to pull away, when he felt her arms wrap around his waist, her hands caress his back, her lips grow soft and pliant. They kissed this way, just lips, no machinations of tongue or jaw, until finally she began to giggle and pulled away.

"Um, thank you," she said, touching her mouth.

*Thank you?* He looked away. Why had she stopped? Had she just forgotten what it felt like to kiss and wanted to know? Did she have no desire for him at all?

Grady turned toward the sink, pretended to rinse dishes that were already rinsed. Did she know what she did to him? *Jesus,* he thought.

"I'll carry your breakfast out to the dining room," Lucie said, and he nodded, waiting for his erection to subside.

Something had to give. He was a prisoner in his body with no outlet. If he didn't at least get to swim soon, he would go crazy. He was banned from the club, but there was a public pool at Green Lake. *Too many neighbors,* he thought, too many people who would notice him and make a fuss over his foot. There was another pool on Queen Anne Hill, just ten or so minutes away by car but a world away in clientele. Grady sighed. It would be weeks before he got the boot off.

And who knew how long before he got another chance to kiss Lucie?

## nineteen

# lucie

~~~~~~~~~~

Her lips felt the warm pressure of his throughout the day: as she showered after breakfast, on her walk to the market, later as she read the *Seattle Times*. Each thought of him made her body react, fizz in her bloodstream, the silly pounding of her heart. The scent of him lingered, triggering the deep, warm sensation of arousal. Of yearning for Grady. Her body had not forgotten that.

When they spoke she felt shyer than she had in one way, bolder in another. Lucie still couldn't believe she'd made him kiss her that way. It had been sweet and tender, but when he didn't take it further, she'd felt like an idiot, backing off to save them both embarrassment.

But he'd opened up so much the night before and she'd felt herself growing closer to him, watching his face as he talked about such difficult things. They were making progress, she'd thought. Had it just been her?

Sitting at the dining table, she heard the office door open, his step-crutch-swing across the living room.

"Hey," he said, poking his head through the door. "You want to go out for dinner tonight?"

And he hated her cooking. She knew he was being nice to her every single time she prepared something to eat, and yet she felt determined to make something he would love, so she kept trying.

"That would be nice."

"There's a good place we like to go just around the corner from the market, next to the yoga studio."

"Oh?" They'd become accustomed to speaking this way of their former selves. She'd ask, "What do we like to do on weekends?" or "Do we have friends?" He'd say, "We don't really do much, other than work and go out to eat." They'd stopped catching themselves to insert the past tense. It was as if they'd decided to go with the status quo until something had been decided.

Lucie was keenly aware of the wedding invitations in the boxes. She'd pulled one out, read it over and over, wondering how they might still be able to show up at the Fairmont Olympic the night of September fourth with all their family and friends. Well, his family. Who knew whose friends they'd planned on inviting; no one had been in touch with her since she'd been home. Didn't she have work friends, at least? Friends from college? But no one at all had been invited yet, and Lucie couldn't imagine how they might still have such a fairy-tale moment.

And Grady had said that it was also her fortieth birthday! Surely this aunt of hers wasn't so evil she'd ignore something as momentous as that.

Or maybe she was. Grady had also said Lucie hated her. Her only family, and they had no connection at all. A now familiar lump swelled in her throat, then receded. She would have a family, soon. Grady's family was her family, too.

At six thirty, they stepped out of the house into a sweltering evening, sun still high enough that Grady wore sunglasses. She'd found a sleeveless silk dress in the closet, and donned the flat sandals she'd worn home from the hospital.

"Sure you want to walk?" she asked, but Grady had become so efficient and nimble on the crutches that sometimes she forgot he was using them.

"I need to move," he said. "I haven't been this sedentary, since, well. Ever."

As they walked past the widower's house, the old man came from the side yard, trickling garden hose in hand. Lucie rarely saw him on her walks, but when she did, she tried to catch his eye, or called out "Hello!" He never answered, or even looked at her.

"Evening, Don," Grady said, and the man nodded, not looking up.

"Wow," Lucie whispered. "He never responds to me."

Grady waited until they were out of earshot before saying, "Well, Luce, the thing is, you two don't like each other much."

"But he likes you?" Why did this hurt her feelings?

"We just have an understanding. It's a guy thing. That was pretty much the extent of our communication."

Lucie walked quietly for a half block, hands trailing in stands of rosemary and lemon balm. She stopped to admire a particularly striking orange rose in bloom.

"Why am I so mean?" she asked.

Grady sighed. "You're not mean. You're just . . ."

"Challenging?"

He shrugged. "Sometimes you can be a little challenging, sure. Sometimes we all are, though, right? It's not exactly like I've been tons of fun since I broke my foot."

"You have a good reason, though."

Grady cleared his throat.

"What?" she asked, turning to look at his profile. He kept his eyes on the sidewalk as they walked.

"I think you have plenty of good reasons for being the way you are."

"You do?"

He nodded.

"Like?" *Please,* she thought. *Just tell me.*

His Adam's apple elevatored up and down his long neck. His crutch glanced off a rock and he stumbled, cursing as he came down hard on the booted foot.

"Oh god, are you okay?" she asked, and he nodded, but didn't say anything more. She'd wait until they were seated and comfortable; then she would ask him everything on the list in her head: what had been wrong between them that made her run? Did he really want her here, now? Did he still want to marry her? These questions were so hard, she realized, because she cared so much about the answers. They'd only been to-gether—again—a matter of weeks, but her feelings for him came from somewhere deep. She flinched with the realization that her love for Grady was ripe and mature, not new at all.

LUCIE HAD SEEN the restaurant before, the first time she came to the little retail area off Fifty-Sixth with Susan. They'd toured the three-block area, Susan pointing out the pub that made great Reubens, the mending lady inside the cleaners, the vegan donut shop. Lucie had asked Susan about the restaurant just up the street, in fact, thinking it looked like a nice place to have lunch or dinner. Belle, it was called.

Inside, it was even more pleasant: small, lots of wood, and lilies of the valley in vases on the tables. Lucie could smell the sharp scent of fresh chives and the comfort of butter frying.

"Oh my god! Hi, you guys!" the young hostess said. Her satin sheet of hair swung in a shampoo-commercial arc around her shoulders as she reached up to hug Grady, who blushed. "You're home!" she exclaimed to Lucie, but did not reach for her, just smiled with large, perfect teeth and carefully made-up eyes. She looked as if she wanted to say more, but turned back to Grady. "Oh, poor you! Crutches!"

A stout older man walked up from the back, impeccable in a starched white shirt, his silver-shot hair molded into place. He looked Greek or Italian, and he threw his hands in the air as he approached.

"Mr. Goodall! Ms. Walker! We are so happy to have you both back." He shook Grady's hand in both of his, then turned and grasped Lucie's hand warmly. He looked into her eyes. "You are better now, eh? No more escaping this big lug?"

"Oh, well, now—" Grady started, but Lucie was delighted.

"Nope, I'm home," she said. No one had said anything like this to her since she'd come back; it was like being tucked into bed. This man knew her and liked her, and wanted her here enough to chastise her for running off.

He scurried ahead of them as the hostess led them to a table at the front window. First he pulled out a chair for Lucie, then on the other side one for Grady, taking his crutches and leaning them in the corner nearby. "You just call for me when you need these, hm? I will take care of you. Tonight, dinner is on me. The usual?" He looked from Grady to Lucie, expectantly.

"Absolutely," Lucie said. "We'll have the usual."

After they'd been left alone, Grady smiled, shaking his head. "I should've known it would be this way. Sorry, I didn't think it through."

"What? I love it here, I love them. It just feels really, really . . ."

Tears welled up. Grady looked surprised.

"Oh, Luce," he said, and tears ran down her cheeks.

"I need this," she said.

She felt embarrassed to be crying in public; luckily the only other occupied table was on the other side of the room. Grady handed her his napkin. "I really didn't know you were so unhappy."

"It's not that," she said, pressing the cloth to her face. "I'm not unhappy. I'm . . . I don't know what I am. I don't even know that." She lowered the napkin. This was all coming out wrong. "Who am I, Grady? What makes me me? Why am I here with you?"

He looked alarmed.

"No, I don't mean it that way. I want to be here. I'm just saying . . ."

"I understand what you're saying," he said quietly. "You're not sure if we, if this—"

"No," she said loudly, then lowered her voice. "I don't know if *you're* sure. And I really need to know that. I want to know everything, every single thing, and we never talk about anything that feels too . . ." She sighed. "I don't know."

"What do you want to know?" His posture was so erect, his nostrils flared. He looked like he was facing a firing squad.

"I want to know . . ." God, how could she do this? How could she ask, when he'd brought her here, to this lovely place, clearly their date place? She bit her lip, considering all of the questions on her list. She couldn't help it; one pushed through, bumping all the others aside. "Who is Helen?" She knew this name, she did, from before—just not what it meant.

The color drained from Grady's face.

"Oh, shit," he said. "Oh no. I wasn't sure when to tell you, or even if I should tell you. I'm sorry, Luce. I really am." Now his eyes filled, and he reached across the table, but Lucie did not take his hand.

Why had she felt so certain he wouldn't be involved with someone else? It hurt him, she could see, but she'd forced the issue, and now, even though they'd had their first kiss just that morning, she'd brought to the surface what had lain ugly and unsaid beneath.

"Do, do you love her?" she asked, knowing it was a stupid question.

"Excuse me?"

"Please, just tell me."

"I don't even know her," he said, his dark eyes glossy. "I just didn't know how to tell you about her. I didn't want to hurt you even more."

*Fuck you,* she wanted to say. *It hurts now.*

"She called me at work. She was trying to get me to tell you about her, and she's just as weird as you always said, and I just wanted to wait awhile before I told you." He looked away, then back at Lucie. "I was trying to protect you."

"You—"

"She's your aunt, Lucie. Aunt Helen. Remember?"

"What?" It sounded so loud, bouncing around the restaurant like that. "You didn't tell me the only living family member I have is looking for me?" Her body jerked to standing so quickly she knocked the chair over.

On a small piece of blue paper a connection to her past existed. A connection to her mother, her father. An aunt who had known her from the time she was born.

And Grady had kept it from her.

The restaurant owner was walking toward them with a bottle of champagne and two glasses, but he hesitated as Lucie threw her napkin to the table. She strode across the floor, past the wide eyes of the other dining couple and hostess, out onto the sidewalk, and through older couples and young families out for a stroll or on their own way to dinner.

She crossed against the light at the busy intersection, mind reeling with even more questions now, but not for Grady. Her step quickened, growing more insistent, another block, and then another, and finally up the walkway to their door, fumbling with her key.

Inside she went straight to the office and Grady's messenger bag on his desk, digging inside it, flinging bits of paper and folders to the floor until at last she came upon the blue sticky note, which she held up to the light with trembling hands as if to ensure it wasn't counterfeit.

Why had he kept it from her? How could he have done that? She grabbed the phone from his desk, trying to dial the number, but her fingers were too shaky, her vision too clouded, the hurt overtaking her until she was crying in big gulps and sobs.

Like sorrow and grief and not knowing, betrayal turned out to be an entirely too familiar sensation.

# helen

Canadian Club sloshed over the rim of the glass, droplets marring the tiny crystal face of Gloria's Timex, the only keepsake Helen had received upon her sister's death. She set the drink on the TV tray and pulled a tissue from inside her brassiere strap to dry the watch and her parchment skin beneath. The doctor had not seemed concerned at her worsening tremor, her debilitating asthma, but she knew they were signs of things to come. Raymond, the casino manager, was already questioning her ability to quickly count the hundreds of liquor-sticky bills she needed to each shift, to sort the ones and fives and tens fast enough to keep up.

The television news had not once shown Lucie after the night she returned home. Helen watched faithfully, hoping for a glimpse of the girl. She'd been so thin and pale, where once she was a robust thing with pink in her cheeks and a bounce in her step. Helen sighed. She'd watch again at eleven, if she could stay awake.

She'd just opened the photo album to the first page when the telephone rang. The only calls she ever got were from police charities and pushy mortgage salesmen, but she'd started answering her phone again once Lucie was found, particularly once she'd given that Grady Goodall her number. As she reached for the green handset, her arm tangled in the curlicue cord and she swore beneath her breath, then brought the phone to her face.

"Hello?"

"Is this . . ." a female voice said, then stopped. It sounded just like Gloria, but it was her, the girl. Helen would know that voice in her sleep, in her dreams, when she was lying ten feet beneath the earth with Edward.

"Oh, Lucie!" She'd meant to play it a little more cool when Lucie finally called, but such emotion surged through her thinning veins, her brittle frame, she couldn't contain it. "I'm so glad to hear your voice." She heard the sound of weeping at the other end, and tears came to her own eyes.

"Am I really your niece?" the girl asked, voice nasal and desperate. "You're really my aunt?"

"Of course you are, yes. I promise you."

"Oh my god, I just . . . I can't . . ."

"Oh, my," Helen said. She had to remove her glasses to wipe her eyes. Her niece was as overwhelmed at finding her as Helen was to have been found. This was not the same Lucie who'd left them some twenty years ago. That Lucie did not have emotion.

"Where do you live? Can I come see you? Please?"

Could she come visit her? Helen thought she might lose

all control of herself. Her tremor kicked in, and she clenched her empty hand into a fist, digging her nails into her palm until it hurt.

"I'm still right here in Marysville. Why don't you come tomorrow morning? I'm afraid I don't have much to eat, but I can make coffee. I had to give up the house, but I'm in a nice little apartment in town now. East of the reservation?" she added, trying to prompt the girl's memory.

"I . . . I don't know what any of that means," Lucie said. "I'm sorry. What's your address? I have one of those things in my car, a navigation thing. Oh god, I can't believe you're there, right there, and I didn't know."

"It is hard to believe, after all this time," Helen said, wondering if perhaps the spirit of Gloria hadn't had a hand in this. "Tomorrow at, say, eleven? I have a shift at one, so that should give us time to get reacquainted." She gave Lucie her address, then precise directions from the highway, even when the girl protested that she could find her with whatever this thing was in her car she kept going on about. It had been hard enough for Helen to find the apartment complex in town the first time, and she was familiar with the area. She was not one to leave things to chance, much less to electronic devices.

"I'll see you tomorrow at eleven," Lucie said. "Thank you so much."

"For what?" The old woman harrumphed, then realized how it sounded. "Lucie, we're family."

After a pause, Lucie said, "Can I ask you one question?"

Helen sucked in a breath. What was the most burning thing this girl wanted to know, now that she'd lost her memories? Surely about the tragedy, something Helen still had a hard time talking about. Lucie had never talked about any of it when she'd returned alone to them, which had suited Helen and Edward fine. The girl was impossible at that point, and they'd had such grief of their own. But this Lucie seemed open and sincere, more like little girl Lucie, the Lucie who'd loved Helen so completely.

"Yes, of course, what is it?"

Lucie paused at the other end. "Did I used to have a piano?"

Helen rolled her eyes. The piano. All this time and distance, and that's what she wanted to know about?

"Yes, yes, your piano. I gather you still have it, then?" She'd better, all the money she and Edward had spent on that thing.

"How did I get it?" Lucie asked. "I mean, was it, was it my . . . parents'?" Her voice wobbled; she was crying again.

"It was our gift to you," Helen said, softening, remembering the day they'd moved it into Gloria's little yellow house near the reservation, the look on the girl's face as she watched the three adults—Helen, Edward, Gloria—struggling it up the porch steps and into the living room. Lucie had radiated a joy so pure that Helen felt her eyes tear over again at the memory.

Later, when Lucie had come back to them, Edward had thought it would be good for her to have the piano, and paid the shipping all the way back from California, but the girl had not played it again, not in their presence, anyway. Edward had insisted she take it when she moved away for good.

Later, in her bed, Helen prayed her usual prayer. "Oh, Edward, give me the strength I need to make it here alone without you." Then she added, "And don't go chasing Lucie away this time. I don't need your protecting. Never did." She lay silent for a long while, then said, "Not that I didn't appreciate your concern, of course, my darling."

She sighed into the darkness. She would be joining him soon, but first she would finally do right by the only living child between her and her sister. Then she could die in peace.

# grady

The morning after the wretched night before, Grady woke in the guest room to no sound at all. Lucie was not making breakfast, or moving about. She had not played the piano during the night. He felt alone in the house again, and the pain of it rushed back all at once.

He'd waited too long at the restaurant before going after her. He'd sat there and drunk his champagne, and then hers, refusing to let Milos bring him food. Then he'd left two twenties on the table when the older man was back in the kitchen and the hostess busy with other customers arriving, and hobbled too slowly with his crutches back home.

Why hadn't he rushed after her, asked Milos to drive him? He felt pretty certain she wouldn't run away again, but what if she had? Here he was an engineer, a professional paid to figure out and solve complex problems, yet he had no clue how to proceed, what to do or how to do it. His current mode of problem solving seemed to be paralysis. What still hadn't gotten through his thick skull?

He was afraid, Grady realized. He was always goddamn afraid.

When he'd gotten home she was in the office on the phone, the door shut. She was crying. He knew she was speaking with her aunt, and that she'd gone through his workbag somewhere along the way. Why was it surprising that she hadn't remembered her aunt's name? She had fucking amnesia.

Rather than face her when she was off the phone, rather than explain, he'd gone to the guest room and lain on the bed, door closed, and listened to every move she made. He'd hoped she'd come knock at the door, but she didn't. Why would she? He'd kept this very important thing from her.

If only she could understand why.

He had to make her understand. Grady got out of bed, determined to be a better man.

After a visit to the bathroom, he prowled the house, as much as one can prowl with crutches and a hard hunk of plastic wrapped around one foot. She wasn't in the office, and there were no telltale signs of the activity of the night before. But what would there be? Puddles of tears on the rug? His things shredded to bits on the desk?

She was not in the living room or dining room, not in the kitchen. No coffee had been made. He went to the front of the house and looked out the window. Her car still sat at the curb. He turned and looked up the stairs. All was quiet.

Grady lifted his good foot to the first stair, then leaned

hard forward, pushing to bring his body and the crutches up to steady himself so he could hoist the booted foot. He didn't fall, so in this tedious way, he mounted the narrow wooden steps for the first time since injuring his feet. As he neared the top, he heard the deep, relaxed breathing that meant Lucie was asleep.

She hadn't left him. He stopped for a moment to recover from the exertion, and the surprise.

At the top, he leaned the crutches against the wall and limped to the bed. She opened her eyes, and it was only then he remembered he was wearing just underwear and a ratty sleeping T-shirt.

"I'm sorry," he said. Words were a preposterous way to try to communicate such a thing, but they were all he had. "I thought I was doing the right thing, protecting you."

She studied his face, looking bewildered and sleepy, then lifted the covers, scooting to make room for him. She wasn't wearing anything. Grady averted his eyes and eased himself and his boot in beside her, not touching her or expecting to be touched. He lay quietly, listening to her breathe, letting his physical excitement at her proximity subside, and then, at some point, Grady began to dream of swimming in a sea of brightly colored birds.

At a clatter downstairs, he jerked awake, alone in the bed. Had he dreamed that she'd been beside him? He reached to where she'd been and felt her residual warmth.

Grady sat up, groggier than the first time he'd woken that morning. It was now nine thirty, later than he'd slept in years. He needed a shower. He needed to call in to work. But more than that, he needed to grow a spine and talk to this woman he loved, no matter who she was now.

He got up and found some shorts and a fresh T-shirt. Getting himself down the stairs proved far trickier than getting up them. Grady kept feeling as though he might fall headlong to the bottom, so he took the crutches in one hand and sat, scooting down on his butt with his broken foot extended. He hoped Lucie wouldn't come see what all the commotion was about.

She didn't. He found her, dressed already, sitting at the small kitchen table reading the paper, coffee and emptied cereal bowl in front of her. There were no other dishes out.

"Good morning," he said.

She looked up and nodded, as she had in bed that morning, but made no move to help him, or to get him breakfast. She looked back down at the newspaper.

Grady poured a cup of coffee, then stood drinking it at the counter, not sure if he should sit across from her or just leave. "So, I think we should talk," he said.

She did not look up.

"Right?" He had no idea how hard to push. What now? He stood, paralyzed, except for the arm that kept bringing the coffee cup to his mouth until he'd drunk it all.

"Maybe later, then?" he tried.

Lucie pursed her lips and flipped the Northwest section of the paper over to read the back.

Grady sighed. "Hey," he said. "Come on. You're gonna have to help me out a little."

Nothing. This was ridiculous.

"Here's what I have to say, then: I did it to protect you. You hate this woman. She gave you nothing but grief when you were a teenager, and you got the hell out of her house as fast as you could. I didn't want her hurting you again, Luce. That's it. That's my crime. Guilty. Guess I'll go shower."

A dramatic exit was impossible. He fumbled for his crutches and got his body turned around, the upside of which was that he caught sight of her face, the confusion and hurt that washed over it in the microsecond she looked up.

*Well, good,* he thought. He'd spoken his piece. If she didn't like it, or if it made her feel bad, well, at least they were in the same boat.

# lucie

T he drive to Helen's apartment took Lucie through scenery she knew she'd seen before, to places she'd known her entire life apparently, and yet it was all new: gracefully dowdy old neighborhoods giving way to newer shopping malls and then layer upon layer of trees, for miles. The navigation unit had said it would take Lucie forty-nine minutes to reach her destination, but she'd doubted it could be true. At minute forty-two, however, the city of Everett punched through the trees, and Marysville lay just a few miles farther.

Lucie was early. She needed to pee. She needed to think. Intermittently, she felt like crying or throwing up at the thought of finally learning her past. She knew Grady was just protecting her, but how could he not see that she needed to know everything? She hadn't told him where she was going that morning, but she had a feeling he knew.

A highway sign advertised a Starbucks at the next exit; she put on the blinker. The heavy traffic on I-5 was unnerving and she found herself being especially cautious. Had she always been such a safe driver? Would she always question every single thing she did, compare it to a time she may never remember? Like, had she ever been sexually desirable to Grady? How was it that a man could crawl into bed with a woman he supposedly loved and wanted to marry, and not touch her?

There'd been tenderness and remorse in his voice when he apologized, and Lucie couldn't help but forgive him. He felt so protective of her, and as misguided as that was, it had made her swoon with desire for him. She'd lifted the covers, thinking *Yes, now, finally,* and he'd lain beside her like a corpse.

Sucking her bottom lip to keep it from trembling, Lucie made her way down the highway ramp, seeing the Starbucks sign to her right. She needed to clear her head before she met her aunt. There were so many things to ask, so many things to finally know and understand about who she was, who her family was, and most especially, what had happened to her parents. She would never be a real person until she knew where she came from.

Inside the coffee shop, Lucie made a dash for the restroom, realizing she knew, innately, the layout of the place. She'd apparently been in many a Starbucks before, knowing already the mood-lit bathrooms at the back, the curving counter, where to order, where to pick up, even the hanging teardrop lights over the espresso machine. A voice sang in Spanish or Portuguese in the background. Mothers sat with strollers, and casually dressed businesspeople conversed or read newspapers.

After using the toilet, Lucie splashed water on her face and looked into the mirror, straining in the dim light to make out

how she would look to her aunt. To Helen. Did she call her
Aunt Helen? Her eyes were puffy and her hair flat against her
head. Why hadn't she gone to a hairdresser yet? Her crazy hair
was just getting crazier: dull brown from the roots to the defin-
ing line where all the action started. She raked her fingers
through it, but that only made her look deranged; she smoothed
her hair back down and went out to order an herbal tea—no
caffeine—before resuming her drive.

Maybe she really should go see the shrink after all. She'd
thought she could do it on her own, given enough time and
friendly faces, but so far, there'd been so few faces other than
Grady's and the only things she remembered were songs and
the image of small hands at the piano. It wasn't much to go on.
But now she had Helen. Everything was about to change, and
Lucie wondered whether it was for better or worse. As angry as
she'd been at Grady, she had listened when he said that the old
woman was a little off, and that they'd had a contentious relationship in the past. Still, she'd sounded so . . . well, so old on
the phone. Maybe she'd mellowed over the years.

At exit 199, Lucie left the highway. At the bottom of the
ramp, a sign indicated the Tulalip Indian Reservation was to
the left and Marysville to the right. She'd hoped she would
have some sense of familiarity when she got there, but it all
looked like small town anywhere: a Dairy Queen and a Burger
King, a Christian bookstore and a JCPenney's catalog store. She
followed the main drag a few blocks, and then she was through
town. *A gasp of a place,* she thought. This was where her family
was from?

At the next left she angled onto the street the navigator indicated, then followed a series of lefts and rights through small post–World War II houses. And then she saw the only apartment building in the neighborhood, faded gray wood, two stories. She parked on the street and got out, looking at the rows of windows, each dressed in the dweller's personality: bent blinds, closed drapes, sheers. Aluminum foil over a surprising number of windows. She was about to walk in when she saw someone in a second-floor window. An older woman. Helen lived in 218. Lucie smiled and waved. The woman backed away from the window.

Inside, the building smelled of fried fish and cat urine. Lucie climbed the stairs at the far end of the hallway.

The door to apartment 218 was festooned in dusty red, white, and blue bunting and a smattering of now deflated balloons. Lucie realized she'd missed the Fourth of July while she was gone, and thought immediately of potato salad, the smell of cut grass. Was this a memory? Closing her eyes, she breathed in, out, waiting. She was about to give up when it came: the flashes of color against dark, the percussive thuds in the chest, the smell of something burned.

"Oh," she muttered, brow tightening. She wanted to bring her hands to her ears, to scream. She opened her eyes, came back to the hallway, the droopy decorations. Had fireworks frightened her that much as a kid?

She took a deep breath and knocked. The door creaked open a few inches, a gray head poking out. "Come in, come in, before all the heat escapes."

It was early August and eighty-one degrees outside, and warmer still inside the apartment. Helen was smaller than

Lucie had imagined, stooped over, polyester beige slacks hanging loose to her white sneakers, a short-sleeved top with sailor motif too large on her frame. She wore pink and gold eyeglasses with thick lenses, her irises cartoonishly large behind them. With crooked arms, she reached for Lucie, soft wing skin undulating with the motion. "Oh, my," she said, "you are the picture of your mother."

Lucie bent to hug her, tears filling her eyes. She breathed in the scent of pine cleaner and boiled eggs, a hint of whiskey.

"Really?" Lucie pulled back, seeing now that Helen had teared up, too. "I look like her? Do you have a photo?"

"Of course, of course." Helen led her to a stained corduroy love seat. The coffee table held cups of black coffee and a plate of sandwiches cut into quarters. Helen picked up a pile of photos from beside a matching recliner and came to sit next to her. "Let's have a bite while we look through my pictures, shall we?"

The hodgepodge stack held old black-and-whites and more modern color snapshots, maybe fifteen photos in all. Helen handed Lucie the photo on top. In it, a woman who looked like Helen stared back at them in black and white, next to a dour-faced old man.

"Your grandparents," Helen said. "My father and mother, may they rest in peace."

"My grandparents," Lucie said, feeling no connection, no sense of familiarity. She wanted to see her parents, that's what she'd come for. "Did I know them?" she asked, to be polite.

"Only when you were real small," Helen said. "They died young."

Young! They looked ancient, Lucie thought. "How did they,

well, pass away?" What diseases were hereditary in her lineage? she wondered, a brand-new thought. What might she die of, one day?

"Sadness," Helen said and took the photo back from Lucie. "Melancholy runs through the family. Daddy couldn't take it anymore and sat in the garage with the motor running on his sixtieth birthday, and Momma just upped and died of loneliness after that." She sighed, hand brushing across their faces.

"Depression?" Lucie asked, alarmed. "Depression runs in our family?"

"Well, I suppose that's what they'd call it these days," the old woman murmured, picking up her cup of coffee and sipping it.

"Did I have it, when you knew me?"

"You were the happiest child," Helen said, carefully setting the cup back down.

"Was I afraid? You know, of loud noises and things, like fireworks?"

Helen clucked. "No, don't be silly. You were anything but a scaredy-cat." She searched through the photos with gnarled fingers. "Here, I have pictures to prove it." She handed over a few yellowing snapshots, and suddenly Lucie recognized herself in unfamiliar settings: a smiling baby in a high chair, a toddler holding an ear of corn like a prize, a small raincoated girl climbing the ladder of a tall slide.

"These are me," Lucie said, knowing it to be true, but how?

"Of course that's you. See what a delightful girl you were? You were not anxious, not melancholic, most certainly not." Helen clucked. "Now, have a bite to eat. You're too thin."

Lucie thought of the letters carved into the piano bench. "Did people call me Lulu?"

Helen adjusted her eyeglasses. "Not that I recall, but I'm old, you know. The memory plays tricks."

*You're telling me,* Lucie wanted to say. "Did I have cousins? I keep thinking that there were other kids with me, or one, anyway, playing piano with me. Is that a memory, or . . ."

The old woman cleared her throat with a loud, phlegmatic hack, then wiped her lips. "No, no cousins," she said and handed Lucie more photos.

There stood a buxom woman in her thirties, outdoors by a car, wearing Capri pants and a tight sweater. She stood alone in one shot, with a smaller woman who had to be Helen in the next, and with a tall, dark-haired man in another. "Is that my mom and dad?" Lucie asked, shocked. The man was as dark as Grady. Was he Native American, too?

"No, that's not your father, but it is your mother," Helen said.

Lucie looked closely at the woman's face, trying to imagine that she loved her, but felt repulsed instead. And the woman looked nothing like her, despite what Helen said. It couldn't be her mother.

"And that's my husband, your uncle Edward. Good-looking son of a gun, wasn't he? It's the Indian in him, I think, makes him so handsome. Those Skykomish are a beautiful people."

Lucie felt close to tears. She'd wanted something more; she'd wanted the faces in the photos to bring it all back, all the love and memory and connection that were missing. She'd wanted to be healed, suddenly and miraculously, but she felt exactly the same. Unclaimed, unmothered.

And how was it that her uncle was also Native American? Did that have something to do with why she'd been with Grady?

"What was my mother's name?"

"Gloria," Helen said. "Gloria Frances. Named for our grandparents on our father's side. I was named for our grandparents on our mother's side, Nancy Helen. Didn't care for Nancy as a kid, probably because I happened to despise that particular grandmother."

Lucie laid the photos on the table. She couldn't look at any more of them. She didn't want to see faces she couldn't remember. "Please," she said, "could you just tell me about her? And my father? What happened to them? What happened to me? I just need to know."

"But, there are more—"

"Please," Lucie said. "Just tell me."

# helen

So distraught, this girl was. So full of emotion and tears, not at all like either Lucie that Helen had known. She was not cheerful and affectionate and carefree. She was not cold and unfeeling. She felt too much, Helen suspected. Her entire past was finally catching up with her.

Helen took the photos she'd selected so carefully for the girl and set them on the table. They held the same power over her. She'd spent many an evening crying over her pictures, and now Lucie was clearly upset by looking at them.

"Now, now," she said. "Eat your sandwich, and your coffee is getting cold. I'll tell you as much as I can."

Gloria Frances was the younger of the two sisters, by one year and eight months. They were born in Everett, Gloria while their father was away in the Navy. Their mother told them he'd been a good man but had come home from the war different. Moody, distracted. "Thank the Lord he didn't take us all with him when he gassed himself in the garage," Helen said. She twisted her crooked fingers together as she spoke, an old habit she'd forgotten she had. Edward used to tease her about it.

The girl looked impatient. Her mother. Of course, she wanted to know about her mother.

Helen cleared her throat. "And then there was Gloria, light of the world." She closed her eyes for a moment, then continued. Gloria had been special. She was not like other girls of the time. She was adventurous, Helen decided to say, as opposed to "wild" or "insensible" or "tempestuous," though all those things were also true. Helen wanted to focus on the good for Lucie, and the truth was, she'd loved all of those things about Gloria, even though they sometimes got Helen into trouble with her parents, too, for not controlling her sister. Helen had been the sensible one, but she'd secretly delighted in her sister's escapades, like the time she climbed the light pole to prove she could, and didn't even get a scratch when she touched the live wire and fell to earth. She just picked herself up and laughed. Or the time she stole Mr. Higgins's Ford pickup and drove all the way to Bellingham before the state troopers got her and brought her home. Their father had beat her for it, but she gave Helen a wink when she limped in from the shed. For which Helen then got whipped, but it only seemed fair.

They'd been inseparable, Helen told the girl now, until 1969, when Gloria met Lucie's father, Gene, who had long, god-awful sideburns and wanted to live off the land or some such nonsense. No, she did not have any pictures of him. They'd run off to Boise to get married after knowing each other less than a month, and lived there in a trailer. Three years later

Gloria came back home without him, but with a little girl—
Lucie. Gene had fallen in with some ne'er-do-wells and gotten
involved in drugs and sex parties, and Helen heard many years
later that he'd died from some sort of cancer. She hated the
look on Lucie's face when she said this, wishing she'd softened
the blow. Even her stranger of a father was dead.

"But I'm still here. This is why it's important that I found
you," Helen said, taking the girl's hand. It was so smooth and
unmarred by veins or age spots, just as Helen's had once been.
"I've had no one, either, you see? And now we have each other."

Lucie nodded, her expression pained. "Please, go on," she
said, latching on to Helen's hand, sending a shiver of pleasure
up the old woman's spine. How many years had it been since
the girl had touched her?

"Well, then you and your mother came to live with Edward
and me," Helen said, "and those were some of the happiest
times of our lives. Ten solid years we had with you here in
Marysville. Oh, we'd go to the beach and dig for clams and
roast corn over the fire, and we'd go to the pictures, and the
Strawberry Festival every summer, and even after you and your
mother moved into your own house, you'd come spend the
night . . ."

So many memories. They clustered and darted in Helen's
mind like schools of fish, coming, going, too slippery to hold on
to long enough to show the girl how it had been between them,
how they'd been a real family, how they'd loved each other.

"You see, Edward and I were not blessed with children, so
having you in our lives was . . ." Helen felt the flush spread
from her throat to her face. She'd promised herself she

wouldn't get this worked up. They'd become like parents to the girl, seeing as how Gloria liked to have her fun at night, which often carried over into the next day, and sometimes the next several days. But Lucie didn't need to hear about that, not now.

"Then what happened?" Lucie pressed. She didn't care how close they'd been, how Helen felt about any of it. No, she wanted to get to the unhappy memories, of course. Helen sighed.

"Well, then your mother fell for this other fellow, and he was far worse than the first one. I tried to tell her, even Edward tried to talk her out of it, but she ended up taking you and moving with him to San Francisco when you were just eleven years old. He had family there, thought he could get a job with his brother selling cars. Oh, it was so sad the day you all drove away, you in the back window waving at us, poor little thing. You didn't want to go."

The girl had cried like her heart was breaking; they all had. The old sorrow washed over Helen, a wave of sea and salt, drowning her as it did, and she reached for her tissue, dabbed her nose. She didn't know if she could do this, after all.

"San Francisco?" Lucie looked stunned. "Where in San Francisco? That must be why I went there." She was growing insistent, and Helen did not like the tone in her voice. "I knew it; I knew I was looking for something. Where did we live?"

"Please, I'm old. Let me gather my wits. This is very difficult for me, and I need to be on my shift soon, and . . . Could you please just eat your sandwich? I went to the store special and got the good deli cold cuts."

Lucie picked up a sandwich but didn't take a bite. "What

happened in San Francisco? You can't stop now, not now that I'm here and you know everything." She looked about to cry.

Helen tucked her tissue back into her décolletage. "Oh dear, now I've upset you, too." She felt calm again. "Yes, I will tell you, of course I will. That's why you're here." Clearly not to get to know her aunt, she thought. Well, then. Just let her share this family burden.

"This fellow was not a nice man, as I have mentioned, and he was even meaner when he was drinking."

She looked at Lucie for her response, but the young woman was sitting with her sandwich in her lap, just staring at it, not taking one bite, and here Helen had also bought the expensive mayonnaise. She sighed and continued.

"Over those four years, your mother wrote me letters intimating that he was what they call 'abusive,' but never quite admitting it. Now, she was no fairy princess herself. Gloria always gave as good as she got, but still. It's never a fair fight between a man and a woman."

Lucie's breathing had gone shallow. Oh, Helen thought, this wasn't coming out right at all, but how else to tell it?

"She was always changing her mind, anyway, breaking it off, taking him back. She put up with that nonsense for four long years."

"He beat her?" Lucie was wide-eyed now. Yes, she was all ears now.

"He did indeed, but she was strong and stubborn. No, the trouble all came about because once you started to mature, he turned his meanness on you."

"He—he beat me?"

"All I know is one day, your mother found those cigarette burns on your leg when she got home from work and he was sleeping off a drunk on the couch."

"Jesus," Lucie said. Her hand went to her thigh, and Helen knew just what was beneath. No, not a birthmark at all, although she'd let the girl call it that, all those years ago. Maybe she should have made her tell the truth. Maybe the doctors had been right about that, but it had seemed easier just to let her begin again with a new story, one that included nothing about what had happened, nothing about anyone who'd died that day.

"Then what happened?" The girl just wouldn't stop, would she? Wasn't she seeing the big picture yet? How could she not remember?

"Well, she called me all hysterical about it, and I tried to calm her down."

Helen trembled, thinking about that conversation, one she'd never shared with anyone and certainly wouldn't now. *Take care of my babies,* Gloria had said, and it scared Helen so much she demanded Gloria leave the house immediately. Gloria didn't hear her, couldn't hear her, Helen supposed, in her state. *Don't let Lucie turn out like me,* her sister had moaned, then hung up. No matter how many times Helen called back, there was no answer.

"Of course, she knew where he kept his gun."

She paused, yet still Lucie looked at her expectantly, wanting to hear some happy ending. Helen sighed, felt her hands tremble. If only she'd been able to convince Gloria to just walk out the door that day, or if she'd thought to call the San Francisco police, but Helen had failed her sister. She'd failed them all. She took a sip of coffee, wishing it were whiskey, then wiped her lips. She'd just have to get it over with.

"She shot him, there on the couch. Dead." And she would leave it at that.

Lucie's gasp sucked the air from the room. "What? She killed him?"

"But not without provocation, don't you see? She was a mother bear protecting her cubs. I immediately arranged for you to come here, to be with us. We were all you had left."

"But my mother—"

"Died, not long after. Her spirit was broken."

The girl crumpled at this, as if she'd held out hope that her mother was alive. It had seemed a miracle that the teenage Lucie had never talked about any of the details of that day, and had never once mentioned any of her family members again. The doctors said she was in shock and speculated that she'd run into a bedroom to hide and saw none of it. Edward had said it was best not to force her to talk about it, and Helen had gone along with him. But what kind of a child doesn't mourn for her own flesh and blood? How on God's green earth could she tell this young woman what an unfeeling monster she'd been then?

This Lucie was human.

Helen shuddered, wondering for the first time if the teenager who came back from California on the airplane might not have had any memories inside her, either.

"Oh, my, it's getting late. My shift starts soon," Helen said, and excused herself to the bathroom, ashamed suddenly at the anger they'd had toward the girl all those years ago. Helen coughed, barely able to breathe; her asthmatic chest had tucked in upon itself. Where was her inhaler?

The girl had the amnesia back then, Helen was certain of it now, remembering Lucie's face on the television when they found her last month, those same flat eyes, that lack of expression. It explained everything.

"Oh, Edward, what did we do?" she whispered, a familiar wheeze rasping at the edges of the words. Her fingertips were going numb. If she looked into the mirror, she would see that her lips were blue. She needed to see her husband again. He would reassure her, tell her that they'd done all they could, that a firm hand was best with children who didn't respect their elders.

It hadn't worked, though. They'd just driven her away.

The inhaler sat next to the tissue box on the commode. Helen picked it up with shaking hands and brought it to her lips, but only after first considering lying her wretched old body down in the tub, where she could wait for Edward Ten Hands to come pull her into the light, where she could be with him and her mother and dad, and with Gloria and that beautiful little boy.

# grady

drying off after his shower, Grady knew that Lucie was gone. He felt it in the stillness of the house, in the clouds that had gathered in the sky. He didn't sense that she'd left him, but he knew that when she returned, every-thing would be different. Again.

She'd gone to see the aunt. Of course. And if he'd had the good sense to replace her cell phone in the past weeks, he could call her now, but he hadn't. She was always home, or in the neighborhood, seemingly adjusting, happy even. The cell phone was like the psychiatrist. It would happen, eventually, when the time was right, only now he realized he should have insisted on both, should have put his foot down and made the appointment with the doctor, taken matters into his own hands and gone to the electronics store for a replacement phone.

He'd been so selfish. He hadn't wanted to share her with anyone, yet, but her recovery hinged on her making her own

way in the world again. He had to help her, and he had to let
her know he was on her side.

Grady limped naked into the office and looked through his
bag for Helen's phone number. It wasn't there. Lucie had taken
it with her.

How many people in Marysville could have the name Ten
Hands?

The Internet revealed just one, a listing for Edward Ten
Hands. Grady had to talk to Lucie; the old woman worried
him. Did she really have Lucie's best interests at heart? Or had
seeing Lucie in the press just rekindled some twisted desire to
hurt her again?

When Helen answered, he said, "I'd like to speak with
Lucie, please."

"And whom shall I say is calling?"

"You know damn well. Just put her on." There it was, anger,
the thing he always tried to deny, and he was glad for it.

He heard murmuring and fumbling, and then Lucie, crying.

"What's going on?" he asked. "Are you all right? Do you
want me to come get you?"

"No," she said, sounding stern, then started to sob. "God,"
she whispered, "it's so horrendous. No wonder I'm such a lunatic."

"You're not a lunatic. Is that what she said? Is she standing
right there?"

"She's gone to get more coffee," Lucie said. "She's definitely
odd, but I don't think she's lying. It's just . . . god. So much
worse than I ever imagined." She blew her nose. "But guess

what? We lived in San Francisco when I was a kid! There was a reason I went there, at least."

"I'm coming up there."

"No, don't. You can't even drive." She began to speak to the old woman, saying, "Yes, yes, everything's fine."

"Everything is not fine," Grady said. "I want you to leave there, now."

"I'm sorry," Lucie said, "but I have to go." She was going to hang up. She was still mad at him, and now her aunt was influencing her. Grady didn't know what to do.

"Dammit, Lucie, I just want to do the right thing, but I don't know what that is. I don't know what you want. I just want to be with you and help you, and . . . shit." His voice dropped, almost to a whisper. "I love you so goddamn much, and I don't know if I should even say it anymore."

"Grady," she said. "I just have to do this."

She was right, and he hated it.

"And, yes." She paused. "You should definitely say it." The line clicked to silence.


GYM BAG IN tow, Grady clumped his way down the front steps to his car. The doctor had said he shouldn't drive, but Grady felt fully capable of figuring out how to make his booted foot do whatever was necessary to get him to the Queen Anne Community Pool. If he left now, he'd be back by the time Lucie got home. If he stayed home and worried, he'd make himself crazy.

He tucked his crutches and the bag in back, then settled behind the wheel. Pressing the accelerator with the boot was tricky, but Grady felt lucky that his left foot had healed enough to work the clutch. If he'd borrowed Lucie's automatic at any time during the past couple of weeks, he'd have made it to work, no problem. He'd known that at some level, but he'd wanted to be home. He'd wanted to be where Lucie was.

"You should definitely say it," she'd said. The commotion this caused in his chest was so visceral he'd have sworn birds were beating actual wings inside him, saying, "See? She does love you, or she will." An exaltation of larks. A flock of fucking seagulls. An orgy of lovebirds, he thought, tapping his fingers on the wheel in time to the Modest Mouse song on his iPod: *That's what I'm waiting for, that's what I'm waiting for, aren't I?*

A new thought occurred to him: he could prove to Lucie how much she'd loved him. He had the data; it was verifiable. Their five years together were well documented in all the mushy correspondence he'd saved, corny romantic cards and love letters. He'd dig them out when he got home and show them to her as he had the photos early on, to help her remember. If she could read the words she'd written to him, she'd have to feel something waking inside.

Grady drove the old Volvo west on Forty-Fifth through the Wallingford retail district to Highway 99, then headed south over the high-arching Aurora Bridge, notorious for its body count from jumpers. All that water, the mountains in the distance. The view alone should be enough to bring even the saddest person to his senses, but Grady could understand the draw. Driving past dried flower bundles and notes attached to the suicide prevention fence, he had to avert his eyes to avoid imagining the leap.

Turning off onto Queen Anne Hill, he realized he hadn't considered how difficult the steep inclines would be to negotiate with a manual transmission, the boot clumsy on the gas and brake pedals. Twice he stalled the engine, but twice he managed to get the car going again without letting it roll back into the impatient Range Rover behind him.

Finally, after navigating the twisty, narrow streets lined with stately old homes, Grady made his way to the neighborhood business district at the top of the hill: a parade of coffee shops, trendy restaurants, yoga studios, and massage therapists. Dodging strollers and runners and kids on skateboards at every intersection, he navigated until he found a spot to squeeze the car into. Despite the neighborhood's cachet, the Queen Anne Community Pool was just another public pool: fluorescent lights too bright, chlorine smell too sharp, and screaming kids too loud. He'd fallen a long way from the executive comforts of Sound Fitness, but it no longer mattered.

Water was water. Life went on, and Grady had a feeling that if he removed the boot but kept his foot wrapped, and if he took it easy, he'd find he had healed enough to get back on with it. Or not. But he had to try.

# lucie

When it was time for Helen to leave for the casino, Lucie walked her to her car in the building's parking lot. She had serious doubts that the old woman should be driving, as arthritic as her hands and fingers were, as much as she wheezed and coughed and trembled, but Lucie knew not to argue with her, and not because Helen was strong willed, although strong willed she certainly was. It was that Lucie sensed the fragility of her aunt's old broken places—the family she grieved, the sorrows she'd carried alone. Lucie had lost her parents and, worse, herself. But Helen had lost her connection to the world, it seemed. She was weird and crazy because no one expected her not to be. No one kept her in check. No one waited at home for her at the end of the day or told her good night before she went to sleep, and hadn't in years.

Helen's old Toyota Celica listed to the left, tires lower on the driver's side. The old woman extracted her keys from her handbag. "Well . . ." she said, looking glum.

Lucie knew she should hug her, but she couldn't bring herself to. Part of her hated Helen Ten Hands and everything she'd revealed.

"You'll come again soon, won't you?" Spittle had formed in the corners of Helen's withered lips. Her glasses were smudged. Lucie nodded, but she hadn't decided whether she would see her again or not.

Finally, alone in her own car, Lucie reclined the seat and closed her eyes, still queasy from the smell of bologna and watery Nescafé, from the photographs she didn't recognize and the people in them she didn't love, the stories she didn't want to think about. Her life had been a series of tragedies, if she was to believe Helen. She had a disaster of a family.

*My mother was a murderer,* she thought. Even though it had been in self-defense, or rather in Lucie's defense, it was crazy, wasn't it? He was passed out on the couch; why hadn't her mother just taken Lucie and left? Gloria still had family to go home to.

*My family,* she thought, shuddering. Had the stories been about strangers, Lucie might have marveled at how bad her mother's decision making had been in all things—men, conflict—but it was that part of her mother she could identify with. Something felt familiar about her desperation. Grady was a good man, though; she seemed to have bucked her mother's trend for losers. He wasn't an alcoholic or abusive. They'd fought, but Lucie hadn't shot him, right? She'd only run. But why? His description of their fight didn't seem that bad.

What was it that tugged at her memory, or was it just her imagination? Such murky sensations, like those she'd felt at seeing the July Fourth decorations, or when playing the piano. The sense that someone was missing. The explosions. The smell of smoke.

A gun firing.

Lucie sat up, eyes wide open. Not fireworks at all.

She sat perfectly still, heart beating fast, one hand clutching the door handle. Did she remember her mother shooting the man? Was she going to freak out, have some terrifying flashback? Lose her mind again?

She waited for the next thing to happen. After a few minutes, her heart slowed back to normal and her body relaxed. She felt a residual shakiness, a deep sense of loss, but she'd been feeling that all along.

She'd remembered something real, finally. Something verifiable, if she could believe Helen. It didn't kill her. It didn't harm her. It left her wanting more.

Clicking her seat belt into place, Lucie started the car. Strangely, she felt better, in spite of her newly discovered family tree. Finally, she had something to look for.


AT HOME, THE house smelled of swimming pool. The sound of whistling came from the office. Grady had never whistled before.

"Hello?" Lucie called, hanging her bag on the back of a dining room chair.

Yes, she was still angry that Grady hadn't told her about Helen, but it was a more academic anger now. In his awkward way, he was trying to take care of her, although Lucie suspected it was the former Lucie's needs he had in mind. But she also understood now that he was capable of keeping secrets, big secrets. If she was going to get better, if she was going to get on with her life, he had to tell her the truth.

Lucie walked toward the office and met Grady in the hallway. He wasn't using his crutches. She looked down and saw that he wasn't wearing his boot.

"What's going on?" she asked.

"Are you okay? What did she tell you? How do we know she's even mentally competent?"

Lucie sighed. "Oh, she is. It sucks, but she is."

"But—"

"But what are you doing? Where's your boot, your crutches?"

"I'm experimenting," he said. "The pain's not really that bad." He winced, taking a step. "Well, not as bad. And I'm supposed to be getting off the crutches soon anyway."

"Please," she said, "for me, put the boot back on."

This seemed to delight him, and he smiled more broadly than she'd yet seen. "Okay," he said, "for you," and turned to hop back to the office. "I swam today," he called over his shoulder. "That's when I got the idea."

"Where?" She followed him and saw piles of cards and letters atop his desk. He seemed to be sorting through them, perhaps cleaning out a drawer. He took a seat in his chair and grabbed the boot, widening its jaws to slip his foot inside.

"At the Queen Anne pool. It's a little small and a lot crowded, but I couldn't go very far anyway. It didn't hurt that bad to swim, so I thought I'd try walking. I don't think doctors know exactly how quickly each person heals, you know? There has to be some statistical variability."

"Grady." Lucie said it quietly, but he stopped talking, looking up at her with raised brows.

"I remembered something today up there."

His smile faltered. "Really? What?"

"First, I need you to tell me the truth, the entire truth."

"I do, I have," he said, frowning. "What about?"

"What did I know about my past? How much did I tell you about my parents, my background? I mean, if I never even told you I lived in San Francisco . . ."

His face relaxed. He sat forward, elbows on knees. "You never told me anything except that your parents were dead. That you hated your aunt and uncle, and had gotten out of their house as fast as you could. I don't know if you knew more, but you never told me any more than that."

She paused, considering. "And you didn't press me? Weren't we the kind of couple who talked about everything? Weren't we completely honest with each other?"

He shrugged. "You just didn't want to talk about that stuff. I always wished you could have opened up with me, but you kept it to yourself. It seemed too hard for you, so eventually I quit trying to make you." He paused. "I thought I was doing the right thing, but now, I . . . I'm not sure. Now I can't help you."

Lucie nodded. "Well, I think I might have remembered something today, in a way. Explosions, like gunshots. Just the thought of them made me want to scream or throw up." She shuddered as she had earlier that day. "I think maybe it was my mother shooting her husband, my stepfather."

"What? Is that what she told you? Lucie, she's senile or something."

"I could feel it, kind of. I could sense it," Lucie said. "I think she was telling the truth." She waited for Grady to ask her questions, but he was quiet, eyes cast down. "I know I wouldn't before, but can I talk to you about this?" she asked.

He looked up, surprised. "Well, yeah. Of course! I'm just not used to—"

"Are you sure you—"

"Yeah, yes, of course," Grady said, securing the boot and standing, then hobbling to where Lucie sat. He put out his hand, and she took it, standing. "Let's go somewhere more comfortable," he said.

Lucie knew he meant the living room, but as she left the office ahead of him, she veered left instead of right and stepped into the guest bedroom. He'd said he loved her. He had no other woman named Helen. There was nothing in their way.

*What am I doing?* she wondered vaguely, but she didn't stop. Maybe she just needed to feel something good after the awful day. Something life affirming, something about now and the two of them and all that could be between them. Or maybe she just needed to connect on a physical level before she could let down her emotional guard again with Grady. She needed to know he loved her this way, and every way. She needed to know she was safe.

Lucie went to the bed and pulled down the covers, neatly folding them back. She turned to see Grady holding on to the doorway for support, sans crutches, looking at her in a way that was new but not. She knew this face, this expression, from somewhere as deep as she knew the explosions. The little hands on the piano. Larger hands on her breasts, her waist, her hips.

Grady's chest rose with deeper breaths, his lips parted. He stared at her in a way that made her feel already undressed.

"Hi," she said, brain turning to fizz.

"Hi," he said. His voice cracked.

Lucie smiled, nervous, and pulled her shirt over her head. She slipped her feet out of her sandals, watching Grady watch her. He did want her; she should have known all along. And she needed him close, as close as people can get, skin to skin and breath to breath, sweet and salt and damp and soft. Before she could talk with him, she needed to know they were capable of cohesion and solidarity, that she was his.

# grady

ucie's lips tasted the way they had from the first time he'd kissed her, like sunset on a hot day, or a sudden rain. Like apples picked from the tree. Her kiss had always woken him from the daily humdrum, from the depths or from the usual, and it did now. She stood naked in front of him, unbuttoning his shirt, helping him hop to the bed, where he sat while she finished undressing him, looking into his eyes.

She smelled faintly of lotion, the same simple lotion she'd worn every day he'd known her. Her hard, lean body was gone, though, replaced by a softness he could not quit staring at. She hadn't gained weight or gotten plump, just feminized without the intense exercise, and he wanted to touch her so much his fingers trembled.

"I thought you wanted to talk," he said, not wanting to ruin his chance at making love with Lucie after so long, but also not wanting to misunderstand. Why was she doing this, now? How was he supposed to respond?

"I do," she said, sliding her hands down his chest, caressing his nipples, then leaning to kiss them. She looked up at him, pink lipped and flushed. "We will."

"Oh god," he said, touching her head, her cheek, sliding his hand down her long neck to her collarbone. "I won't be able to talk much longer," he said.

"Shh," Lucie said.

She tugged at his shorts and underwear, and he lifted his hips while she pulled them down and off over his boot. When her hand glanced over his erection, his body convulsed so hard that she drew away. "Did I hurt you?" she asked.

"No," he groaned, pulling her to him. "No, not at all. You are amazing." And she was. This Lucie was bolder, taking the initiative and undressing him. He'd always loved having sex with her because she enjoyed it so much once she loosened up, but he'd been the one to instigate, to caress and kiss her beyond inhibition. This woman seemed to have none, kneeling between his knees, and now, god, she had taken him in her mouth, something she'd done previously only on his birthday or after too much wine. The top of her head was different, her hair darker, smooth, not spiky, and it suddenly felt as if he were cheating on Lucie. His Lucie.

He cringed as he realized he was losing his erection. Jesus. How could that be happening? It felt so good to be doing what they were doing. "I'm sorry, I . . ."

Her mouth slid off him; she made a sound like wind in the desert. Rocking back on her heels, she stood and began to pick up pieces of her clothing.

"Luce, wait, I'm sorry, I—"

She wouldn't look at him. "I'm not her anymore, am I?"

Grady flushed hot with embarrassment and grabbed a pillow to cover himself, wanting to protest. This Lucie was everything he could ever want in a woman. She wasn't needy or demanding or complicated. She was patient and kind and easy to be with, and so damn sexy he couldn't stand it. How on earth could any red-blooded man go limp with her doing what she'd been doing?

But she was right; he did miss the old Lucie. He grieved for the woman he'd worked so hard to make love him, then chased away with his insecurities and defensiveness. If only he could have loved her better, if only he'd been able to prove himself to her as a worthy man, she never would have run. He'd never have the chance now.

"I'm sorry," he said, knowing he should stand on his stupid broken foot and take the living, breathing Lucie in his arms, but he lay back on the bed, hand over his eyes, and waited for her to leave the room before letting himself roll over and succumb to the grief at the demise of his first, most precious Lucie, whose approval he would never now earn.

THAT NIGHT, AS Lucie played some kind of classical piece in the basement, Grady crept back into the office. He needed to read through the cards and letters from the woman who'd loved him before it all went wrong. He picked up a card on top of the pile, with a beautiful Japanese print of waves and foam, trees on mountains in the distance. Inside, Lucie had written in her careful script:

*Grady,*

*Of course I know you love me. Obviously I love you.*
*That's not what this is about. I just have so much to do*
*and there's never enough time. I know you're busy with*
*the redesign, too. Can't we just agree that we love each*
*other and not get so caught up in how much time we do*
*or don't spend alone together?*

She'd signed with a big looping *L* and added a P.S.: "Are you going to make it to the Tech Night at the Opera thing next Friday? It would be really nice if you could. I put it on your calendar and took your suit to the cleaner."

Grady opened a few more cards. They weren't love letters. They were instructions and guidelines to a coupled life with Lucie, peppered with her side of their ongoing struggle, written to assure him that all was well but that she was going to do whatever she was going to do and she would appreciate it if he would comply. Why had he thought of them as proof of something more tender, more real? He tried to remember what his letters to her said. Had she saved them as he'd saved hers? He had always tried to get her to agree to special nights they could spend at home together, "date nights" he'd called them, but she'd thought date nights should be spent out at restaurants and events around town. Always multitasking, handing people cards, making sure to say hello to this or that human resources manager or potential client across the room.

Grady swept the pile back together into the box of keepsakes he stored beneath the bookcase. Why had he saved them? Other than the stylish works of art Lucie chose and the neat, pretty script she wrote in, they were simply memos to a cohabitant.

And then he crept out into the dining room, where a shaft of streetlight hit the white boxes of wedding invitations stacked on the floor. He couldn't stand to look at them anymore, these reminders of what had never really been. Tomorrow was recycling day. Something had to change. He had to change. He lifted the stack of boxes and headed for the garage.

THE NEXT DAY, there was nothing to do but go back to work. Grady had proven he could drive. He could swim. He could live his life the way he had before breaking his foot, before finding Lucie, before losing Lucie the first time, as he feared he now had again.

Sitting in his cubicle with his foot propped on a visitor chair, he dialed Dory's cell.

"Hey, G! How goes the honeymoon?"

He'd usually just have said "Fine," but this was why he'd called her, wasn't it? To confess, to be chastened and brought back to reality.

"The honeymoon is over," he said, knowing he was pouring it on, but that was his role, too. Gloomy Gus, his sisters called him.

"Oh no, what happened?" Grady could see her, settling back in her own cubicle, even though she'd have clients a mile deep to wade through.

"I totally screwed up, and now she thinks I don't love her anymore. She's so different than she was—it's hard to believe she's the same person. But she's so, well, so Lucie, too. Just like a more relaxed version or something. Lucie in an alternate universe, only I'm still in the normal one."

"Jeez, sounds kind of ideal to me. She always was wound a little tight. What'd you do that was so terrible?"

Grady rubbed his brow, closed his eyes. "She wanted to do it."

"God, TMI," Dory said. "No details. But I'm guessing you didn't want the same thing."

"No, I did, I do. I really do. I miss her."

"Then what's the problem? She's still your fiancée, she's still the same person, Grady, I promise you. Trauma victims—"

"What trauma? See, that's the part I'm not getting. Losing her parents never bothered her before, not in the whole five years we were together."

"Come on, Grady. That's called 'repression,' not emotional health for god's sake. Dissociative fugue is set in motion by big emotional trauma. Soldiers on the battlefield kind of stuff, you know?"

Her mother shot her stepfather. Good god. If that wasn't traumatic . . . why wasn't he telling Dory that part?

"What happened the day she left, Grady?"

He felt the tightness in his jaw. He'd told Dory more than anyone else, and now he was regretting it.

"Well, you know, I told you. We had a fight. A really bad fight. But, I just don't get how they correlate. I'm not her crazy-ass family. I mean, a lot of people go through a lot of bad shit, but they don't just erase their lives because of it. You and I didn't have the easiest lives, either. You don't just leave someone you love."

As he said it, he heard what Dory heard, and he'd never let himself say the words aloud before because they were so ridiculous and selfish.

"Wait, who's this about, Dad or Lucie?"

"I know, I know."

"Listen, it's wiring, pure and simple." Dory was always so sure of things. "Biological, nature, nurture, whatever. We each have our own personal clockworks, and hers happened to go kablooey. You can't penalize her for a mental illness any more than you could if she were diagnosed with cancer, Grady. It's not fair."

"She doesn't have a mental illness!" Grady looked up to see who might have heard, then lowered his voice. "She's just . . ." There was no way to finish the sentence.

"I'm afraid the *DSM-IV* classifies dissociative disorders as mental illness, sweetie. She's been ill. She's now recovering. Can you think of her that way?"

Grady sighed. "I know. I should."

"How's it going with the psychiatrist?"

"She doesn't want to go."

"What? Grady . . ." He knew Dory was rolling her eyes. "Think of it this way: if she did have cancer, say of the brain, and was mentally impaired, would you leave that decision up to her?"

"You know Lucie. No one can tell her what to do."

Dory sighed. "So, she is the same Lucie."

"Well, yeah. In some ways. But did I tell you she plays the piano now? And she's cooking. And making *friends*."

Dory chuckled. "She sounds pretty damn healthy to me. If that's not to your liking, maybe it's your problem, not hers."

There it was. That was what he'd come looking for, and Dory always delivered. "I hate that," he said. "And I hate it when you're right."

"Of course I'm right. And I'm right about the doctor. If you don't make Lucie an appointment soon, I'm going to."

Grady laughed. "Yeah, yeah. Fine."

"Hey, I have to get back to work. I'm fighting with PUD over a client's electricity bill, even though it's not in my job description and my boss will give me hell when she finds out. I mean, at least it isn't winter, but how can you expect people to live decent lives in the dark?"

Grady dropped his head to the back of the chair. "Yeah, well, I know what it's like."

"Then just turn the light on, honey. I guess I'm seeing you Sunday at Mom's, right? What's up with that?"

"I don't know. Lucie really wants to see everyone, for some reason. Who knows what will happen now, since she can barely stand the sight of me."

Dory snorted. "Why wouldn't she want to meet us? We're awesome! And hey, I'll put in a good word for you, little bro."

Grady shook his head, but hung up with new resolve. He would turn on the light in his life. If Lucie could be a new and better version of herself, maybe he could try it, too. Grady 2.0.

ARRIVING HOME THAT evening, he found her at her desk in the office, engrossed in something on her laptop. He hadn't seen her near it since she'd been home, hadn't realized she even knew how to use it, in fact, but she was clearly surfing.

"Hey," he said from the doorway, half expecting her to ignore him, but she turned. "For you," he said, indicating the
dozen hot pink gerberas in his hand. He'd also brought home a
roasted chicken and the cucumber salad Lucie used to love, all
tucked away in the kitchen.

"Is it that late already?" she said. "I haven't even thought
about dinner." She got up and walked over, taking the flowers
and bringing them to her face, but of course, gerberas have no
fragrance. He should have thought of that. She was always
smelling the flowers in the neighborhood. She used to like gerberas because of the way they looked.

"Dinner's taken care of," he said. "I brought home a roast
chicken."

He waited. Did she know that was her favorite? He'd pictured them at the dining table, a candle burning, a bottle of
wine, talking about everything she'd learned at her aunt's
house. She'd shut down, and it was almost as though he'd gotten what he wished for; the old Lucie had been big into the silent treatment.

"What are you working on?" he tried.

"Research," she said, pulling her mouth in a tight, noncom-
mittal, non-happy smile, then moved past him. "I'll put these in
water."

They'd moved back many, many steps. How could he turn
it around?

Grady followed her into the kitchen and watched her find a
vase in a high cabinet and carry it to the sink. She knew the
kitchen better than he did, once again, as she had before she'd
blotted it out.

*No,* he thought. *Before her brain misfired.* He would try to take Dory's suggestions to heart.

"Lucie," he said to her back. She didn't turn. "I really need you to know how sorry I am about yesterday. I'm just muddling through this whole thing, and not very well, apparently. Please . . ." He faltered.

She turned her head slightly toward him. "Please what?"

"Please look at me."

She shut off the faucet and faced him. He knew her well enough to know she was trying to keep her face impassive, but it was no longer so easy for her. *Thank god,* he thought.

"Please don't give up on me," he said.

"Why did you throw out our wedding invitations?" she asked. "I saw them in the recycling bin. You could have at least told me." Her chin quivered. She rolled her lips together, then looked away.

"Shit," he said, and she carried the vase of flowers out to the dining room table.

# lucie

~~~~~~~~~

he empty silence while Grady was at work was good, Lucie thought the next morning, pouring herself a cup of coffee. Dinner the night before had been awful, Grady trying to explain that he thought it would be best not to have the expectation of the wedding hanging over them. But why hadn't he even asked her? He didn't have an answer.

The worst thing for Lucie, though, was the mortification of having tried to have sex with him, only to be rejected. She felt stupid and overexposed whenever they were together now, especially face-to-face across the table. She had a hard time looking at him anymore.

How had she so completely misread the signals? That wasn't even the first time he'd had an erection in her presence. But then he went and did such sweet things, like bringing her flowers, and asking her not to give up on him.

It was enough to drive anyone crazy.

She carried her coffee into the office and opened her laptop. She hadn't gotten any satisfying information so far from her Google searches on "Gloria Walker," "shooting," "San Francisco." She tried to think of other keywords that might work.

As her computer whirred to life, she noticed a folder on the desktop, "Photos/Videos." She hesitated before clicking it open.

Hundreds of image files cascaded in a long list of numerical file names. There was no way to know what was what, so she clicked on the first one. It was a dull, grainy shot of what looked like a conference hall, display tables in rows. The next image confirmed that it was some kind of trade show or conference. *Boring,* Lucie thought, jumping ahead a few files, clicking randomly. And then, there she was, in full makeup and hair, smiling widely next to another woman, in one of those self-portrait shots taken at arm's length that make everyone's noses look too big.

The two women had a look of confident success that Lucie couldn't imagine possessing. They seemed to be cookie-cutter images, in their costuming, the carefully constructed makeup, hair shellacked into place.

"That's me," Lucie said aloud, trying to convince herself, but nothing about the woman's expression or demeanor felt familiar. It was like looking at her long-lost twin. *Separated at birth,* she thought.

She clicked through dozens of shots, all businesspeople doing business things in business places. Where was Grady? Were there any shots at home? Did she ever not work?

The videos, at least, were titled. "2009 Breast Cancer Fund-raiser," "2008 Mariners Opening Day Brunch." At the bottom of the list was a file called "2006 Gala, Dancing." *Dancing* . . . She selected and opened it.

Dark at first, eventually a dining table set for many people came into view, in a sea of other tables. A ballroom. The camera panned across the room to a dance floor bathed in colored lights, packed with gyrating bodies. "Look at everyone go," she heard herself say, loud against the music.

And then Grady: "Go ahead. No one's dancing with partners up there. You don't need me."

The view whirls across the room until stopping at Grady's face. He shrugs for the camera, hair shorter, a blue striped tie around his neck—the same night as the photo on her bedside table. "Believe me," he says, "you do not want to dance with me. I have no sense of rhythm, and big feet. Both left." She can see reflections in his black eyes, his eyelashes even, the camera is so close.

*Don't make him,* she wants to tell this woman.

"Oh, but I do want to dance with you," her voice says, only it's not her voice, it's the voice of someone flirty, someone trying to get her way. "Come on. I'm sure you dance just fine. You have all those sisters. They must have taught you something. Besides, this is my favorite song."

Lucie strains to hear the music, but there's only rhythmic noise. What was her favorite song? She never wondered before, but now she can't stand not knowing.

Grady's lips tighten and he nods. He looks away, then back at the camera. "Well, then I guess we have to dance," he says. "But only if you don't bring this."

The camera jostles, and then, voilà, the former Lucie appears on-screen. She is laughing, a little drunk maybe, and so pretty. Her eyes are glistening, her lips lush and plummy, and the neckline of the sparkly thing she is wearing reveals the tops of her breasts. "Fine," she says. "I won't document our first dance for posterity. But, believe me, you'll regret it." She reaches forward, and then it is over. The screen goes dark.

Lucie's face grew hot, and she felt like crying. *I'm jealous!* she thought. She hadn't quite believed this other woman really existed, but there she was, exactly as she knew she'd be from all of the evidence she'd collected. The sex toy now made sense. The designer clothes and expensive cosmetics, the brochures for how to stay beautiful. And most of all, Grady's infatuation—his love and lust—for this far more glamorous woman who no longer existed.

Lucie closed the laptop, breathing steadily to calm herself. It was impossible to be jealous of yourself. It made no sense. She swallowed. Her stomach growled. She wanted breakfast, a hot breakfast with eggs and potatoes and pancakes and syrup and too much of everything to fill in the empty spaces, but she was such an abysmal cook. How could she not know anything, like how to make pancakes or how to make her own fiancé love her?

*Scrambled eggs,* she thought. *Who can mess up scrambled eggs?*

In the kitchen she broke two eggs into a mixing bowl, then spent an inordinate amount of time fishing shells out of the slime. The pan she'd put on the heat was smoking; she switched the heat off, wondering if she should wipe out the melted butter that had turned brown. She was starving.

Lucie decided to just leave the shell in the eggs. After whisking briefly, she poured the mixture into the pan, then turned the burner back on and went to make toast.

While buttering the toast, Lucie smelled something wrong and rushed back over to the stove to stir the eggs. The creamy yellow mixture had scorched on the bottom. "Dammit," she muttered, switching off the burner.

After scraping the burned eggs into the waste bin, Lucie dialed Susan's number. "Hey," she said when her friend picked up. "Want to go out for breakfast?"

AT SUSAN'S HOUSE, the front door sat half open. Lucie knocked on the door frame and walked in. "Hello?" she called. "Why does it smell like bacon in here?"

"I'm in the kitchen," Susan yelled back, and Lucie walked through the house to the push door and eased it open.

"What are you doing?" she asked, but it was obvious. Every burner on the stove was lit and topped by a pan filled with something that looked and smelled delicious. "I thought we were going out."

"Get in here." Susan handed Lucie a floral apron. "Cooking lesson number one," she said. "Today we make omelets."

Lucie held the apron up to herself, then shook her head. "But I can't even make scrambled eggs."

"They're more difficult," Susan said, moving to tend to the bacon. "Scrambled eggs require a kind of sixth sense. Omelets, on the other hand, are rules based. Follow a few basic instructions and they come out perfectly every time."

Lucie squinted at her. How could that be? But Susan seemed to have mastered everything domestic in her life, from gardening to decorating to baking and, no doubt, cooking eggs.

"Fine," Lucie said, tying the apron around her. She took a closer look at the pans on the stove: bacon sizzling in one skillet, potatoes and red peppers in another. Mushrooms bubbling in butter in a small saucepan.

"You did all this in the time it took me to walk here?"

"The first rule of cooking: Always keep good ingredients on hand." Susan lifted the mushrooms from the heat, gave them a shake, then set the pan back down, turning off the burner. "Leftovers, like last night's baked potatoes, make great ingredients when repurposed for future meals."

"You know, you really are very nice," Lucie said. "Not a bitch at all." If she wasn't careful, Lucie thought, she'd get all gooey, and Susan was not a fan of gooey. Her friend shrugged, but Lucie could see this pleased her.

"Okay, so, I've got the side dishes going, but you, my dear, are responsible for the main course. Ready?" Susan opened the fridge.

"As I'll ever be," Lucie said, taking the carton of brown eggs Susan handed her.


SEATED AT A small table in Susan's back garden, Lucie took a bite of what, indeed, looked like a perfect omelet. "Mm," she said. "This is so good." The taste, the texture, the softness in her mouth; she closed her eyes. Eggs were her comfort food, had always been her comfort food. She knew this, now, though she hadn't until taking that bite.

"See?" Susan took a taste, then added a pinch of the sea

salt she'd brought to the table. "Even though delicious, a little salt enhances flavors."

Lucie nodded and swallowed her first, perfect bite. She had to remember how to do this again. "Okay, I should have written down what we were doing. First, use only farm eggs. Real farm, not factory farm."

"Directly from the chicken's butt when possible." Susan speared potatoes on her fork. "In the winter, when the farmers' markets are closed, it's a little more difficult, but they're worth searching for."

"Two, nothing but a dribble of water in the eggs, then beat them into submission."

"Well, that's kind of violently stated, but yes. Hand-mix until you no longer see any separation between the whites and the yolks, then mix a little more. You want the two to become one."

Lucie wondered if Susan was doing this on purpose, folding her little life lessons into the cooking instructions, but she continued. "Rule three: no more than one, maybe two extra ingredients."

"Too many flavors overwhelm our senses," Susan said, covering her mouth full of food, then swallowed. "I mean, the eggs alone are so succulent, the olive oil or butter you cook them in divine. Herbs, sure. A little cheese? Okay. Mushrooms, well, yes. In my omelets, there are always mushrooms."

"Four, plenty of lube in the pan—"

"Ew." Susan grimaced, waving her fork. "I never said 'lube.'"

"You did, actually. You said, 'It doesn't matter if you use butter or oil for your lubricant, but if you use butter, make sure it doesn't burn.'"

"Fine. Okay, after the lube?"

"Five, low to moderate heat, a lid."

"And, six?" Susan prompted.

"Patience."

"The most important ingredient of all." Susan raised her coffee cup to her lips. "Okay, so if the edges get even a hint of brown, what do we do?"

"Turn down the heat."

"Check."

"Use a rubber spatula—"

"Heat resistant."

"A *heat-resistant* rubber spatula to gently lift the omelet to allow uncooked egg to run under it, making sure the bottom stays yellow until the top has stopped quivering."

"Then and only then—" Susan coaxed.

"Gently roll onto a warm plate."

Susan lifted her cup to Lucie. "Congratulations. You are my best student."

Lucie raised her cup to clink it against Susan's. "I believe I am your only student."

"True." Susan smiled. "So, what do you want to learn next? I make a pretty decent piecrust. Also rules based."

Maybe there was hope for her culinary skills, Lucie thought, if she gave it a little time.

"Thank you," she said. "Pie would be perfect."

\*   \*   \*

BACK AT HOME that afternoon, Lucie wandered into the office and turned on the box fan in the corner. The day had turned muggy with a storm due in from the Pacific. Lucie folded her arms, looking around. She wanted something in here, but what?

*People,* she realized. Susan had become a friend; surely there had been other people she could reconnect with now that she'd been home for a while and gotten her bearings.

The first time she'd opened her e-mail, it had felt disorienting—the unfamiliar names, the crush of people wanting her to be the old Lucie and help them with their problems.

Maybe she'd overlooked someone who was kind, someone who might talk to her about what she'd been like, what she'd done in her work—exactly the things she hadn't wanted to know at first.

She opened her e-mail program, surprised to see new messages, with far friendlier subject lines:

Best wishes on your recovery
Welcome home
Glad to hear you're back

She sat silently for a moment, just looking at them. People did remember her; they had cared what happened to her. As she read through the messages, she discovered that they were businesslike notes, but they were nice. Maybe, as with Susan and the other neighbors, she'd been the one who created the distance with work acquaintances.

Ten or so messages down, she smiled at the sender's name: mfgoodall@aol.com. It was titled "When you're ready . . ."

"Oh, Motherfucker," Lucie said. "Here you are." She clicked it open and read.

Dearest Lucie,

Grady has shared with me that you are recovering well but that you feel the need for some privacy, and I can certainly understand that. I'm very excited you'll be visiting us this weekend, because I've missed you and worried about the both of you. I don't want to impose, crazy old mother-in-law that I am, but I will say that I'd be happy to talk with you anytime about anything, by e-mail or on the phone, if you feel it might help you regain your memory. (Which Dory says it will.) Or even if you just want to talk. Grady might not be too happy that I've reached out to you, but I know in his heart he wants what's best for you. He's just scared to death of losing you, as he did his dad. Well, that's what Dory says, anyway, and it sounds reasonable enough.

Much love to you,
Mary Faith

Mary Faith Goodall. Lucie felt shame at having called Grady's mother "Motherfucker," but she loved each word in the note. She hit Reply and typed:

Dear Mrs. Goodall,
I am overwhelmed with happiness at your

Shaking her head, Lucie selected and deleted the text, then tried again. But it didn't matter. Everything she wrote gushed onto the screen like a prepubescent girl's diary entries. Finally, after staring at the screen far too long, she wrote:

> Dear Mrs. Goodall,
>
> Thank you for reaching out. It means so much to me. I can't wait to meet you and the rest of the family on Sunday. I know that sounds weird. You already know me, but at this point, for me, it will be like meeting you for the first time. Of course, I've seen your pictures, and I know how wonderful you all are, through Grady's stories.

Here she hesitated at the white lie, but decided to go with it. She typed, "See you soon," then, "Love, Lucie."

A few messages below Mary Faith's was from another Goodall, dorothy.goodall@piercecounty.wa.gov. Dory, Grady's favorite sister.

She opened the message. "Hi Lucie," it began.

> Remember me? (Sorry, bad joke!) I just want to tell you how happy I am that you're home. Grady says you've taken up some new hobbies, which is really great. Just remember that seeing the psychiatrist will help you the most, so I hope you'll schedule an appointment soon. We're looking forward to seeing you on Sunday. I'm sure Grady has told you all about us, good, bad, and worse. We are a wacky group, but everyone has a good heart, even Eunie. She may be a little, well, let's just say "prickly" when you meet her, but it's only because she cares so much about Grady. She was our little mother hen after Dad died and Mom went back to work. No other warnings, I'm happy to say! Just be

prepared for a lot of people, and a lot of noise. Oh, and there will be crying. And too much food.

Then, she'd typed a smiley face and the words "Love, Dory."

Lucie read the e-mail over and over. She'd never thought about trying to contact any of the sisters before meeting them. She wondered which one Dory was, and went to look at the photos on Grady's corkboard. It was impossible to know. They all resembled one another with their dark hair, and most wore glasses. One of the sisters seemed smaller than the others, her hair in a short style while the others all had long hair. Lucie put her finger on the smaller woman's face. *Dory,* she thought, but why? A strange sensation swept through her, little bubbles in her bloodstream. She stared at all of the other faces, but they remained mysteries.

She went back to the computer, hit Reply, and wrote: "Dear Dory, Are you the one with short hair?"

Then she hit Erase and sent a friendly note as she had to Mrs. Goodall. She would be talking with them both that weekend. What mattered most was that these women had wanted to talk to her, and probably would have come to see her if Grady had let them.

*If Grady had* . . . she had to let that one billow up in anger for a moment before putting it back away with all of the other things that were going wrong between them. For now, she could concentrate only on moving forward, one little step at a time.

# grady

When he was a kid, Sunday mornings meant many things to Grady. Big family breakfasts with pancakes or waffles, or crepe-like Dutch babies filled with apples in the winter, berries in the summer. Extra swimming time at the pool or Dash Point. Going to church, more so after his dad died. As an adult, Sunday had simply come to mean a day spent at home instead of work, although he did check his e-mail less frequently. He and Lucie hadn't had any special Sunday rituals like big breakfasts (too many carbs, she said), and certainly not church. Not that he wanted to go somewhere and have someone tell him what to think and who to pray to.

But he realized now, lying in bed in the guest room, that he would really like some kind of way to mark the end of one week and the beginning of another, to be grateful for things, even to notice what was lacking in life. Being busy left no time for taking stock. Maybe that was why they'd filled their time with remodeling the house, improving this and that; everything but their relationship. If Lucie ever came back to him, really in her heart came back, he would ask that they have special, quiet Sundays together.

That didn't include his family.

Grady groaned and rolled over. It was the day Lucie was going to meet them, for the second time.

The first time, it had been his idea for them to make the trek to Tacoma for a family barbecue. He and Lucie were getting serious, after all. He hadn't realized what putting two such dissimilar elements together would do.

Lucie had been nervous that morning, and dressed too formally for the occasion in a navy blue dress and low heels, but how could he tell her that? She was just trying to make a good impression, but it was like she'd never been to a barbecue before. He'd dressed in shorts and a T-shirt, then changed when he saw the panic in her eyes at his clothes.

And she insisted they stop on the way and pick up wine and flowers. How could he tell her that his mother grew county-fair blue-ribbon flowers in her garden, and that the house was always full of them in summer? That no one in his family really drank wine; that he hadn't until he met her. He'd wanted her to think of him as worldlier than the beer drinker he was. What love-struck guy wouldn't? He just hoped they wouldn't turn up their noses at Lucie's carefully chosen Pinot Gris, her store-bought peonies.

When they arrived, the dumb dogs jumped on her with their dirty paws, scaring her half to death, and that was before she even met anyone. Then the sisters descended, all checking her out, raising their eyebrows at each other when they thought she couldn't see. But Grady knew she did.

Dory had rescued Lucie, of course, as only Dory could, giving her a hug, taking the wine and thanking her for it, promising to open it right up and have some. It wasn't just her psychology training that made her so good at defusing sticky situations, and not even her determination to defend the wronged. Dory had always been the "different" sister, the one who turned left when the others turned right, who cut off her hair, who traveled to exotic destinations, who hadn't married. Dory chose her own path in all things, and her kindness toward Lucie was no doubt also a gift for Grady.

And his mother, well. Mary Faith Goodall had a way with gentling shelter dogs and friends abused by their husbands, offspring who got kicked around a little too much by life. Even now, at eighty-two, she was their rock—more solid than the rest of them put together. She'd taken Lucie by the arm that day five years before and led her around the gardens, made a fuss over the peonies because they were the exact shade of pink she never could coax from the ones she grew.

When they'd all assembled back in the house, too many of them standing in the kitchen as they always did, the questions started flying. How had they met, how long had they been dating, why hadn't Grady told them he'd found someone? And was that why he was dressed halfway decently? The cackling was earsplitting.

Then they turned on Lucie, asking her about her work, though they didn't even pretend to understand a thing she said about it. One of them, Renie maybe, made a comment about how it must pay well, looking Lucie up and down. Then, of course, they asked about her family and, hearing that her parents were dead, gave each other those same little knowing glances.

Of course their brother would find someone whose parents had died; to them, only one thing defined Grady, and he was sick of it. Weren't they the ones who always told the same old stories about life-after-Dad every time they were together? Eunie, the eldest, was about to turn fifty-four and she was *still* pissed off that she hadn't been allowed to read a poem she'd written at the funeral. It was an awful poem, and sure, Grady laughed along with everyone each time Eunie took it upon herself to recite it, just to prove that she still could. *Trees* and *bees, flowers* and *showers*—those rhymes were to be expected, but when Eunie got to the parts about *fishing* and *wishing, salmon* and *rammin'* (to describe the accident at sea), well, no one could help themselves. They'd snort whatever they were drinking through their noses and wind up howling and slapping the table. Their mother would shush them, then turn her back to laugh herself. It was ridiculous and pathetic, and yet *Grady* was the one who couldn't get over it.

By the time they'd left that day, Lucie was nearly in tears, and Grady numb. It took three days to get back to normal between them. It took Lucie and his sisters many visits to find a way to get along when they were all in the same place, but most of them warmed to her. Just not Eunie, who didn't have the patience for anyone who wasn't the way she thought they should be. Grady had always told Lucie, "That's her loss. Don't worry about it." But of course, Lucie had.

Grady got out of bed and limped without crutches to the bathroom to get ready for the day, wishing it could be over before it started. How would he and Lucie endure it all over again, especially when the two of them were barely speaking? Why had he thrown out their wedding invitations without even asking her? She had such a good point on that one. He'd felt suddenly that everything was hopeless, and acted impulsively.

Water from the upstairs shower coursed through the pipes overhead, and he could imagine her nervous excitement, because this time, Lucie really was eager to meet everyone. One thing was for sure; she wouldn't overdress. He hadn't seen her in any of her dressy clothes since the day she left. In fact, they'd probably all raise their eyebrows now at this Lucie in her casual, new style, and ask her too many questions. But he'd make sure she was okay this time. Even if she wasn't speaking to him, he'd make sure no one hurt her again.

# lucie

a desertscape of beige and gray lay strewn around the bedroom: the former Lucie's clothing. This Lucie wanted to appear friendly and inviting for the Goodalls. They were her last chance at having any kind of normal family. If she could just dress in the colorful, fun way they did in the photos, but nothing in the closet looked like that to her. She remembered the tangerine T-shirt, the words "I am a noun" not overly large across the chest but a definite statement. Would Grady hate it if she wore it to his mother's house? His sisters liked to laugh. Wouldn't they think it was funny? She felt pretty sure Dory would.

"Well, I like it," she muttered, going to the dresser. She could wear it with the white jeans she'd taken a liking to, rolled up at the cuffs, and the flat sandals from the hospital, and the earrings she'd bought in one of Wallingford's little shops. She might even put on makeup, which she hadn't tried again after the night of the ill-fated dinner out.

At the bathroom mirror, Lucie dug through the drawer that housed cosmetics. Anything marked "concealer" or "cover-up" she lobbed into the waste can next to the toilet, each metal clang satisfying.

The old Lucie had spent so much time and effort just trying to blend in, to disappear, almost, into a neutral background of nothingness. She had been more of a blank than this Lucie, trying to disappear, and finally, well, she had.

Chewing her lip, Lucie took stock of what was left: foundations, powders, shadows, blushers, lipsticks. Anything that resembled her skin tone was history. She kept the prettiest blush, the darkest eye pencil, a tube of mascara. Next she tackled the lipsticks.

Inspired now, Lucie dug through the rest of the drawers, the cabinet beneath the sink, and the medicine chest, throwing away things she'd never use, the potions and promises and miracle cures for living an authentic life.

Oh, to rid herself of the old Lucie's things, to claim those she wanted as her own—it was good. In the end, the items she kept took up one drawer and two shelves in the cabinet. Grady would be so surprised when he . . .

She looked up as her forehead crinkled in the mirror. Grady didn't use this bathroom anymore. He didn't sleep with her; he didn't want to have sex with her. He no longer wanted to marry her. He hadn't even wanted to take her to his mother's house. She'd forced him to arrange it.

Her nose and cheeks burned a dark pink. She tried to relax her brow, but the hurt didn't leave. It settled into the back of her throat, the place that made it hard to speak to him. They'd regressed, and Lucie didn't know how to shift forward again. She wanted what wasn't hers: the love he held precious for the old Lucie.

She bared her teeth, snarled into the mirror. She could be mean and nasty; she could be hard and cold. That's what it seemed old Lucie was. From someplace inside her, she could almost wrap her fingers around what it had felt like to be that way. Her trip to Helen's had illuminated just what she'd been up against her whole life. No wonder she'd been so disconnected. Who wouldn't be, with a past like that? And how was it that a kid of fifteen could withstand that, only to lose her mind after a fight with her boyfriend twenty-five years later?

Her skin prickled.

*Oh Jesus,* she thought. *Oh shit.*

"Are you almost ready?" Grady called from the bottom of the stairs.

Helen had said she'd been quiet and reserved when she came to live with them. A normal girl would have been distraught and grieving the loss of her mother, processing the carnage she'd witnessed, wouldn't she? Wouldn't that memory have scarred and defined her? Yet, she'd never spoken of any of it with Grady.

"Luce? We need to leave pretty soon."

She leaned forward over the sink, gripping the counter.

"Lucie?" Grady called again.

Her hands trembled on the porcelain.

"I'm coming," she said, then turned on the faucet and splashed water on her face. So much for makeup—she'd run out of time—but she picked through the remaining lipsticks, reading the tiny print at the bottom of each until she found the one she was looking for—Raspberry Kiss. She opened the lipstick and applied it, smacking her lips. There: bright. Cheerful. Lucie forced a smile in the mirror, wiped a smudge from her tooth, and headed down the stairs.

IT WAS A long, quiet drive south on I-5 to Tacoma in Lucie's car, which Grady insisted on driving. At the curb of his mother's house, two old dogs came running as they stepped from the car. Lucie knelt down to take their happy faces in her hands, to scratch their ears and say hello.

"Oh, you remember them?" he asked, and she looked up.

"No, I just like dogs." The way he nodded told her this was yet another new character trait. *Get used to it,* she wanted to say.

And then everyone was streaming out of the house, coming across the lawn, a crowd of women chattering, laughing, calling out to them:

"Oh my god!"

"Hello!"

"Finally!"

Lucie stood, smiling nervously. She hadn't thought she'd be scared, but she was. There were so many of them, and they looked so different from the people she'd gotten to know in Wallingford, who were all pale and slim and wore black athletic clothing or muted natural fabrics, whose hair was all done as plainly as possible: straight, bobbed, smoothed.

These women swirled together in flowing, bright colors

and scarves and bracelets, perfume and long hair and big earrings. Like Grady, they were mostly tall, but rounder, and had
such warm shades of skin, from light golden tan to as brown
as Grady. The smallest of the bunch, the one with short hair,
reached them first, heading straight for Lucie, and when
Lucie offered her hand, the woman laughed, pulling her in for
a hug.

"Oh, just come here," she said. "I'm Dory." She had tears in
her pretty hazel eyes.

"Dory, hi," Lucie said, a funny knock in her heart at saying
the name. She *had* recognized her, after all! And then the next
sister was upon her, and then the next, hugging her or squeezing her arm or offering a teary smile. One laughed at her
T-shirt, another admired her Guatemalan bag. Florence and
Isabel and Nanette, Irene—the names like butterscotch in
her mouth. By the time she got to the last one, Eunice (the
sister Dory had warned her about), Lucie was almost relieved
that the eldest sister kept a stranger's polite distance.

"Well, welcome back." Eunie avoided her eyes, then turned
to pick up a toddler who had a hold on her leg. "Remember my
grandson?"

Lucie smiled at the little boy, all big eyes and baby teeth.
"Hi, Davy," she said, reaching to squeeze his chubby knee. She
saw Grady watching her carefully.

"Davy?" Eunie said. "Where'd you get that? This is Sam."

Lucie flinched and shook her head, dropping her hand. "I
don't know, god. He's such a cutie. You must be so proud."
Shaken by Eunie's tone, Lucie kept babbling. "I'm really sorry, I
don't know why I said that."

"I bet you don't know why you do a lot of things," the older woman said, already walking away.

*"Shame on you, Eunie."* Lucie heard the whisper; it could have been from any of the sisters in their midst.

"Shame on you," Eunie shot back. "He's your brother, too." Grady fell in step with Eunie, whispering furiously in her ear.

*God,* Lucie thought. She'd already caused a problem. Why had she said "Davy"? It just came out.

The remaining sisters didn't seem to hold it against her. They were all smiling, chattering, fussing over Grady. They teased him mercilessly. His embarrassment and enjoyment at this was new for Lucie. He acted like a twelve-year-old with them, and Lucie wondered why he wasn't that way with her. Did he used to be more fun loving, before she ran? She had a hard time imagining it.

Teenagers and kids poured from the house and hovered in the background with a handful of nervous-looking men. Then Lucie saw Grady's mother, practically skipping over to slide herself inside the curve of her son's arm, replacing his crutch with her shoulder. So much smaller than her offspring, so slight and light skinned compared to them, but she was just as lively. She had to be at least Helen's age, but where Helen brought to mind decay, this woman was the fountain that had poured forth all this life. Had borne Grady, had saved him from the water. Had been with him from birth, and would be to her death. Now she smiled at Lucie with bright blue eyes, beckoning her over.

Unexpected tears began to stream down Lucie's face as she walked toward her. Everyone hushed around them, perhaps thinking they might be witnessing the return of Lucie's memory in this moment of emotion, but it wasn't that. Lucie just suddenly missed her own mother in a way that made no sense, but there it was. She didn't recognize her face in the photos, couldn't remember anything about her, but she missed her. She had never missed someone so much.

"Welcome home, honey," Mary Faith murmured and hugged her with surprising firmness.

Lucie relaxed in her embrace, grateful. "Thank you for writing to me," she said. "I only opened it the other day or I would have called or something."

With small, weathered hands, the woman reached up and cupped Lucie's cheeks. "It's so good to see your face."

Lucie sobbed. Why would her brain do such a cruel thing, erase her life and everyone in it? And how many times? She waited until she could speak, and then whispered, "What do I call you? Mrs. Goodall or Mary Faith?"

"Well, you call me Mary Faith," the woman whispered back, "but I'm hoping that after the wedding you'll call me Mom."

Lucie nodded, wiping her face, and saw Grady watching them. Again. Was he nervous she was going to screw everything up?

The rest of the crowd was advancing, all of the offspring and husbands, their kids and others of indeterminate relation. She was introduced to each person, and she knew she'd never remember all their names, but it was thrilling to meet so many people who knew her, who smiled shyly or broadly, who seemed to like her or even just acknowledge her as a part of the group, whether or not they really understood what had happened to her.

There were those who wanted to ask her questions about what had happened, what it was like to not remember anything. Some of them wanted to be the one who would help her regain her memory, and shared stories of things they'd done together. The Halloween that they'd caught Mary Faith's oven on fire when they drank too much and forgot they were roasting pumpkin seeds. The Labor Day picnic at Dash Point when they ganged up on Grady and threw him off the dock. A nine-year-old niece named Hannah showed her the silver bracelet Lucie had apparently given her for Christmas, just the year before.

As daylight faded and evening set in, Nan's oldest son, Adam, brought out his guitar and began to strum chords, and everyone shushed to listen. Lucie had heard from one of the husbands that the young man was about to be deployed.

Mary Faith stepped through the sliding doors and kissed the back of his shorn head as she passed by.

"Gram," he protested, but smiled at the ground. "Okay, I'll play your song, but just one time. Not everybody likes those old cowboy songs, you know."

Everyone laughed, and the sister named Izzy leaned over and whispered to Lucie, "My dad sang this to Mom on their honeymoon, and we had Adam learn it for her eightieth. Now she won't let a family occasion go by without the poor kid having to sing it."

Adam had a sweet tenor voice, and Lucie closed her eyes to listen. It was a sadly sentimental song about being parted from the one you love, and she heard a few sniffles around her at the chorus: *Oh, I'm thinking tonight of my blue eyes who is sailing far over the sea . . .* Her lips started to move, and she realized she could sing along, word for word. She knew this song, and not just generically. She could remember the sound of Adam's voice singing it.

She opened her eyes in surprise and looked around. She knew these people from somewhere deep and blurred inside her. No knowledge of events or dates or places came with this knowing, but it was comforting all the same. She looked over at Grady sitting with his mom, the two of them holding hands, tears flowing. *They are the sentimental ones,* she thought. No, she remembered.

Was that why he wasn't telling her the truth, the entire truth, about what happened the day she ran? Oh, he was a maddening creature, she thought.

THAT EVENING, AS Grady drove home, Lucie leaned back and pretended to sleep. She felt too exhausted to deal with their impasse. She yearned to be home in bed, flat on her back, waiting for sleep.

She'd fallen madly in love with Grady's family. Just after the meal, as Lucie had been scraping plates in the kitchen, the artistic sister, Floss, had come up and hugged her. "I don't know what happened to you, Lucie, and I'm sorry you've been through so much, but I think this has brought us all a lot closer together. And now it's like we have a whole new sister." Even Eunie had said a civil good-bye at the end of the night.

Lucie gathered that was the general consensus: new Lucie

beat the pants off old Lucie. *See?* she wanted to say to Grady. *I'm worthy.*

Her eyes filled behind her closed lids; her mouth became thick with saliva. It had been a day of crying, but they'd been mostly happy tears. She'd found her family. But these tears had nothing to do with that. The more she tried to stop, to still her hiccuping, the deeper the claw ripped into her chest. It was so old, this feeling, so dark and familiar. It preceded everything, all that Lucie knew, but she could now guess where it came from.

The explosions. A murder. Her mother being led away and leaving a young Lucie to fend for herself. Someone was missing, someone so vital as to be almost physically connected. This she had known from the days just after waking up, but she hadn't known who it was. Didn't it make sense that it would be her mother? The little hands must be Lucie's playing next to her mother's. The explosions, smoke. Terror. She gasped.

"Are you all right?" Grady asked, and when she couldn't speak, he pulled off to the side of the highway. "Lucie, what? What's the matter? I thought it went really well today."

He put the car in park, then turned to pull her to him. She pushed against his chest, elbowed her arms against his embrace. She wanted to open the car door and run.

"No!" she cried into her palms. "It's going to happen again! Stop it, stop it!"

"What?" Grady said, letting her go. "What's happening?"

"You tell me!"

"What do you want me to tell you? I've tried—"

"You've lied to me, you've kept things from me!"

"Jesus, what?" He was angry now. "I don't know what's

going on! Come on, give me a break. What am I supposed to tell you?"

"You're supposed to—" *Fuck!* she wanted to scream. "You're supposed to tell me what happened the day I ran away, that's what. Just fucking tell me!"

Grady fell back against his seat as if someone had shoved him, breathing hard. In the dark she could make out his profile, his jaw hanging slack, his eyes staring straight out at the night. He was afraid; she could see that. But Lucie was more afraid of what would happen if he never told her.

She used her sleeve to wipe her face, her nose. "I know it was bad. Why would I have done it if it wasn't?"

Grady closed his eyes.

"You have to," she said. "Please."

# grady

~~~~~~

grady felt Lucie watching him, her breath still labored from the struggle. He'd almost thought . . . but no. She'd stayed. And if she'd run, he'd have run after her.

But she hadn't. His Lucie was still in the car, waiting for him to speak, and he might not ever have another chance.

Where did he start? How far back did he go? They'd always depended on each other so much: Grady grateful to her for helping him become someone he actually liked being, and Lucie, well. It was hard to know exactly what she'd needed him for, but he suspected it was a certain sense of safety. If Grady was anything, it was stable. And Lucie wasn't quite as self-assured as it appeared from the outside. She could be fragile, she could be frightened of things that no one would suspect if they only knew her from the distance of a business associate or social acquaintance. Lucie didn't have sisters or a mom or girlfriends, not the kinds of girlfriends he imagined

most women had, who went out and had coffee and shared secrets. Lucie hadn't shared secrets, not even with him, but
she'd depended on him. He hadn't realized that though, not
back then; she'd needed him. And she needed him now. She
needed him to be honest, even though it might still break
them apart.

Heat swamped his face; suddenly his entire body was too
hot. He opened the window a crack, letting in the roar and die-
sel of a passing truck, the damp intimation of a coming rain-
storm. He exhaled, then said, "I just let you down. Pretty much
completely."

"How?" After the crying and shouting, she now sounded so
small.

See, that was the whole problem. The old Lucie had never
sounded vulnerable. Even if she felt that way, she'd always
come off strident and challenging.

Grady winced. "I lost faith in us. I gave up."

"Oh!" This surprised her. Of course it did. "You dumped
me?" She twisted in her seat to see him better.

"No, of course not."

"But, what, then? Was it my fault? Did I do something?"

He shook his head. "No, it was me. That last fight we had?
I was a complete asshole. I'd been out most of the night drinking because I was too much of a wimp to come home and tell
you I was having doubts."

"Oh," she said again, processing the new information.
Would she hate him? It didn't matter. As much as he'd thought
he could employ a little revisionist history with the new Lucie,
the truth had been ticking away, the timer running down. Bet-

ter to lay it out, let her see all of it, and make her decisions from there.

"I should have just come home after work that day and talked to you about it, but by then you were so . . ."

He could hear her swallow in the dark. She was just as scared at being revealed as he was.

"You were on a mission, man. You were gonna get us married. You had it all figured out and planned and ordered, and everything was over the top and crazy expensive, and . . . I don't know. I just thought I'd gotten lost somewhere along the way."

They were quiet, then Lucie said, "You mean *we* got lost? The you and me of it?"

Grady closed his eyes, nodded. Oh, the way she said that. *The you and me of it.*

"I'm sorry," she said. "I wish I had been different."

"No." He turned to face her, his knee constricted by his boot and the console or they would have been touching. "No, that's the thing. I loved you. I loved the way you were, and then I lost my nerve about all of it. I regressed, I became one of those guys who freak out when the going gets tough. I turned into this stupid jerk and, I don't know. I guess I was trying to push you away, to make you not love me anymore. To make you leave me."

God, that was it. He'd wanted to leave her but he was such a coward he'd left it to her to do the leaving.

She wrapped her arms around her ribs. "I need to know the bad part. Because there is a bad part, right? I mean, Grady, come on. Amnesia?"

"Yeah," he whispered.

A procession of logging trucks thundered past. Drizzle specked the windshield.

Grady cleared his throat. "You're right, it was pretty bad," he said. "Can we at least go home and have this conversation?"

"No," she said. "I'm on the verge of losing my mind again, here. I need to know, now."

Was she kidding him? He squinted at her in the dark. She wasn't crying anymore. She was just sitting there, looking sad but pretty. He found the dome light overhead and turned it on, revealing them both, suddenly, in unflattering yellow light and long shadows.

"Hey," he said. "I just needed to see your eyes."

"Jesus," she said. Was she angry, or what? Her chin quivered. Her eyes welled. "So, what, are you going to leave me? Have you just been waiting for the right time to, um, to—?"

"Lucie, no! I love you. That's what I wish you could remember most of all, just how much I love you."

She flinched at the words, but tears spilled down her face.

How was it that even traumatic emotion made him want to tear off her clothes? He wanted their bodies to merge, to slide into each other and twist and turn and contort until they weren't two bodies but one. He wanted to enter her, to come inside her and plant a baby, and take care of her for the rest of her life.

He looked at her for a long moment, drinking her in, so real, so open to anything now. His heart was pounding.

"That morning, I was lying on the couch, so hungover I was probably still drunk. I was being a total asshole. You'd gotten all dressed up for your appointment, and you should have been so happy, but how could you be? I was shitting on your parade. It was one of the things you'd been looking forward to most, this dress thing."

He paused, reaching to push damp hair off his forehead. This was the part he hated, but he had to tell her. "Just before you were going to go, you came and sat next to me on the couch. You asked me point-blank if I wanted out of the relationship, and I said . . . shit."

"Please, don't stop."

"I said I didn't really give a fuck anymore. About any of it." He swallowed. "About you."

To him that was it, the worst part, but Lucie only said, "Then what?"

Rain struck the windshield steadily now. "You attacked me." Her eyes widened. "I . . ."

"Just, I don't know, all of a sudden you were all over me on the couch, punching me and kicking me, and I was just so shocked. You had this look on your face that was so alien or something. Like you didn't know me, or like you hated me."

It was so vivid, all over again. Grady rubbed the scar on his neck. "The diamond on your ring cut me. You didn't mean to do it, I don't think, but when you saw all the blood you made this awful sound, this wailing sound like some wild animal that was being tortured. God, Lucie. It was just . . ."

"But I wasn't like that, usually, right? I mean, I wasn't violent."

"No, god no. This was something completely bizarre, like you snapped. I mean, they always say that, but it was exactly like that. You snapped."

Lucie reached to turn off the overhead light. She shivered, even though the night was still warm, and turned to look out the window.

"And then I ran?"

"Yes."

"Did I say anything else before I left? Was I crying, or . . ."

Grady shook his head. "Nope, just that sound, and then you left. Boom. Outta there. I should've run after you."

"It wouldn't have mattered." She looked back at him in the dark, her eyes round, unflinching.

"I could've at least caught you and . . ."

She shook her head. "I was already gone. It had already happened."

How could she be so certain? He'd been trying to piece it together for weeks. At what moment had her actions ceased to be decisions? Exactly when did the real, cognizant Lucie leave him? On the couch? As she ran? At the train station? In San Francisco? He hadn't asked, because she couldn't know, and she was already so tortured by it all. He knew that; he knew her pain was worse than his, even though you'd think not remembering would be a blessing. But it haunted her. If she never remembered anything, she might never feel like a real person again.

"Grady," she said. "I think I'm figuring it out. I need to tell you the rest of the story. About Helen. About me, and my mother. About why I'm the way I am."

He reached for her hands, held them inside his. "I want to know," he said. These were the details he'd yearned for when they first met, the ones he'd pressed too hard to get. And now

that she was going to tell him, finally—now that she *could* tell
him—he felt something inside him crumbling. He held her
hands to keep her as close as possible as she revealed what
she'd learned from Helen—the ugly, the poignant, the mun-
dane. The things that had made Lucie the woman she was now
and had been when he first met her, for better, for worse. He
could handle these truths, he realized, because the sum of
them was Lucie.


LATER, AT HOME in the entryway, they stood awkwardly,
Lucie about to head up the stairs, Grady to the guest room.
He didn't know how dissociative fugue worked, exactly, but he
wondered if she simply hadn't known what happened to her
parents when he met her five years earlier. Maybe she'd blotted
out that horrible thing, too. But knowing now what she'd been
through so many years before he knew her, before he could protect her, felt devastating, as though he had personally failed her.
He wanted to follow her up to their bedroom, to lie down beside
her, to pull the sheets and blankets up and around her, to hold
her and watch her fall asleep.

They stood looking at each other. He wanted to kiss her
again. She looked exhausted, but she hadn't walked away.

He was so tired of always wondering what he should do.
He swallowed, then moved closer until he could feel the
warmth of her. She looked up and he leaned down, kissing
her lightly on the lips, their breath stale from the long day,
skin scented with sweat and barbecue smoke. She looked so
young, so like a kid, freckled and tousle haired, in her funny

orange T-shirt. He thought he probably loved her more than he ever had. *Please,* he prayed. *Ask me to come up to our room.*

"I had an engagement ring?" she asked instead. "Probably an expensive one. I lost it, didn't I?"

He shrugged. She would have found out somehow.

"Oh god, Grady. I hate that I hurt you."

"I know, but . . . you know. We hurt each other."

She nodded, but there was nothing more to say. Lucie turned to climb the stairs. When she'd gotten to the top and switched on the bedroom light, Grady tested putting pressure on his right foot. A dull sensation, not quite pain. *Good enough,* he thought, and propped his crutches against the wall. Tomorrow he'd stash them in the basement with everything else he no longer needed.

LATER, MUCH LATER, waking in the guest room in the dark, Grady felt for a moment like everything was normal, like none of the bad things had ever happened. He realized, then, what had woken him—the absence of piano music drifting up from the basement—and the heaviness seeped back in.

Lucie had trusted him enough that night to tell him everything she knew about herself, more than she ever had in the past. She'd revealed things worse than he could have imagined, but no matter what had happened to her, he realized, none of it was her fault. The events of her childhood—the way adults had acted and reacted—were out of her control, and she'd been forced into simply reacting in whatever way she could, to survive.

To survive. That was the drive of all life, right? From the time it had emerged from the water.

The weight of water upon him; Grady felt the pull toward it as strongly as he ever had. Figures disappearing into hazy shapes, the absence of sound, the darkness at the bottom. Breath squeezing from lungs, bubbles rising upward, one breath after another until . . .

Until it was all gone, he realized. He'd never let himself think that before, had always stopped just shy of the finality of it. But he'd wanted to stay beneath the water, had been drawn to that from the day his father drowned. *Pish pish,* Grady thought. *I didn't really want to be a fish; I just wanted to stop being a boy.* To swim was to be dead, in a sense. It was an act of disappearing.

Grady didn't want to disappear anymore.

He rolled over, the old ache to see his dad like lead in his bones. Would Harry Goodall like who his son had become? Grady had a good profession, which would be important, but was he the kind of man his father would be proud of? Did Grady even know how to be that? How could he?

His father was a ghost.

Lucie was just as haunted by her mother. She hadn't known how to be herself, either, just a month ago, and look at her now, becoming Lucie Walker again. Because that's what was happening.

There weren't two Lucies. Just the one.

The Lucie he'd known before had been protecting herself from the world the only way she knew how, by creating a big, hard shell, and now she'd shed it. He'd watched her with his family during the day and evening, and she'd been so open and herself that they fell in love with her, as they should have the first time.

Grady rolled over and faced the wall. He wished she were lying there with him. Barring that, he wished she would get up and go play the piano. He didn't know how to get to sleep anymore without it.

# lucie

~~~~~~~~~~

t he next morning, Lucie woke to the sound of someone knocking, downstairs. Was it the front door? Why so early? She rolled over, pulling the sheet over her head.

"Luce? You up?" It was Grady, at the bottom of the stairs, rapping on the wall. Lucie looked at the clock. She'd slept late, nine o'clock. The day before had exhausted her: the family visit, the emotions, the talk in the car, revelation piling upon revelation.

"Mm hmm." She tried to mumble loud enough for him to hear.

He clumped halfway up the steps and stopped.

Lucie rubbed her hands through her hair and down her face. "It's okay, I'm awake." She sat up and pulled the sheet around her to cover her chest.

He arrived at the top of the steps with no crutches, a mug of coffee in his hand.

"Hi," he said, handing it to her. "Happy Monday."

"Wow, room service." Lucie took the cup, warm and smooth in her hands, and lowered her face to breathe it in before taking a sip. Grady made excellent coffee. "Thanks."

"I was just heading out, so . . ." His hands fished fruitlessly in his pockets. "So, okay. Have a good day."

Lucie looked up and into his eyes. What did he want? Something, she knew, but it was the detail of it that escaped her. "You, too," she said.

He nodded and started toward the steps.

"Hey," she said, to make him turn back around. "Has it been four weeks already?"

He looked at her blankly.

"The crutches? You're off them?"

His face lightened. "Oh, yeah. Legally, even."

"So, what do you have going on at work today?" She still didn't understand what exactly he did. She knew it had to do with airplanes and high-tech stuff.

"Well, mostly meetings. We're in design review crunch time, and behind, as always. You know."

She didn't know. But she used to.

"So," Grady said, seemingly encouraged by her interest. "What are you doing today?"

"Research. I think I'll call Helen again." Might as well tell him, she thought, even though he'd probably object.

But he said, "Good idea," then gave a little wave and made the arduous journey down the stairs: boot clump, step, boot clump, step. She heard him gather his things and leave.

Lucie sighed and got up, pulled on clothes, then carried her mug downstairs. Every time she thought she knew how

Grady felt or what he wanted, she was wrong. He advanced and retreated, over and over. When he'd come to San Francisco, it was the old Lucie he was after. It was obvious now that, no matter what memories returned, she would never be that person again. Had she always been this unsure of him, of his feelings? Had she always wondered if he loved her enough? Maybe that wasn't new. Maybe that was just the way they were.

*Is that enough?* Lucie shook her head. She hadn't thought this way before, that maybe the relationship wasn't worth reclaiming. She'd counted on Grady for everything at first, for food and shelter, and just for the simple comfort that someone knew her. But now she could survive on her own, she felt pretty sure. Susan had a brother-in-law who needed help in his chiropractic office should she decide to work. She'd made her way in the world before, knowing very little and figuring it all out, and Lucie knew she could do it again if she had to.

*No,* she thought. *If I want to.*

Overnight, in her sleep and musty dreams, so many thoughts and fears and desires had coalesced into some kind of plan. She grabbed her laptop from the office and carried it to the kitchen. She was so close to understanding—academically at least—why her brain had shorted out and cleared away all memories, the good along with the unbearable. And not just a month ago—if her hypothesis was correct, it had done the same thing twenty-five years earlier. The two triggering incidents weren't that dissimilar.

Her mother shot her husband on the couch.

Lucie attacked Grady. On the couch.

To the primitive brain—the emotional one as opposed to

the intellectual one—those two things could look a lot alike. In her own violence, Lucie might have scared herself literally out of her mind, just as she had been shaken from it back then.

Hearing Grady's account of what happened the day she ran had been a relief—knowing that it was momentous, not just a lovers' spat. That she had become physically violent, drawn blood even, was almost the best news she'd heard. It made seemingly disparate pieces fit together, even though it painted an ugly picture of who she'd been. But Lucie thought of her former self as another person anyway and, if she was honest, one she didn't much care for. To know her fate, to understand her undoing, might help bring her new self more to life.

And it was so much easier to think about it from that academic place. She'd been working the emotional side since she'd come home, and it had been painful and unsatisfying. What she needed was evidence, cold, hard facts. Names and dates, reports and accounts. Grady's story had whetted her appetite, and now she hungered for more.

If she could find corroborating evidence that what Helen said was true, it would all make sense. Absently, her fingers went to the scar on her thigh, where the man had burned her, provoking her mother to shoot him. What was his name? She hadn't even thought to ask Helen when she'd visited her. And she'd used her mother's first married name in her Google searches. No wonder nothing had shown up.

The burns had to have been excruciating, she thought, marveling at how much pain even a young girl can endure. And then, the very same day, the gunshot—the last and most horrific act in a string of violent acts in an abusive family. When did fifteen-year-old Lucie go blank? Did she even know it was her mother the police took away? Or was it the blast that sent her mind spiraling into nothingness?

Would there be notations of Lucie's behavior in police records? Had there been a psychiatric evaluation of this traumatized girl? Did she stay with foster parents or in a facility until custody with her aunt and uncle was arranged? Wouldn't there be paperwork on file somewhere, about all of these things?

Helen Ten Hands would be happy to hear from her; Lucie knew that much as she punched the old woman's number into the phone. It rang three times, four, and Lucie tried to think of what message she would leave. At the seventh ring, Helen answered. Lucie didn't get the impression that her aunt was someone who would sleep late on a weekday, but she sounded groggy.

"Are you all right?" Lucie asked. "Did I wake you?"

The old woman wheezed. "I'm fine, I'm fine. You just caught me in the john. I don't move as fast as I used to."

"I want to come see you today," Lucie said. "I have so many questions."

"Well, I'm sorry, but today is not a good day for me. I have my volunteer work at the Boys and Girls Club." She coughed into the phone and then, Lucie could tell, held the phone away until the coughing had subsided.

"Are you sure you're okay? Maybe you should call in sick if you don't feel well."

"No, no. It's just asthma, I'm used to it. And the children are the highlight of my week, I'll have you know. They need me."

Lucie could imagine, if not hear, the little harrumph at the end.

"I need you, too, Aunt Helen."

"Oh?" Helen sounded pleased. "Well, perhaps you could come visit tomorrow then. I could make us a nice lunch before my shift at the casino."

Not another bologna sandwich. "Please, if I can't come today, can you just talk to me for a few minutes? I'm . . . well, I need someone to talk to. Someone who knows me."

"Your fiancé, perhaps?" Her aunt wasn't quite so happy to hear from her this time.

"I mean from before. You've known me my whole life." It was true, and saying it brought thick, salty emotion to the sur-face. "Please," Lucie said. "I'm sorry, I just . . ."

"Now, now. Fine, we can talk for a few minutes, but then I have to get ready. I like to be punctual."

There were so many questions, but Lucie needed to slow down. Like everyone, Helen just wanted to be appreciated. To be loved. No matter who you were, or whether or not you were anyone, anymore, that was what really mattered.

"Tell me again about when I was younger, when we all lived together in Marysville before we moved to California." That wasn't why she'd called, but it was what she suddenly most wanted to hear. Happy stories.

"Oh . . ." Helen faltered, coughing. "Oh my. Those were the best times."

Lucie listened, eyes closed, as Helen recounted picnics, rowboating on Silver Lake, strawberry picking in Marysville's "U-Pick" farm fields.

"Every year we took you to the Strawberry Festival, just you and Edward and me," the old woman said. "Your mother, well . . . she worked a lot." She paused. "Your uncle and I did most of the picking, but you'd sing your little songs for us and hold the pail till it got too heavy."

*Yes,* Lucie thought. The sweetness of a sun-warmed berry plopped into her mouth. "Little baby bird," her uncle would say, feeding her. She'd felt special—but wait. Helen didn't say anything about that. Lucie knew this taste, this sensation of doted-upon pleasure. A memory had eased through.

"You had an orange car," Lucie said. "With a rip in the back-seat."

*The color orange,* she thought. *The sweetness of strawberries. The sound of women's laughter in another room.* Her mother and her aunt, maybe others.

"The Dodge," Helen said. "Now, how do you remember that? You were only five or six years old when we got rid of that car."

"I don't know," Lucie said, "but I remember being in it." She'd played with the edges of the ripped fabric, the unraveling weave. It felt normal, knowing this. No bells or sirens or fire-works or nausea. This was nothing like remembering the explo-sions. This was a ripple in calm water, a quiet flutter. She wanted more. "So, we lived with you that whole time?"

"At first you did. Do you remember the big house we lived in, up by the reservation?"

"Kind of," Lucie said. "Almost."

"You had your own bedroom, the blue one with the floral curtains, remember? And you liked to play house in the big coat closet downstairs. My land, you could play house for hours if someone had the patience for it. Your mother and I, well, we'd get tired of it after a few minutes, but not your uncle. He doted on you."

Lucie trembled at this, wishing she could remember all of it, every second.

"After a while, Gloria got work at the new Thriftway and you moved into a place a few blocks from us, but you still liked to sleep over at our house because your uncle made you biscuits in the morning. Remember?"

"I still like biscuits," Lucie said. "Maybe that's why."

Helen was quiet for a moment, then she said, "Everything was fine until your mother took up with that son of a bitch who worked at the Chevy dealership."

Lucie shuddered. "Was that . . . was he the one?" This was why she'd called. This was what she needed to know.

"Oh yes, that was him all right. If it wasn't for Ron Douglas, my baby sister would still be here, I have no doubt, right here in Marysville in her little yellow house, and you never would have moved away, and . . ." Lucie heard her crying.

"Are you all right? Helen?"

She heard fumbling, then the phone clicking off. It was too much for the old woman. Lucie had forced her to remember too much, but she'd had to, hadn't she? In order to remember anything, Lucie needed information only Helen had.

Ron Douglas.

Fingers trembling, she opened the browser on her computer and typed into the search box: "Ronald Gloria Douglas murder San Francisco 1986."

And there it was, from SFGate, home of the *San Francisco Chronicle* archives:

"Double Murder Suicide in Richmond: Mute Girl Only Survivor."

CONCRETE THRUMMED BENEATH the tires; Lucie's hands gripped the steering wheel as she fled the city. Traffic was moderate, the sun brilliant as if it were a normal day. Her mind was intact, and she wasn't exactly fleeing. She was flying toward something.

She wasn't crazy. This was real.

The drive north was more familiar now, but Lucie didn't see the passing signs or landscape, only the words scorched in her mind.

*Double murder.*

Double . . .

*Ronald Douglas and three-year-old son . . .*

Small hands next to hers on the piano.

*Apparently distraught, Gloria Douglas turned the weapon on herself.*

Helen had lied, and who knew about what else.

*Mute girl placed in custody, released to relatives in Washington State.*

Mute. Gone, baby, gone. Lucie wiped her face, but it kept getting wet. Her nose was running, tears a silent relief after the sounds she'd heard coming from her own mouth, her chest, her gut, as she read the story, one she now kept repeating over and over in awful snippets, a mantra of disbelief, of knowing but not knowing, because it all felt too familiar, somehow.

Ronald Douglas was shot as he slept on the couch, and his three-year-old son, David, killed by the same bullets as he lay beneath a blanket with his father.

*Bullets.*

Explosions. It had always been explosions, Lucie realized, as in plural. She felt them now, deep in her chest, *boom* and *boom* and *boom*. And each boom a life: her stepfather, then, oh god, her baby *brother*! Killed in front of her! She saw a woman's terrified eyes looking straight into hers, the woman in Helen's photographs, and Lucie's body convulsed. Was it real? Or was Lucie imagining this, fueled by the article?

She reached for her bag in the passenger seat, keeping one hand and her eyes on the road. Pulling out wadded dollar bills and assorted loose hard candies, she sifted through the pieces of paper and photos she'd been collecting. At the bottom, she found the paper where she'd written the letters from the piano bench.

D A Y Y.

*V,* she thought, *not Y,* paper trembling in her hand. Davy, the name she'd called Eunie's three-year-old grandson. Davy and Lulu. Her little brother must have called her that: Lulu. Those were his hands on the piano keys, and yes, she knew them, small and dimpled, tiny fingernails cut unevenly. She could feel the stocky warmth of him next to her on the bench, smell his baby-shampoo hair, and hear the banging sounds he made to accompany her. And here again, all at once, the feelings that had torn her insides apart from the time she woke up in the San Francisco Bay: horror at not being able to save him. At living on when everyone else had died. She could drown in this feeling. Why did Gloria leave Lucie all alone to fend for herself? Why hadn't she just taken her, too?

*It's too much,* Lucie thought. *I'm feeling too much. Something is going to happen.*

She couldn't breathe. Choking and sobbing, she steered quickly off the road onto the bumpy shoulder, braking hard until the car was still. Why had she run out so fast without calling Grady? If she just had a cell phone, she could call him and hear his voice. She could ask him to come and get her because she was afraid to be alone with these thoughts, these things she now knew were memories.

How could Helen not have told her the true story?

"God!" Lucie yelled. "I hate this!"

But she could breathe now. She wasn't suffocating anymore, and her head cleared enough to notice she'd parked in a no stopping zone.

She knew what she had to do, like it or hate it. Marysville wasn't much farther.

Lucie wiped her face and tucked everything back into the bag, then started the car. She looked over her shoulder for oncoming traffic and pushed forward until she was back in the slipstream, flying up the highway three more exits, then two, then exit 199 to Marysville. She turned off, and at the bottom of the ramp turned left this time, toward the Tulalip Reservation.

She followed signs west, wondering if she'd arrive at the Boys and Girls Club before Helen did. After passing a shopping center and small casino, Lucie crossed over a small river and the world changed. The only businesses on this side were an open-air fruit stand, a dilapidated drive-through espresso shack, and someone selling hand-carved bears. Thick stands of trees created a canyon on either side of the road, with small wood houses in various states of repair popping up occasionally. A blue-green body of water flickered through the trees on the left. Possession Sound, a sign said.

Vibrating now with nervousness or excitement—she wasn't sure which—Lucie wondered if she'd been on this road before. It felt more like returning than discovering someplace new. After a few miles, a large pedestrian overpass loomed above the road. To the left, playground equipment sprawled across a grassy open area and an old totem pole rose from the grass in front of the Tulalip Elementary School.

*Yes,* she thought, knowing that, as she made the turn, the expanse of emerald meadow with low-slung school buildings would lead to shimmering water and forested banks on the opposite side. Tulalip Bay. This was a special place. All this beauty meant something, and she had known that for a long time.

Just past the playground and a small vegetable garden, she saw the big blue shed of a building that was her destination. The Boys and Girls Club of Tulalip, with children's drawings and Native American artwork in the windows. The parking lot was dotted with cars, including Helen's old white Celica. Lucie pulled in and parked, pulse racing yet again. Could someone have a heart attack from so much pounding? she wondered. Her hands were clumsy at the seat belt latch.

This was it. She would make Helen tell her everything or

threaten to never see her again, she thought, swinging the car
door closed and walking into the building.

"May I help you?" An older woman with long silver hair sat
at a reception desk. "Are you the new tutor?"

Lucie started to speak, then stopped. She could hear children singing in one direction, an adult talking in an unusual
language in another. There was laughter coming from somewhere, and outside a crow cawing, and then a cacophony of
them in a tree towering above her as she pumped her legs on
the swing, dirt covering the half-moon toes of her sneakers.

"Are you all right?" the woman asked, rising to come around
the desk, concern on her face.

Lucie shook her head but couldn't speak. It was another
memory, a snippet of time from so many lives before, forgotten
once, or twice, or who knew how many times? She'd gone to
elementary school here. Of course she had.

The woman wrapped an arm around her, leading her to a
chair against the wall. Once Lucie sat, the woman knelt in
front of her, holding her hands. "What is it? Do you need help?"

"I . . . I know this place," Lucie said.

"Oh, are you a parent, or . . . ?" The woman was being so
nice, and her hands were so soft. Lucie remembered the swimmers in San Francisco when she was in the water, how warm
their hands were, how kind their voices.

"No, it's just . . . I just haven't been here in a very long
time."

"Yeah, it's a special place." The woman stood and smiled at
her. "People who've been away for a while often have powerful
memories."

Lucie nodded, swallowing hard.

"Did you just want to look around, then?"

"No, I'm sorry." Lucie stood. "My aunt is here, volunteering. I just needed to talk with her."

"Ah, Miss Helen. I wish my aunties had half her oomph." The woman walked back around her desk and wrote "Visitor" on a sticker, then handed it to Lucie. "She just started her story time, but if you'd like to go in and watch, she's in room 106, down that hall on the right. Here's a badge, so you're official."

Lucie removed the backing and stuck the rectangle to her shirt.

"She'll be so happy to see you," the woman said, smiling. "She talks about you all the time."

# helen

t he small girl, Raelene—Albert Coy's granddaughter and the latest object of Helen's affection—was absent today. Helen looked around the room at the children tumbling over one another, trying to choose a special helper. She should really choose a boy, she knew. One day someone would catch on and accuse her of, well, who knew what, but she didn't care. Her need for little-girl sweetness was acute, almost as bad as the palpitations that didn't go away anymore, her heart knocking against her old ribs like it wanted to be set free.

Helen stroked the inhaler in her pocket; she needed to take a puff before reading so she wouldn't run out of breath. She turned her back, sucked in one chemical hit, then another just to be on the safe side. Her head grew light, her vision extra sharp, and she turned back around to clap her hands.

*One, two, one-two-three.* It reverberated loudly in her ears.

The children quieted and stood to face her, clapping the rhythm back.

"Take a seat, please, on the carpet," she said, reaching for her stool to steady herself. As the children sat, there was Lucie, sitting behind them in a yellow plastic chair meant for a six-year-old, looking so much like she had as a little girl that Helen was afraid she might be hallucinating. She adjusted her glasses. The doctor said if she used her inhaler too often . . .

But no, it was Lucie, who was giving her a little wave and smiling that crooked way that Helen had once thought she'd never see again. She waved back, trying to hide the tremor, but she knew everyone could see it now, no matter how she tried to disguise it. Helen wished she could be at her best for Lucie, but, well. Perhaps this was her best, now.

She cleared her throat and picked the book of the day, one the children loved and asked for over and over again.

Her voice sounded unnaturally high and tremulous as she began to read: "If you give a moose a muffin . . ."

A sea of small hands went into the air, waggling furiously. Helen looked up. "What is it?"

"You need to pick someone to show the pictures!" an older boy said, and the children all nodded and repeated after him.

Well, of course she did. She knew that.

Helen looked around the room. She generally made a big show of picking the most obedient one, the least wriggly or chatty. She looked up, and her eyes met Lucie's. "Lucie? Would you please help me show the pictures today?"

The children turned to look at Lucie, gasping and exclaiming. "Aw, no fair!" the older boy said.

"Boys and girls, this is our special guest today, my niece, Lucie. Please make her feel welcome."

Cheeks coloring, Lucie rose and walked to the front to stand next to Helen's stool. The children settled, and Helen continued to read, handing the book to Lucie after each page so she could hold it up for view. Lucie held herself just far enough away—taking the book from her aunt at its opposite edge, never meeting her eyes—that Helen knew everything was not yet right between them. But she wouldn't stop trying, not as long as she was still alive.

At the end of the story, Helen asked the children if they had any comments or questions about the book. Raelene's older sister raised her hand.

"What's a niece, Miss? Is that like a cousin?"

"No, Bertha," Helen said, weary with impatience. A sudden wave of fatigue threatened to pull her under, but her shift didn't end for another thirty-two minutes. "Your cousin is like your brother or sister, only his parent is the brother or sister of your parent. Understand?"

The girl shrugged. "But what's a niece?"

Helen coughed into her Kleenex. She needed another puff; she needed to reapply her lipstick so no one would see how blue her lips surely must be.

"I'm her sister's daughter," Lucie said to the girl. "So I'm more like . . ." She looked at Helen, willing her, it seemed, to say the words.

"So you're like her daughter," the girl said, and Helen felt the sweet stab of the word, the pain and the pleasure it brought.

Bertha jumped up with the rest of the children, who had taken Helen's momentary inattention as a sign of release. "You be my daughter," she said to another girl with ruddy cheeks and untied shoelaces. "And I'll be your cousin."

"Mother," Helen said quietly among the din. "You'll be her mother." The children didn't hear. Helen stood and walked stiffly to the bookshelf, where she tucked the book away, then sat in a chair at the back of the room. Lucie came to sit next to her.

"Are you all right?" Lucie asked, leaning over to touch Helen's arm.

*Warm,* Helen thought. *I am so cold, and you feel so warm beside me.*

"Soon," Helen said. "I will be soon."

# lucie

So many intent little faces had watched her aunt as she read the story, rather artfully, Lucie thought. Helen was good with children. They respected her and, Lucie thought, actually liked her. No wonder this was the highlight of Helen's week. She had no family, no husband, and a lousy job, but she had twenty or so children who loved her every single week. This was the family she'd made for herself, and Lucie felt a new admiration for the old woman. *What it must be like to have them look at you that way,* Lucie marveled. There was an intensity in their faces she never would have imagined.

At the end of Helen's shift, Lucie offered to drive her home, expecting her to refuse, but Helen nodded and gathered her things. Once in the car, the old woman closed her eyes, her breath like leaves rustling.

"Are you sure you're okay?" Lucie asked. Her aunt's skin was pale gray, and no matter how many times she used her inhaler, her breathing didn't improve.

"I just need to rest."

Lucie found Helen's address in the navigator's memory and selected it. The electronic voice said, "Proceed east on Marine Drive Northeast."

The old woman perked up and leaned over to look at the display. "Oh, my," she said. "So that's what you were going on about." She adjusted her glasses to have a closer look, then leaned back. "You always did like electrical gadgets, just like your uncle Eddy."

"Eddy? I called him Eddy?"

"You did, and the two of you could spend hours together pulling apart a transistor radio or the kitchen clock, just to see what made it work."

"What made it tick," Lucie said.

"That's exactly what he'd always say," Helen murmured. "Nothing ever worked quite the same again once you two had your way with it."

Lucie smiled. How could she not like this strange person? It wasn't just that she needed her for information, although every snippet felt diamond encrusted. Uncle Eddy. She didn't remember the radios and clocks, but the sound of Uncle Eddy was soothing, a warm flannel shirt, the smell of pine and gasoline.

They drove in silence for a while, through the green, filtered light and old souls of the towering trees. Lucie glanced at Helen in the passenger seat.

"We need to talk about the rest of it, you know."

The old woman stared straight ahead, but didn't resist.

"I read a newspaper article about the murder," Lucie said. "Why didn't you just tell me the whole story?"

Helen blinked hard, then said, "It was too much."

"No, it's not. It's what I need to know." Lucie tried not to sound angry.

"I meant it was too much for me," Helen snapped.

"How could you not tell me I had a brother?"

"Half brother."

"How could you not tell me my mother committed suicide?"

"Because she didn't mean to, don't you see?" Helen tried to twist in the seat to look at her. "She couldn't believe what she'd done! What a terrible mistake, to kill your own child!"

All at once, Lucie was crying, her face wet, her breath choking. This sorrow was old and deep and heavy, as if her organs had been concreted together inside, the pain now growing sharper, uglier.

"Why didn't she just kill me, too?"

*A room, murky dark, only a television for light. A burned smell in the air. Something bad has happened—something really, really bad.*

"Never!" Helen cried. "She didn't mean to kill the little boy. It was an accident. He must have crawled up under the blanket after his father passed out, that damn drunk. Gloria would never kill her own child."

*Her mother at the couch now, lifting the blanket, blood everywhere, the boy in her arms, torn open on one side like an animal hit by a car. Blood on her mother's arms and hands, her blouse. Blood on her cheeks after she buried her face against the boy.*

Lucie couldn't breathe. She couldn't see. She pulled to the side of the road, jammed the gearshift into park.

*The mutilated boy hanging limp and heavy from her mother's left arm, the gun shaky in her right hand.*

"So much blood," Lucie moaned. The smell of rust, a sweet, sickening kind of rust.

"Oh, please just stop." Helen wept, her glasses steaming over before she removed them.

*Her mother raising her arm.*

"She pointed the gun at me."

"No," Helen insisted. "She loved you."

"She pointed the gun at me, too," Lucie repeated. "I screamed."

*Mom! Don't!*

She could hear it, still, all of it echoing around in her skull as though it had always been there with the volume turned down. The first three shots, the screams. And she'd wanted to run as hard as she could to get away. Running was the only way to survive.

But she'd just stood there, paralyzed, believing she was about to die.

"And then . . ." Lucie swallowed, shuddering. "Then she pointed the gun at herself." She remembered now. And that was where it stopped.

"Oh, my lord, no, no." Helen reached for Lucie's hand. "Please, say it isn't true."

"You know this."

"We only knew she'd shot herself in her torment. You were the only one who knew all of it, and you didn't say a word when we got you back." Helen's fingers dug into Lucie's palm, anchoring her to this time, to this place. "Not one word! Not about your mother, or your poor baby brother, about what you had to see. We thought you were a monster, but you were gone . . . Your mind was gone." Each word bent the old woman lower until she'd curled upon herself like a shell, convulsing with sobs. "Oh, I'm so sorry, so sorry . . . oh dear god."

Lucie shook her head, trying to catch her breath. No, they couldn't have known every detail she witnessed, but how could they have not known something was wrong with her and gotten help?

Yet, she was now guilty of the same thing. She'd never called the psychiatrist.

"Yeah, I was gone," Lucie said, still trembling, but her mind felt clearer now. She'd shown herself some mercy and blanked out at the moment of her mother's death, wiping her memory clean for the next twenty-five years. "I was gone for a long time, forgetting."

No wonder she bore so little resemblance to the Lucie that Grady knew. It was starting to make a weird kind of sense. She'd been reset by amnesia two months before, when she ran, but not to the life she'd just left. Lucie wondered if she'd started over as her fifteen-year-old self, before she'd witnessed the events that left her shell-shocked and hardened off to the world, even mute at first, according to the article. When did she start talking again? She'd ask Helen another time, when she hadn't already put her through so much.

The old woman clutched her hand, along with yet another tissue fished from her bra. Lucie suspected she kept an entire box in there. She comforted her aunt instead of the other way around. It was the way it was. Helen was elderly and frail. She needed someone to care for her.

"Ready to go home?" Lucie asked, finally, but the old woman remained hunched over. "Aunt Helen?"

She didn't respond, but she'd begun to pant, almost.

"Helen?" Lucie said louder. "Are you all right?" Still no movement. Lucie leaned the woman back into her seat, palms on bird-bone shoulders, looking into her blank eyes for some kind of light, but her aunt seemed to be off somewhere else, as if some switch had been flipped, even though she was breathing so rapidly. Her face was gray, her lips almost blue.

"No," Lucie said, saliva thickening. "Shit shit shit."

A hospital. She needed to get to the closest hospital. The navigator. Quickly tapping the commands on the display, she found a way to search by category. Sure enough, a hospital icon led to a list, with Valley General Hospital in Monroe the closest, nearly thirty minutes away. Would Helen be alive by then? Lucie started the car and glanced over her shoulder. *Help me,* she thought, *please,* spinning the wheels on gravel before the pavement took hold.


AT MILE SIXTEEN Lucie looked down and saw she was doing ninety. The road was long and rolling, with no dangerous curves. If cops chased her, she'd let them, all the way to the hospital.

"Are you okay?" she tried again, glancing at Helen as long as she dared to. Lucie couldn't hear her aunt breathing over the road noise but detected movement in her chest. The old woman had her head back and to the side, saliva trickling down her chin. "Oh god, please. Hold on just a few more minutes."

How could this be happening? Was Lucie supposed to witness each of her family members dying? Was it some kind of curse?

Lucie gripped the steering wheel tighter. Well, it was happening, and she wasn't running away from it. Even though she was scared shitless, she was in control and she'd do anything it took to get Helen to the hospital alive.

And then there were signs for Monroe, and then the hospital, and the wide driveway of the emergency entrance. Lucie didn't know whether she should park and run inside to find someone, or just honk until an attendant came out; she lay on the horn. Two men in blue scrubs looked out from the wide double doors to see what was happening. Lucie jumped from the car.

"She's unconscious," she said. "She's having trouble breathing."

One of the men came and opened Helen's door. He knelt beside her, checking her vitals, speaking to her, telling her what was happening even though she was out cold. The other hurried a gurney outside, and the two extracted her from the car, limp and dead looking as they placed her on the gurney.

"How long has she been out?" one asked.

"I don't know, half an hour at the longest, maybe?"

"You family?" the other man asked.

"Yes," Lucie said. "I'm . . . I'm her niece. Is she okay?"

"Park right over there, then let admissions know you're

here," he said as they rolled her away. "We're going to get to work on her, but we'll need her info."

Lucie was relieved to have tasks to complete. After parking the car, she hurried with Helen's handbag into the emergency room and dug through it to find identification and insurance information for the admissions clerk before she was led to the examination room.

Helen now wore a pale blue gown. The hospital staff worked over her, adjusting monitors, drawing blood, inserting an IV. Her face was dull beneath an oxygen mask.

Lucie shuddered, remembering when she was first led from the water, how they placed the mask on her. How frightening it was. Was Helen afraid? The old woman mumbled something, and Lucie drew a deeper breath. She wasn't dead. Lucie's legs felt ready to buckle.

A tall, silver-haired woman in a white coat stood at a laptop on a rolling cart. "I'm Dr. Bryant. You must be Mrs. Ten Hands's niece." She smiled briefly as she tapped the keys.

"I'm Lucie. Is she okay? Is she awake?"

"We're getting some oxygen into her, and running labs, and we hope to collect some history from you. Okay?"

Lucie shook her head. "I'm sorry, I can't tell you much. I barely know her. But, I have her purse and her medications are inside." With shaking hands, she pulled out an inhaler and several prescription bottles, handing them to the doctor. Lucie wished she'd eaten more that morning.

"Another inhaler? We found one in her pocket, too." The doctor read the label. "Okay, good. Let's see what else she has here." She looked up at Lucie. "You okay hanging out in here? There's a chair in the corner."

Grateful, Lucie went to sit in the chair, still holding Helen's purse to her abdomen. Her limbs felt disconnected, rubbery and strange. Maybe she should put her head between her knees.

"So," the doctor said. "Tell me what happened."

"Um . . ." Lucie took a deep breath, then another. "She wasn't feeling well after her volunteer work at the reservation, so I was driving her home. She was having trouble breathing, you could tell. Then she just stopped talking, stopped responding to me." When was that? Lucie looked for a clock. "We were talking . . . well, about really stressful stuff. I kept making her tell me things she didn't want to." Lucie blinked her eyes. She didn't want to cry, not here, not yet.

The doctor looked up. She had a pretty face, bright blue eyes. "It's not your fault," Dr. Bryant said. "Promise. You need to take a few more deep breaths."

Lucie nodded, inhaling deeply before she continued. "It took about a half hour to get here, and sometime during that I realized she'd really passed out."

"Okay," Dr. Bryant said, entering information. "Seems we've seen your aunt here many times over the years, so we've got some good background information to go on."

A young woman in pink scrubs entered the room. "Ready for us?" she asked the doctor, who nodded. The woman wheeled in a large gray machine.

"Chest X-ray," Dr. Bryant told Lucie. "We'll see what's going on in there, okay? You can just hang out in the waiting room. I'll come find you. It may be a while."

Lucie thanked her and left with Helen's bag. She sat near a window, wanting air. Lots of air. This waiting room had been refurbished in the past year, she guessed. Everything was clean and new, warm maple furniture and light olive fabrics. The magazines held no interest for her though, or the people coming and going in their various states of distress.

Too many thoughts swirled and collided inside her. The news article had reported that Gloria Douglas was forty at the time of her death. Grady had said Lucie was terrified of turning forty. Could her impending birthday have triggered the amnesia?

And she'd lived with her family in Richmond, across the bay from San Francisco. A small map had accompanied the article. Was that what she'd been looking for when she walked into the water?

How could she ever know what she'd been thinking, or what she'd done, how she lived, while she was gone? Would she ever remember everything, or would her mind spare her the best of it, along with the worst?

There were things she wanted to know: had her mother lived a happy life? Had Lucie been a good daughter, a good sister? Had the little boy been scared before he died, or was it just like a light switch snapping off? Lucie shuddered. She knew her mother was frightened. Lucie could still see it in her eyes, and she wished she could reach through the ether and tell her mother that her daughter, at least, had survived. That she was on her way to being happy, even with all the work of becoming whole and healthy again lying in front of her.

Lucie lifted Helen's beige faux-leather purse from the seat next to her and settled it back in her lap. She'd already had to violate her aunt's privacy, going through it for information. Helen's wallet had been thick with photos in plastic sleeves at the back. How horrible would it be to look at them?

Lucie dug through the purse, finding Helen's wallet and holding it in her hands for a moment. It was battered and dated, the kind with a little clasp at the top, like a purse. She'd seen Helen's driver's license earlier, when she gave it to the admissions clerk, marveling at how different her aunt looked in the grainy little photo from years before. Her birth date was May 20, 1942. Helen was only sixty-nine, but she looked as if she were in her eighties.

Lucie opened the clasp and saw the first photo. A studio portrait of middle-aged Helen and Edward, looking in the same direction, smiling. They both wore glasses; they looked contented. Was this before or after she'd been with them? The next photo was of young Edward, shirtless in a snapshot outdoors. He was tall and thin, buzz-cut hair, dangling a fish from a line. *How amazing to love someone for so long,* Lucie thought.

The next photo stunned her to tears: another studio shot, a mother and two children. A tired-looking Gloria and awkward-age Lucie with bangs and pimples. Between them sat a sturdy blond toddler, showing off his new top and bottom teeth in a drooling grin, holding a stuffed toy lion.

*Yion,* she heard a little voice say.

Lucie closed her eyes, listening. Waiting for more.

\* \* \*

AN HOUR AND a half later, Dr. Bryant walked out and took a seat next to Lucie.

"Your aunt is breathing a little better now," she said. "We've gotten the results back on a few of the tests. Mrs. Ten Hands is battling some chronic issues with her lungs, and she has congestive heart disease, but we're pretty sure this emergency was the result of medication misuse. Operator error."

"Oh," Lucie said, sitting straighter in the chair. Her back ached from slumping.

"It's not unusual with seniors. She'll improve once we get her back on track, but she'll probably need help staying organized, and taking her medications properly. And she was severely dehydrated. Has your aunt been more forgetful lately?"

Lucie shook her head. "I don't know. This is only the second time I've ever seen her."

"Right." The doctor nodded. "Do you know if she has someone nearby who can check in on her? Kids, relatives? Neighbors?"

Lucie chewed her bottom lip. "Not that I know of. I live in Seattle."

"Well, then, she may be better off in a care facility."

"Oh, god." Lucie sighed. "She'll probably hate that."

"At some point," the doctor said. "Don't worry about that just yet. You okay? You want to see her? She looks much better than she did."

Lucie nodded and followed the doctor back to the exam room. Helen looked as defenseless as a newborn, Lucie thought, so small beneath all of the equipment. But the doctor was right; her color had brightened, and she wasn't struggling to breathe.

"She's pretty wiped out," Dr. Bryant said. "Her blood oxygen levels were low. We've given her a breathing treatment, and we'll continue with those tonight and for the next few days. She may need to be on oxygen when she leaves here."

"Permanently?"

The doctor nodded. "Probably. We have your number, but feel free to call to check on her, okay? We'll be moving her to ICU soon. Hopefully, by tomorrow, she'll be doing well enough to be in a regular room."

Lucie sighed. How was she supposed to just leave her here?

"I doubt she'll wake up," the doctor said, "but you're welcome to stay."

Lucie thanked her and walked to Helen's bedside, gripping the side rail, watching the old woman's blue-veined eyelids flutter occasionally, in dream perhaps, or just the involuntary twitching of sleep. Her nostrils were pink where the oxygen tubing rubbed her skin; dark bruises spread wherever she'd been given an injection. She'd been through too much that afternoon.

"I'm sorry," Lucie whispered, reaching to untangle the old woman's fingers from the IV line, then holding her hand. "I won't ever do that to you again."

She would stay until Helen was conscious enough to find out what happened to her from someone she knew. Everyone deserved that much.

# grady

is team understood when Grady said it was going to be a rough day for Lucie, and that he needed to skip the afternoon meeting to be with her. His techs and engineers had been considerate about everything all along, and it occurred to Grady that he'd never have found a place to work that fit him so perfectly if it hadn't been for Lucie. She'd read him like a damn book at that job fair.

The parking gods must have been on his side, too, because he found a spot on the street right in front of the market Lucie loved.

Without crutches, everything was so easy now, even though he walked like a peg-leg pirate. He picked up a handbasket and made his way up and down the small aisles, searching for things Lucie would like. He wouldn't make the mistake he had before, choosing healthy foods she'd preferred in the old days. He filled the basket with sweet things and luscious things, then found the best smelling flowers he could in the buckets near the register. Rather than just one clump, he stuffed the entire bucketful into a plastic bouquet bag and tucked them under his arm. Sweet peas, they were called. *Perfect,* he thought.

He had to admit it seemed like the best picnic ever, no matter where they ate it. He imagined them sitting in the park overlooking the Lake Union floating homes, or maybe down at Shilshole Bay on a blanket in the sand, but even just the kitchen table would be fine for the evening he had in mind.

AS HE PULLED up to the house, Lucie's car was parked in a different spot than when he'd left that morning. So, she had gone up to Marysville to see Helen Ten Hands. Grady sighed. How would she be feeling this time?

He got out of the car and scanned the windows of the house, wondering where she was, what she'd be doing at four forty-seven in the afternoon. He should have called to let her know he was coming home early, that's what he should have done, but he'd wanted to be spontaneous. He strapped on his messenger bag and grabbed the grocery bags and the huge bundle of flowers, then bumped the car door closed with his hip and limped up the steps. What if she wasn't in the mood for all of this?

The bags were heavier than he'd gauged, and at the second to last step before the top, the toe of his plastic boot caught, lurching him forward, everything falling, flowers scattering across the concrete, watermelon splitting with a thud, peaches bruising. He caught himself with his right palm, pain shooting through his wrist and forearm.

"Fuck!" he yelled, rolling onto his side, holding his arm. No way did he break his stupid arm now, too. He sat up and held his wrist in his other hand, squeezing and releasing. It still moved fine, as did his arm. It just hurt like hell. He looked at the neighboring houses. Thank god no one was outside.

The front door opened, and Grady looked up. There stood Lucie wearing a pair of his underwear and a tank top, barefoot, a look of incomprehension on her face. Her eyes were puffy, her nose red.

"Hi," he said. "I was going to surprise you."

She tilted her head at him and stepped out onto the concrete. "So I see." She came to sit next to him on the step and took his hurt wrist in her cool hands, studying it. "Are you always this clumsy?" she asked.

"Pretty much." He enjoyed the closeness of her, her hair so near to his face, the way his underwear looked on her.

"I think you'll survive this one without a trip to the hospital," she finally said and let go of his arm. "Thank god."

"Are you all right?" he asked. "Did you go see Helen?"

She nodded. "She almost died on me." Her chin wobbled.

"What?"

"I was driving her home, and she passed out. I took her to the hospital up there, and, um . . ."

"Is she okay?"

"Well, no, but she just got her medications mixed up, they said." She rubbed her forehead. "We had this intense talk about everything that happened to me and my mother, and . . ." She paused, staring into space.

"Luce? You okay?" Grady brought his good hand to her cheek, and she shrugged.

"There is so much more horribleness than I ever imagined," she said, then looked at him. "It's too much for me. I have to go see the psychiatrist, I know, I just never . . ."

"It's okay . . ."

"No, it's not. I thought I could do this, and I can't by my- self, and it's so—"

"You're not by yourself. I'm right here with you."

Tears ran down her face; she wrapped her arms around his neck and whispered, "Thank you," before pulling away. The warmth of her stayed imprinted on him, everywhere their bod- ies had touched.

Lucie turned to survey the contents of the grocery bags strewn across the stoop and reached for a chunk of broken wa- termelon to pop into her mouth.

"Oh, god," she said. "So sweet." She picked up another piece and offered it to Grady. There would be no beach, no view, not even a kitchen table. It was now or never.

"I love you," he said, then leaned in to eat the watermelon from Lucie's fingers. "I want to marry you."

Her face crumpled, turning dark pink as she began to cry. "God, I just finally stopped," she said.

He reached to gather as many sweet peas as possible, then clumped them together. "For you," he said, and she took them, burying her face in the bright colors.

"I love you, Lucie," he repeated, so she would hear him. "I have so much to tell you, but I do better in writing."

She looked up, face wet, and he pulled the messenger bag

around to his lap, rummaged in it, then pulled out the letter he'd worked on most of the day and handed it to her. She let the flowers spill across her lap and onto the concrete, like the most beautiful damn painting Grady had ever seen. She took the paper and looked at it for a moment before handing it back to him.

He felt the weight, the going under, the silence, the awful pull. She had too many other things going on in her life to care about this, about him and his feelings. He had to be patient, but he didn't know how much longer he could be. Seconds passing were lifetimes, familiar and excruciating, and he didn't know why he hadn't expected that she wouldn't be ready for this, and then she wiped her nose and shrugged.

"Will you read it to me? I like your voice."

*Jesus,* he thought, trembling, but he took the letter.

"*Dear Lucie,*" he began, sweat breaking out all over him. He cleared his throat, took a breath, and began again in earnest.

> "*You might have guessed by now that I don't talk a lot about certain things, but I want to change that. I know you also think that I might not love you as much as I did before you left, or that I had stopped loving you, but the truth of the matter is I love you, maybe more now than I ever did. That is the main thing I want you to feel and to know and to be certain of. Even if this doesn't work out, and you feel you have to leave again.*"

He heard her sudden intake of breath—a sob—but kept reading.

"It's true that you're different now, but I am, too. I'm realizing that maybe it was time for everything to change. We were only able to get so far before all this happened, because you and me, well, we hadn't figured out how to connect in the right way, you know? Sure, all of this is hard and it's going to take work to get through it, but I know you're strong enough to do it. The truth is, I'm figuring stuff out, too.

"The main thing I've learned is just how sad I've been my whole life, and I don't want to be sad anymore. I don't want to keep pulling away from everything. When I lost you, I learned how much I needed you to stay a part of the world. You're different in ways now, but you are the same, too: you lift me out of the darker places where I tend to sink. You bring light into my life. I know that sounds so corny, but it's true. You've always done this for me, from the day we met.

"I want to tell you everything. I want to tell you about my dad and how hard it is to be a dead man's son. I want to tell you what it feels like to swim. I want to go swimming with you, and to play in the water with you like I did with my sisters when we were just kids. Do you even know how to swim? I don't know, it never came up before. Do you want to go with me? I could teach you if you don't know how.

"This is a weird letter, I know, but I want it to be the beginning of something. I want to talk with you forever, Lucie. I hope you want that, too.
"Love, G"

He looked up. Lucie was staring at him, her green eyes glossy, lashes matted together.

"Yes," she said.

"Yes?"

"I want to go swimming." She reached to take the letter from him.

"Now?" Grady looked around at the groceries, ice cream melting through its carton, peaches releasing their sweet scent in the heat. It had to be close to ninety degrees, and it would stay hot long into the evening.

Lucie gathered the flowers together and stood. "All of this will keep once it's put away. Green Lake is so close; Susan takes her nephews there all the time."

Grady hesitated. None of this had gone the way he'd wanted it to, but did she understand? Did she see what he'd been trying to do? Was she going to marry him?

"I think this might be the best day of my life," she said, opening the door. Just before she stepped in, she turned to look at him. "No, I know it is." And then she pressed herself into him, sweet-smelling flowers crushing between their chests, and kissed his mouth with watermelon lips.


HALF AN HOUR later, they were wading into murky lake water. Grady had always dismissed Green Lake as a place for kids to play before Lucie brought it up. Sure, it wasn't the sound, with its ocean tang and lulling currents, and it wasn't the pristine, clean blue of a pool, but it was a large and welcoming body of water, with swim beaches and diving docks in the middle.

Grady longed to run splashing into the water, diving forward when it became deep enough, but his bum foot wasn't the only reason he hung back with Lucie. The cool water enveloped them ever higher, buoying them, holding them safe.

At chest level they stopped. "Look how beautiful it is here," she said, turning in a circle to view the ring of trees around the large lake, the lily pads floating in the distance, the burning blue of the late afternoon sky striped by white jet contrails. A V of geese flew overhead, honking occasionally, and the water gave off an earthen smell, a hint of the muck that sucked their feet to the bottom, but it wasn't unpleasant.

Grady wondered if Lucie would be able to swim. Why had they never been in water together before? She owned three swimsuits, all black, and she'd chosen a simple tank suit, although it fit her like skin. Grady had, of course, noticed.

A large wooden dock floated a few dozen yards away from them, scrawny teenagers climbing its ladder and jumping off, over and over, screaming and laughing each time as if it was the first time. Grady remembered how much he'd loved that, too, at that age: the sensation of leaping into the air, hitting the water with as loud a slap as he could manage, and quickly descending among the bubbles. Pushing his feet into the bottom and streaming back to the surface, breaking through, throwing water from his hair with the fling of his head, and then reaching for the rusty ladder again.

"You want to jump off, don't you?" Lucie said, not so much a question as an affirmation. "Go ahead. I'll be fine." She held her nose and dipped beneath the water, coming up, face to the sun, hair slicked back like a seal.

"Don't you want to come, too?"

She smiled, then turned toward the dock, arms reaching in front of her. After a brief hesitation, she sprang forward with a serviceable kick and breaststroke.

Grady watched for a moment, her body as strong and lithe in the water as on land. *Pish pish,* he thought, smiling, then launched after her, pulling long strokes to catch up.

THAT NIGHT, LUCIE called the hospital. Even though she was using the phone in the kitchen and Grady sat in the living room with his laptop, he could hear her speaking with someone about her aunt, asking how she was doing, how long she would be hospitalized.

He knew where this was leading, and sighed. Just more family to come between them, he thought, then, *No.* Family wasn't the problem, had never been the problem. It was his re-action to family that created the tension.

After hanging up, Lucie came into the living room and sat on the couch, tucking her leg beneath her. "I'm going to go see her tomorrow," she said.

Grady put his computer on the ottoman. "Okay."

"I know you don't like her much and—"

"Luce. She's your aunt. I get it."

"She doesn't have anyone else," Lucie said, her eyes pained.

"As long as it's what you want to do . . ." He shrugged. "That's the important thing, for me."

"I love you, too," she said. "I didn't say that earlier today."

"But you did say yes." Grady smiled.

"Yes to swimming." She looked embarrassed. "To everything. In time."

Grady closed his eyes so she wouldn't see his disappointment, and nodded. "Of course," he said, then opened his eyes. "In time."

# helen

rough bedsheets chafed her skin, and the pillow was too hard against Helen's head. They ought to know that old people had special needs, she thought, pressing the call button again. She couldn't even find her eyeglasses.

How was she supposed to sleep when she couldn't get comfortable, and with the lights on all the time, for pity's sake? At least they'd paid attention to her in intensive care. Now that she was in a regular room, they'd forgotten her.

Why hadn't they just let her die? She'd been nearly gone; she could have just slipped away. All she wanted was to see Edward again, her parents, her sister. Death would have been preferable, she thought, if Lucie hadn't been with her. The girl had watched enough of her family die. And now Helen would probably never see her again, either, and that would be her niece's last memory of her.

If only Helen had been strong enough to help Lucie remember, to help her heal, but she was old and decrepit, and not worth much to anyone, not anymore.

What did she have to look forward to now? That female doctor had said she might need to go on oxygen, full-time. How was she supposed to go to her job at the casino, to the Boys and Girls Club, even grocery shopping, lugging oxygen everywhere? With that awful tube across her face? And the doctor had the nerve to suggest she give up her driver's license. What on earth would she do if she couldn't drive? Oh, she knew what every-one would say: there were buses to the casino, and the grocery market was just five blocks away.

"Hmph," the old woman said to those who would try to paint this picture rosier than it was. Being old was a curse, something no young person could endure. And she was none too happy about the caliber of nurses at Valley General, either. How did they know she wasn't having a coronary when she rang the button? She pushed it a few more times for good mea-sure. They were ignoring her, she knew it.

And then, what do you know, there was a knock, and some-one coming in. Finally. "Haven't you got any pillows that aren't made of bricks?" Helen asked.

"Um, hi," a voice said.

Helen squinted, her worn, old heart pounding like a ghost had entered the room. It was her girl, coming closer.

"Oh, Lucie," Helen said, trying to push herself into a sitting position, then giving up and lying back. "I . . . I thought you were the nurse. Oh, where are my glasses?"

"Right here on the bedside table," Lucie said and handed them to her.

Helen slid them into place, and her niece came into focus.

Helen's heart ached for her sister, seeing Lucie standing there at her bedside. She'd become a fine woman and, in truth, looked nothing like Gloria, even though she was about the same age as her mother was when she died. Maybe that's why Helen kept thinking of Gloria, every time she saw the girl. Lucie took after her father's side, she supposed.

"Well, you look better than you did the last time I saw you," Helen said, reaching for Lucie's hand. They'd each been so upset, so distraught. Helen had a hazy memory of Lucie being in the emergency room with her, but she couldn't quite piece it together.

Lucie laughed. "Me? Well, so do you. You had me pretty scared there for a while. But they say you're doing much better today."

"Did they tell you I might need oxygen?"

"They say it makes you more comfortable," Lucie said, "and more energetic, more able to do things you used to do. Wouldn't that be nice?"

Helen started to harrumph, to protest, but stopped. Something washed over her, a tingling, cool river from her toes to her head. Was it Edward, telling her to look at the gift in front of her? Was it Gloria, crying at the sight of her daughter, alive and healthy? Lucie had come all this way from Seattle to see her and was trying to cheer her up, holding her hand and smiling. If wearing a damn tube up her nose the rest of her life was all Helen had to pay for that miracle, well, then. Perhaps it wasn't so costly a price.

"Thank you for coming," Helen said. "These drugs they have me on make my eyes run."

"Aunt Helen," Lucie said, and the old woman had to close her eyes, there were so many tears. Just at the sound of those words.

"I feel awful about yesterday," Lucie said. "I'm sorry I made you talk about, well, everything. It was so selfish of me."

"No!" Helen's eyes flew open, tears be damned. "I should have talked to you long ago about it, about all of it, but Edward thought—Well, I shouldn't have listened to him, even though he was my husband. I should have taken you in my arms and made you listen to me."

Lucie's eyes began to pool.

"I should have told you that your mother and brother were gone, but that you always had us, no matter what. You didn't know any of it; you were in shock, you'd made yourself forget. Oh, I am so sorry for it, for treating you so poorly. If your uncle were alive today, he'd feel just as bad as me, I know he would. We didn't know how a mind could break so badly. We just didn't." Helen removed her eyeglasses and wiped her face.

Lucie grabbed tissues from a box on the windowsill, handing some to Helen, using the others to wipe her own nose. "No one knows this stuff until it happens to them. No one knows how awful some things feel until they're forced to."

"No, no they don't." Helen shook her head. She'd never talked to anyone but Edward about her sister. After he passed, not one soul on earth had known how she felt, what she carried, what she'd lost.

Until now.

Helen blew her nose, then put her glasses back on. "That's enough crying for one day."

Lucie smiled and nodded. "Okay. Yes. Enough." She tilted her head, almost shyly it seemed to Helen, and asked, "How would you feel about another visitor?"

"Oh, I don't . . ."

"But he's out in the hall. He wants to meet you."

*Oh good lord,* Helen thought. Here she was all rummy eyed, and wearing such a thin cotton gown.

"Do you happen to have a hairbrush?" she asked Lucie, reaching to feel her hair. Who knew what kind of shape it was in.

"No, but I can just kind of . . ."

The girl reached and smoothed Helen's hair, combing it with her fingers. The old woman closed her eyes at the sensation. No one had touched her head in such a long time, not since she'd stopped going to the hairdresser. Edward used to stroke her hair, and she'd go and ruin it by teasing that he was petting her like a dog.

Lucie finished, then folded her arms. "There, that's better."

"And do you think you could find my, well"—Helen lowered her voice—"my brassiere?"

Lucie turned to open a closet behind her. Helen's clothing sat nicely folded inside, and Lucie extracted the bra, handing it to her, then pushed the button that raised Helen into a sitting position. "Want help?"

Helen shook her head. "No, thank you. I can manage."

"I'll go out and wait with Grady, then, till you're ready," Lucie said. "Just let us know."

Helen nodded and, once the girl was outside, fumbled with

the straps and clasps and the tie at her gown. *Oh, for goodness' sake,* she thought, hands shaking. *You'd think I'd never put on a bra before.*

When she had herself in order and her gown wrapped back around her, she said as loudly as she could, "All right, I'm decent."

It sounded feeble to her ears, but Lucie entered, pulling Grady Goodall by the hand. Tall like Edward, he was one to duck through the doorway, just in case. The resemblance didn't stop there, although Edward always wore his thick, dark hair cropped short and slicked back.

"Aunt Helen," Lucie said, "this is Grady."

"I believe we've talked on the phone," he said, moving toward her, reaching for her hand. "It's nice to meet you in person, Mrs. Ten Hands."

Oh, it was embarrassing, her mangled, old hand in his big, strong brown one, but he held it for a long moment, and looked down at her with familiar black eyes, and smiled the gentle way her husband always had.

"Are your people Skykomish?" she asked, squinting up at him, for surely they must be. "Flathead?"

"My dad's side were mostly Puyallup," he said. "But my mom is all Irish."

And then there was a racket at the door, a nurse wheeling in equipment, moving Lucie and Grady aside, asking Helen what all the button ringing was about, like it was a big joke, but Helen didn't care anymore about any of that.

"My family came to visit," she said, as the nurse wrapped a blood pressure cuff around her arm. "This is my niece, Lucie.

You may have seen her on the news recently. She was missing, but this young man found her."

The nurse turned to smile briefly at Lucie and Grady, then pulled her stethoscope around to place the cold disk in the crook of Helen's arm.

"He's my niece's fiancé, Grady Goodall. He works for Boeing, you know. And you'd be surprised to know how much he looks like my late husband, Edward Ten Hands."

Helen reached inside her gown for a Kleenex, but of course there wasn't one in there. Her vision blurred and she sniffed loudly, then felt a tissue being tucked into her palm.

Lucie was the most thoughtful girl.

# lucie

I f possible, Helen's apartment smelled even worse than it had the first time, Lucie thought, seeing the place through Grady's eyes now: the sagging furniture, stained carpet, grimy surfaces. Everything needed scrubbing. Helen probably hadn't been up to cleaning for some time.

Lucie walked to the window and looked out at the tired, old houses, brown lawns, and broken sidewalks. "Everything is so dismal here," she said, pushing the window open. It wouldn't be that difficult to air the place out, to get in there and clean and fix it up as a surprise for Helen's homecoming. In fact, Lucie could imagine coming up to Marysville every so often to help Helen, maybe taking the old woman to doctors' appointments or grocery shopping. Maybe out to the lake she loved so much.

Besides, Helen was a talker, that was for certain, and eventually, Lucie would learn most of the details about her childhood.

"Okay," she said, taking a deep breath and turning back to

Grady. "I'm going to go grab her some clothes. It should only take a minute."

The bedroom was dark and small, thick drapes drawn against the world, bed linens fusty and in disarray. Lucie switched on the light. The bedside table spilled over with pill bottles, half-empty glasses of water, and wadded tissues. No one had been in this room but Helen, probably ever, and Lucie felt like an intruder. Clothes. She'd come to get clothes.

Inside a small dresser, Lucie found worn nylon underpants, most with holes at the seams and elastic so stretched that she wondered how Helen kept them on. New underwear, then. She checked the size and brand, then searched through drawers for pajamas to replace the hospital gown.

As she dug deep into the bottom drawer, Lucie heard the rustle of paper. She hesitated. She'd searched through so many drawers in recent weeks, finding things that disappointed her, or scared her, or occasionally delighted her. Should she quit snooping and just take Helen's things and leave?

Lucie bit her lip. The best secrets were always at the bottom or back of a drawer.

She pushed the clothes aside, revealing the bottom half of an old clothing gift box, holding something wrapped in yellowing tissue. It reminded her of all the unused, new clothing in her own closet, and Lucie wondered if the tendency to buy and not wear ran in her blood.

Beneath the paper nestled a garment in a familiar orange and brown plaid, a little girl's dress with puffy short sleeves, an orange sash at the middle. Lucie pulled it from the box, the soft fabric burnished with time and wear.

"What's that?" Grady said from the doorway, startling her.

"My dress," she said, turning to show it to him. "I loved this dress. I can't believe she kept it all this time."

"You remember it?"

Lucie nodded. She did. "It was my favorite."

"And . . ." He seemed wary.

"She made it for me." Lucie studied the stitching of the hem, the homemade buttonholes in back. "It was supposed to be for special occasions, but I wanted to wear it all the time. Oh! I tore it once." Lucie slid the fabric through her hands, searching the skirt until she found a quarter-size patch ironed on from beneath. "She fixed it for me, and didn't tell my mom or anyone."

She turned to Grady. "I remember that. We were always in cahoots."

"Wow," he said. "That's . . . something." He held three photo albums. "What else do you remember?"

Lucie tried to think of more. "Just that feeling of . . ." She closed her eyes. "Of being part of something," she realized. "Not alone." And that was that. The memories that returned to her were in these brief snatches, but complete with emotion and sensation. They nourished her like milk.

"Oh," he said, a catch in his voice. "That's . . . wow. That's good."

"Yeah." Lucie tucked the dress back into the drawer, leaving it the way she'd found it, and pulled out a worn flannel nightgown to take to the hospital.

"So, what've you got there?" she asked, standing.

"Helen said she wanted her pictures." He shrugged. "I've

never seen any photos of you from before we met. Can we look?"

Lucie wrinkled her nose but nodded. Even though she knew it would feel strange, she couldn't say no to searching for the familiar, looking for answers. How long would she be searching like this? Would a time ever come when she felt satisfied with the present?

Grady held out his hand. "Come on. If it's too much, we'll stop."

They moved to the small couch in the living room. There they sat with the first album laid open on their thighs. As they leafed through the pages, Lucie narrated as best she could, seeing now the holes where Helen had removed the pictures she'd wanted Lucie to see. Surrounding each empty spot were photos that filled in the blanks, scenes of houses and tall trees and beaches and people, a family, moving through their lives from one photo-moment image to the next, seemingly happy, content.

She turned the second to last page over. "There it is. The moment everything changed."

"What?" Grady asked. "Which one?"

She pointed at a picture of a car with a man loading suitcases into the trunk, Gloria and an almost chubby eleven-year-old Lucie standing off to the side. She knew what moment it was—she could remember the picture being taken.

"That's my stepfather," she said, but how did she know? It was in the way he commanded the scene, she thought, in the repulsion she felt. Not in the sense of remembering, but in the sense of knowing from some deeper place. She studied the man, his face in profile, his chinos and short-sleeved shirt, his build and stance. His hands on the luggage, hands that had struck her mother, had burned Lucie's leg. He looked like any other man. His cruelty wasn't visible to the naked eye. "That's us going to California," she said, sighing.

Her mother looked stressed out, but like any mother moving her family a thousand miles away would. She smiled for her sister behind the camera. Gloria thought she was heading off to a better life. California! A new husband! It must have felt like a dream.

The girl had been crying, Lucie could see that, studying her child face. She was sad to be leaving Helen and Edward, and the only home she knew, but at that point, she was still a child accustomed to being happy and well cared for.

She had no clue what was about to come.

Lucie closed the book.

"Want to get out of here?" Grady asked, putting his hand on her leg where the photo album had laid. She nodded, but made no move to stand. *Not just yet,* she thought, waiting until he pulled his hand away.

# lucie

Summer in Seattle peaked in late August. Ninety-plus-degree days became common, finally, in this brief burst of dry heat, and the usually luscious landscape dried to tinder. Grass crunched underfoot, left to die off before the rains began again in autumn; flowers slumped and shriveled.

Lucie knew this about August, walking down her front steps one afternoon and out onto the hot sidewalk, where she also knew her child self had imagined frying eggs in such weather. Maybe every child had, but Lucie remembered thinking it outside of a little yellow house, adults in webbed lawn chairs surrounded by clover, a blue inflatable pool in the yard. The promise of an eventual ice cream truck, or a Popsicle from the freezer.

This was how it was now, brief views into a past that had only been temporarily obscured. As soon as Lucie remembered such a thing, it was part of her, and always had been. The more she remembered, the less she might obsess about the last, ter-rifying memories she had of childhood, she hoped.

Her neighbor Don sat in a green plastic Adirondack chair in the shade of his front awning. As she passed, Lucie looked up to see him watching her. "Don," she said, nodding as Grady had. He nodded back, and she smiled at her success, but then he cleared his throat and said, "Good to see you made it home safe and sound."

"Thank you," she said. It was so hard not to say more, but she knew that was enough. She continued on to Susan's house.

That night, eating strawberry-rhubarb pie at the kitchen table, windows open wide and fans blowing the heat of the day across the room, Lucie told Grady about the day's small discov-eries: the pie-making lesson, the flashes of her childhood in Marysville.

Life gaped wide in front of her, with both possibility and a blank space she wasn't sure how to fill. She was about to turn forty, and she had such a long way to go to discover who she was, but Dr. Seagreave assured her that most forty-year-olds felt pretty much the same. At their first session, she'd said, "Not everything that feels like a mystery in life is from a miss-ing memory. Life is full of things we can't figure out."

After dinner, while Grady handled a work emergency in the home office, Lucie sat on the floor in the bedroom closet, star-ing at the dozens of packages she'd been ignoring, all of the things she'd purchased in her previous life but never used. What if there were things in those packages that she actually wanted? Whatever she didn't, she'd return. And if the return-by dates had expired, well, there was always Goodwill.

It took many trips up and down the steep steps, but eventually Lucie had hauled the packages out of the closet down to the living room, where they now spread before her like Christmas presents. She wiped sweat from her forehead with the bottom of her shirt, thinking how nice it would be to have more space in the closet. Maybe she'd start going through her clothes, too, whittling them down to those she actually wore. Someone ought to get some use out of them.

Lucie chose a small package to open first, one from Saks she hadn't looked at before. She pulled out a long white cashmere scarf, soft and plush. It would look lovely wrapped around Mary Faith's shoulders that winter, Lucie thought, smiling and putting it aside. Next she opened a shoe box from Zappos, delighted to see that it contained men's shearling slippers, Grady's size. So, she hadn't only shopped for herself. A lump formed in her throat, and she nodded in relief. Each package was a small surprise, an item perfect for someone else: a tea cozy for Susan, beaded bracelets for at least one of her many sisters-in-law.

The final package contained a handbag that Lucie couldn't imagine having chosen—not for her neutral-loving self—even though it was Prada and had cost nearly four hundred dollars, a price that staggered her. But it was pretty. It wasn't gray or brown or black. It looked like a painting of poppies on silky fabric, red against white, with red leather handles and shoulder strap, and a big, gaping red silk interior.

Lucie had to admit she loved it. She'd been stuffing her little Guatemalan bag for weeks and had outgrown it. With this larger bag, she could carry all kinds of things: candy by the bag instead of by the piece, a paperback for when she sat in waiting rooms. A phone for when she needed to talk to Grady. Photos of people she loved. A cherry red lipstick to match the poppies.

Why had she ordered this, though? Was it a gift for someone else? It would have had to be a pretty special someone, with the price.

And then she knew. *Thank you,* she thought, embracing the bag. If she couldn't be her former self, she could at least appreciate her.


LATE THAT NIGHT, Lucie lay awake in the upstairs bedroom alone, fingers playing piano chords on her belly: the Gershwin song she'd played the first night she was home. She felt too tired now to go play. The desire had become less compelling as other memories had started coming to her. It was as though it had been a portal, the music—a passageway to let the rest in. Grady was probably sleeping better now, too, down in the guest room, without all her late night performances.

Her fingers stopped moving. The empty place inside her yawned wide, the old ache from gut to throat. She missed sleeping with Grady, the two of them lying on their sides like parentheses, their bodies as familiar to the other as their own, his hand twitching on her hip as he relaxed into dreams.

But how did she know that? Her heart tapped quickly until she took a deep breath, then another. It was just the ease of memory slipping through, the comfort as present as the physical sensation of it.

*What is love,* she wondered, *and what is memory?* Where

did the two intersect, and when would it no longer matter which came first?

She slipped from the bed, naked, and made her way in the dark down the stairs, around the corner, and along the hallway. There was where she'd found him sleeping that first night, listening to her play piano; there, in the kitchen, was where he'd first kissed her. She walked back toward the guest room, where he'd rejected her.

Stepping inside the doorway, she watched him sleep. He lay facing the wall in his underwear and a T-shirt, even on this hot night. She remembered now that he'd always slept nude before, and she'd worn his old T-shirts. That he covered himself was probably Grady's way of showing respect as she got to know him again. That she slept naked now was just another mystery.

Quietly, she moved toward the bed and eased herself onto it, trying not to disturb him, but he rolled toward her as soon as she lay down and draped his arm around her.

"Grady," she whispered, but he hadn't woken.

She was too excited to sleep, her heart thudding at what she'd just done, but Lucie knew that eventually she'd calm down and drift off, and in the morning . . . well.

She'd see what happened next.

# acknowledgments

This book is in your hands because of Stephanie Kip Rostan, who put her faith in me and championed this story into print. Her kind support, intelligence, humor, and generosity allowed me the time and energy to write the book I wanted to write, and I am ever grateful. Thanks also to Karen Kosztolnyik at Gallery Books for her enthusiasm and guiding hand in making this the best it could be, and to Heather Hunt, Jen Bergstrom, Jennifer Robinson, Mary McCue, Natalie Ebel, Ellen Chan, and everyone at Gallery Books.

For technical assistance, special thanks go to Tim Mooney for the virtual swimming lessons and assistance with research, and to Tim, Jay Miazga, Stan Matthews, Garth Stein, and Matt Gani for helping me write the truest Grady I could. Kaila and Scott Raby clued me in on the world of Boeing. Margaret Meinecke and Lynne Kinghorn assured that Lucie's dilemma rang true. So many others kept me on track as I wrote, including my writing partners, Erica Bauermeister and Randy Sue Coburn, whose encouragement and discerning ears and eyes were invaluable. And, as always, hugs to those who read for me along the way and shared their thoughts: Sherry Brown, Cindy Grainger, Alison Galinsky, Tricia Hovey, Drella Stein, Jeri Pushkin, and Tegan Tigani. Gratitude to Amber James for her keen eye and to Natalia Dotto for her photographic magic. Thanks to Howard Wall just because. And to all of you who let me borrow your favorite grandparents' names in tribute for every character name in this book, I'm grateful for your trust.

Thanks to my buddies in Seattle7Writers who help in ways they'll never know mean so much to me, including Kevin O'Brien, Stevie Kallos, Maria Headley, Laurie Frankel, Mary Guterson, Carol Cassella, Kit Bakke, Dave Boling, Tara Weaver, and the above-mentioned Erica, Randy Sue, and Garth. Thanks to everyone at Hedgebrook, the best place for a she-writer to hole up for a couple of weeks and revise. Gratitude to my family for their continued love and support. And my love and thanks always to Matt Gani, for making my dreams come true.

And to all of you, dear readers, who waited more than three years for this story, thank you for sticking with me.